no rules

JENNA McCORMICK

no rules

𝒜
APHRODISIA

KENSINGTON PUBLISHING CORP.
www.kensingtonbooks.com

APHRODISIA BOOKS are published by

Kensington Publishing Corp.
119 West 40th Street
New York, NY 10018

All Kensington titles, imprints, and distributed lines are available at special quantity discounts for bulk purchases for sales promotion, premiums, fund-raising, and educational or institutional use.

Special book excerpts or customized printings can also be created to fit specific needs. For details, write or phone the office of the Kensington Special Sales Manager: Kensington Publishing Corp., 119 West 40th Street, New York, NY 10018. Attn. Special Sales Department. Phone: 1-800-221-2647.

Aphrodisia and the A logo Reg. U.S. Pat. & TM Off.
ISBN-13: 978-0-7582-8757-1
ISBN-10: 0-7582-8757-7
First Kensington Trade Paperback Printing: September 2013

eISBN-13: 978-0-7582-8758-8
eISBN-10: 0-7582-8758-5
First Kensington Electronic Edition: September 2013

10 9 8 7 6 5 4 3 2 1

Printed in the United States of America

Dedicated to
Everyone who ever craved the ability to be in two
places at once.

Acknowledgments

Going from a wisp of an idea to a finished book is not an individual task. Many people helped keep me on track, at times pressing my nose to the grindstone. Thanks to my magnificent critique partner, Saranna DeWylde, who listens to the madness of ideas flowing through me, makes a little bit of sense out of it, and keeps telling me it's not as awful as I think it is. This time you get to be right!

Thanks to my agent, Jessica Faust, and the staff at Bookends for keeping the communication going even when I can barely string a sentence together.

Of course to everyone at Kensington, especially my editor, Audrey LaFehr, and Martin Biro, who help make the magic happen.

To Candi Wall for beta reading and pimping this book like a two-dollar manwhore online. Hugs, babe!

Much love and gratitude to my family, especially my dear husband, for reminding me that writing on a deadline and having a life outside of whatever universe I'm mucking around with are not mutually exclusive propositions.

And to you, the readers: Thanks so much for willingly strapping in for another wild ride with me. I couldn't do it without you.

1

Alison Cartwright missed many things about her life as an Illustra executive. Her personal vehicle—a Pegasus EXC that could break the sound barrier and came in a sexy cherry red with buttersoft leather seats. The apartment overlooking New Central Park and the self-sustaining smart house on Martha's Vineyard she'd purchased when she'd been promoted from pleasure companion to management. She longed for her wardrobe containing designer suits, cocktail dresses, and hand-painted undergarments for every occasion from demure to dominatrix. And her shoes—all the latest styles in every color of the rainbow—some she'd never even worn.

But more than anything else, Alison missed her perfect body. Staring at her reflection in the dingy bathroom mirror, she assessed the changes. Her lip curled when she saw that not only was the cellulite back on her stomach, hips, ass, and thighs, it'd brought friends and was having a kegger. The carefully sculpted six-pack was long gone, as was the glorious definition in her shoulders, biceps, and calf muscles that she'd paid contouring surgeons a pretty penny for every three months like clockwork.

The damage wasn't just to her body either. Her face showed lines of strain and anxiety, her lighter blond highlights had completely faded, and her hair had returned to its original dirty dishwater color, stuck in some gawd-awful limbo between blond and brown. She hadn't had a decent cut in months and the layers had grown in raggedy. Picking up a strand, she couldn't suppress a grimace at the texture. Limper than a whisky dick at last call.

She'd gone from a high-maintenance demigoddess to stressed-out soccer mom, complete with lumpy, dumpy tennis ball butt. The only things missing were the hole-riddled sweats and the minivan full of urchins.

How the hell was she supposed to seduce a wealthy man looking like something the cat dragged in, shat upon, and then abandoned? Assuming a decent man ever *came* to this armpit of the universe. She'd been stuck on Pental for over a month and hadn't seen one yet.

The johns who blew through here, hoping to score at the *demjong* tables, were usually one-shot wonders, with no money for much more than a consolation quickie. She'd lost count of how many hand jobs she'd given while sweaty, grimy men with eighty-proof breath pawed her. No one had purchased her services for the entire night in weeks. It was one thing to be a whore, another entirely to feel like a desperate one.

In her darker moments, she wished Illustra's assassin would hurry up and put her out of her misery.

She shivered as she recalled her last encounter with the assassin. He hadn't physically touched her, but icy tentacles had wrapped around her major organs and squeezed, giving her a taste of his power. It was a dish she never wanted to sample again, no matter how ugly she became or how many losers she had to jack off.

Using the bucket of tepid water she'd dragged up to her one-room rental, she washed herself as best she could and tried not to think about the clean efficiency of a sonic shower back on Earth. She was never able to completely remove the slick oil Madam Brizella had given her. Some of it saturated her hair until it clung to her shoulders. She left it there. With nothing to secure it back it would only stick again every time she moved.

The collar went around her throat next, the mark of a woman for sale. The corner of her shirt—or at least what passed for a shirt—was secured to the collar right at the hollow of her throat. From there the shiny fabric skimmed over her breasts and abdomen until another corner tucked into her utility belt, containing the tricks of her trade. She secured the other corners at her sides with some glue-like substance, which she would have to reapply after every tumble, at least if her patron paid to see her breasts.

Most didn't want to cough up for that pleasure, were content to grope her through the fabric. She tried not to take it personally, but the girls *were* hanging lower than they had even a year ago. Wishing she'd invested in an augmentation to perk them up now was a waste of time. She needed to focus on the positive.

She was still alive. Had money for a little food and a safe, warm place to sleep. She was surviving, if not really living.

Ignoring the wild bush at the juncture of her thighs, she fastened the metal panels to her waistband. Luckily she'd had the hair on her underarms and legs genetically demolished so those areas were smooth, but she couldn't get past the idea of having a highly concentrated genetic beam zapping away anywhere near her pussy. The hair was there to stay. Though the panels reached down to her ankles, the way they shifted as she moved exposed her every imperfection.

Once dressed, she started smoothing the oil over her exposed skin. One of the other working girls would coat her bare back before she hit the floor, but she wouldn't seek them out until the last second. Despite her constant loneliness, Alison avoided spending time with the other ladies of the night. They were nosy, asked too many questions, and she had too many secrets to hide. Better they think her a stuck-up bitch than for one of the working girls to whisper her name in the wrong ear.

Leaning close to the mirror, she studied her face again. Her meager makeup box wasn't designed to fix damage of this nature. She had nothing to adequately cover the age spot beneath her right eye or smooth the fine lines at the corners of her mouth. In this part of the galaxy, whores had no power, no money, and very little hope.

An aging whore was just plain screwed.

"Think positive. Visualize a rich man taking me away from all this," she instructed her haggard reflection. It didn't seem impressed so she turned and headed down the rickety staircase to the ground floor of the brothel, the panels of her skirt clinking with every step.

"Alien girl, come here!" Brizella, the proprietor of the gaming hell, beckoned her over with a frantic wave of her bejeweled sausage fingers. Brizella's translator chip was faulty at best, definitely an older model, but Alison had learned to catch the gist of what she said.

She wasn't sure exactly what species the madam was, her purple-tinted skin was unique and she resembled a toad more than a person. "I have special man for you tonight."

Brizella's definition of "special" resided on the opposite end of the spectrum from Alison's. Most of the gamblers were humanoid, even if certain parts were relocated. "Missing limb? Testicles on his chin?" she guessed as the madam dragged her down the pokey hallway behind the casino. Sounds of talk and masculine laughter filled the air, and Brizella pulled back a shimmering tapestry to reveal the low lights of the main room.

"There!" Brizella pointed at the closest *demjong* table. "He is most famous patron; family owns half of the Tibiath System. He likes the exotic girls, like you."

Alison had no idea where the Tibiath System was located and honestly didn't care as long as it was a *long* way from Pental. She'd remained here too long already. Following the madam's bulky digit to the source of her excitement, she studied the players, hunkered down over their cards. Unlike *yugnie*, *demjong* was a game of skill, not chance. Alison had picked up enough to know it was some complex form of poker, though the images on the cards made no sense to her, as they held no numerical value.

Though the table was crowded, she caught a glimpse of a dark head bent low over his cards. His profile was hard, as though carved from the dead surface of the moon they occupied, and though his shoulders were rounded, she got the impression he was only feigning relaxation. A predator lying in wait for the perfect moment to pounce.

The man to his right said something and he turned toward her.

Alison took an instinctive step back as a pair of icy blue eyes swung her direction. *Bam!* She couldn't remember the last time she'd experienced such an instant attraction. Desire pooled low in her belly as he held her gaze with his. The feeling was so foreign, she almost didn't recognize it.

He was horrifically scarred. A nasty jagged line ran along the left side of his face, giving him an almost sinister look. But the truly frightening thing about him was his unwavering focus on her, a cold precision so intense it practically burned her with frost, even as her body warmed from the inside out.

He eyed her up and down, his attention lingering on her lips, her breasts, and the skin exposed between the metal panels. He hid it well, but she saw his flare of interest, as molten and unstable as her own. This powerful and alluring man wanted her imperfect body, the same way she wanted his.

Abruptly, he turned back to his cards and she started as she realized he was shielding his ruined face from her gaze. Feminine power jolted her, another long-forgotten friend she greeted eagerly. The feeling was why she'd become a pleasure companion in the first place, to experience such a strong desire focused on her and her alone. The blue-eyed stranger was a far cry from the dregs she'd been servicing to survive. Hell, he was more appealing than most of her regulars back on Earth.

She wondered if he was any good in bed. Handsome men rarely were, too used to being fawned over to bother learning how to please a woman. And this one had money as well as his striking looks. No doubt she'd have to do all the work, but it might just be worth it to spend one night feeling the way she used to feel.

Desired.

"You go to him now," Brizella urged, slathering the noxiously sweet oil across her back so her skin would glisten under the low lights.

Alison moved forward, then paused. "What's his name?"

"Larshe," the madam warbled. "Mig Larshe."

Alison practiced saying it back a few times, to ensure she had the sound correct before moving forward. Her knees actually shook as she approached the table, the man. Perhaps her luck was changing.

He didn't turn when she reached his side so she said, "Mig Larshe?"

"That's me, beauty."

She turned and faced the speaker, the man seated to the right of her scarred heartthrob. Pushing his chair back quickly he stood, only attaining eye level with her breasts. She fought to hide her disappointment. The scarred man wasn't her target, this orange midget was. He was as wide as he was tall, bulbously round like one of those dolls that got knocked down and bounced up again. Two tufts of deep green bushy hair stuck out over large ears with thick, hanging lobes. His teeth were sharp, almost like a tiger's, and he eyed her lasciviously.

But he might be her ticket out of here.

Plastering a smile on her face, Alison moved toward him. Well, she'd asked for a wealthy patron and the universe had delivered. She hadn't asked for a pulse-pounding sex god, so she had no right to be disappointed. As she kept reminding herself, beggars couldn't be choosers.

Without looking at the other player—the one she wanted—she bent low and greeted the man she needed. "Welcome to The Nebula. My name is Alison. Let me know if I can do anything to make your stay more pleasurable."

The whore had been crying.

From his seat at the octagonal table, Fenton had an unobstructed view of the clean streak along the side of her face where her tears had washed her makeup away. He shuffled his cards, feigning pondering his next move in the game, when really all he wanted was to figure out why that clean streak captivated him.

Why *she* captivated him.

He'd made her as a working girl the second he'd felt her gaze roving over him. Even without her degrading outfit, she had that lean, hungry look Fenton associated with camp followers and women who sold their flesh to survive. When she'd approached, he'd been tempted to leave this important game to spend a few hours learning every dip and curve of her luscious body.

Then she'd asked for Mig—the little dung heap—and he'd tried to concentrate on the game. Tried to forget about her, which was damn near impossible with her seated on Larshe's lap.

Her pale skin glowed in the low light of the casino floor like moonflowers. Though she was coated in some kind of oil, Fenton imagined her clean, dewy fresh from a bath. He'd seen one of her kind before, knew what planet she hailed from. The question was, what the hell was she doing out here on Pental, millions of light-years away from Earth?

"Get me another drink." Mig slapped her bare back and she jumped up to refill his glass at the bar. Fenton tried to catch her gaze. He wanted to know more, to find out what she was doing here, so far from home. He wanted to help her.

"Del, my man. You gonna play those cards or just hold 'em all night?" Reed, his second-in-command, slapped the table, pulling his attention away from the whore.

"She's quite the prize." Mig tugged on one of his ear tufts and looked to where his paid companion had gone. "I was going to keep her all to myself, but what say you we raise the stakes?"

Fenton sat stock-still. He needed to win this game, needed the winnings to buy a new identity out of the Hosta System. And Mig, regardless of his personal flaws, had currency to burn. "What do you propose?"

The Hibariate studied the small fortune on the table in front of him, then Del's meager pile. "You're part of the old regime, are you not?"

"Xander's dead. He no longer rules Hosta." For which Fenton was eternally glad.

"Yes, yes, but I need someone to take me to the ruling planet, into the main palace." Mig's beady eyes gleamed. The whore returned with his drink, and he bade her stand beside him. "I'll bet you the girl for a guided tour."

She gasped and her gaze flew to Fenton's. Her lips, colored unnaturally red, parted but she was well trained in her trade and knew better than to interrupt. Fenton forced himself not to react. Despite his wealth, Mig didn't have enough money to force Fenton to return to the crown planet. No power in the galaxy would do that. So why was he considering making the bet?

"Why would I do that when I have more than enough to

buy my own bedmate?" Fenton cocked an eyebrow at the pile before him.

"Because she's unique. And all mine." Mig held his gaze as he gripped her arm, bringing it to his lips, sinking his teeth in. She cried out in pain, but didn't pull away, just closed her eyes and endured it. Fenton knew that if he lost, or didn't take the bet, Mig would sink those teeth into her tender flesh over and over, getting off on her pain, as Hibariates customarily did. By morning she'd look like a chew toy.

Fenton made the mistake of looking at her face again, his mind superimposing the bastard's bite across her creamy flesh. He'd betrayed one human woman, leaving her to a cruel fate. He hadn't been able to help her any more than he could save his own family. Late at night he saw their faces as the guilt pressed down on him, crushing his lungs until he couldn't take a deep breath. At the time he'd had another, higher priority concern and no alternative. Would the whore's face haunt him too?

But he couldn't cave so easily. "All in or no deal."

Mig released her arm and she snatched it back, her breasts rising and falling quickly as she looked from him to her tormentor and back again. Mig ignored her, though her blood still coated his lips, and studied his credit chips. "I have over a million *drachmas* here."

It would have to be enough. "Those are my terms. Take it or leave it."

Reed whistled low and placed his cards facedown. "Too rich for my blood. Think I'll rustle up some company of my own. See you in the morning, Del."

Fenton nodded once. If Lady Luck was on his side, he would never see Reed again.

Mig studied him and he blanked his mind as he stared back, the moment stretching out endlessly.

"Agreed. All in and the girl, for a guide to the palace on

Hosta and back again." Mig pushed his drachmas to the middle of the table. "Let's see your cards."

Fenton pushed his own neatly regimented stacks forward. "Your grand idea, you go first."

Mig licked his lip. The whore held her breath. He winked at her as he laid down a glider streak, with a Regent on high. "Sorry, buck-o, only one hand beats that."

Fenton stared at the cards impassively. "You're right." He looked up at the woman. "I'm sorry."

"Not your fault." Clutching her injured arm, she wavered on her feet.

Laying down his cards without any theatrics, he continued, "Sorry, but you've had a change of plans this evening."

"Impossible!" The Hibariate raged as he studied the complete cataclysm, Overlord to Slave. "The odds of drawing that hand are astronomical! You must have cheated!"

Fenton was already on his feet, with his arm around the woman. "Careful, Mig. I'm part of the military contingent here on Pental. Accusing a soldier of cheating is the equivalent of issuing a dueling challenge. And I am an expert marksman."

The Hibariate seethed as Fenton led the whore to the cashout table. Issuing an order to have his winnings transferred to his credit account, he then retrieved his coat. "Do you have a cloak?"

"Upstairs." Her voice was faint.

Absently touching the scar along the side of his face, he muttered, "You don't have to come home with me. He's paid for you either way."

She pulled herself up out of her daze, squared her shoulders, and extended a hand to him. "My name's Alison."

"Alison." He brought her thin, white hand to his lips, enjoying the smooth texture of her soft skin. "The pleasure's all mine."

2

Though she knew better than to leave the casino with a john, Alison didn't look back as Del Fenton led her out of the main gambling area, toward the exit. Staying at the brothel didn't seem like the best course of action anymore. Her heart still pounded frantically after her near miss with the little bastard and his shark-like teeth. She cradled her aching arm against her chest. Fenton draped his coat around her shoulders and took her uninjured hand in his as he led her out the door into the street. She didn't know why he was being so nice to her—it certainly wasn't common on Pental for a man to treat a whore with respect—but she was smart enough to accept it for an hour, a night, a year, or however long it lasted.

He'd just won a million credits. By Alison's recently re-assessed standards of care, he could afford to keep her for a very, *very* long time. Ignoring the part of her that chafed at the thought of being kept by any man, she set her sights on doing her damndest to make sure she made herself worth his trouble. Pride had no place in a game of survival.

"Thank you for saving me. When Madam Brizella told me to entertain him, I had no idea what he would be like."

Fenton released her hand and she immediately missed the warmth. "Brizella is one of the only madams who will cater to Mig and his unusual . . . appetites. She's always looking for new blood to throw his way, because he can pay for it. With diplomatic immunity, the military can't stop him. I'm surprised her girls didn't warn you that Hibariates enjoy inflicting pain during mating."

"They don't like me very much." Her own fault. If she'd just made friends with the other prostitutes she would have been warned about the sharp-toothed troll. Making female friends had never been her strong suit, especially now that she had so many things to hide.

Fenton didn't answer her as they made their way through a steamy alley jammed with vendors hawking food and souvenirs to the visitors. The air in the atmosphere dome was full of spice and frenetic energy. Alison hadn't spent much time outside, and she drank in the bustle and buzz of life happening all around her. In a way it reminded her of New New York, and a pang of homesickness made her oblivious to the cracks in the sidewalk. She stumbled and would have gone sprawling if he hadn't caught her.

"Careful." Fenton's solid grip held her up. He didn't linger, just made sure she was steady before turning to resume his course. His shoulders took up almost the entire span of the narrow walkway between the carts and she pressed deeper into his side. Safety was an illusion, but right now she needed to trust somebody at least a little bit. The man had gone out of his way for her, and she figured he would continue to do so, at least until he got what he wanted.

An entire night with him. Her body tingled in anticipation. Hopefully he'd let her patch her arm up before he set in on her, but she wouldn't complain either way. Once activated, her germ shield would eradicate anything that might lead to an infection, as well as protect her from sexually transmitted diseases and pregnancy.

"You just flinched." She started, unaware that he'd been watching her. Fenton didn't require an explanation but his eyes asked the question.

"Just a random thought. The worst-case scenario." A baby was about the only thing that would make her life harder. Even the thought of a child made her twitchy.

"I won't hurt you." Those icy eyes assessed her. "By the looks of you, you've been hurt enough."

It was almost impossible not to take offense to that. Alison was a realist, but knowing she looked like hell and hearing a potential lover say so were on opposite ends of the universe. What was she expecting anyway? Fenton said he was a soldier and he'd saved her ass. Envisioning him sweet-talking her into bed was overkill.

Fenton ushered her out of the alley and across the road jammed by thicker congestion of military and civilian vehicles that idled in the early evening traffic and toward a small bridge spanning a long, dry riverbed. Even with the bioluminescent light fixtures tethered to trees surrounding the crossing, she could barely make out the edges of the arched walkway. With no railing, nothing prevented a one-hundred-meter drop to the long-dead stream.

Seeming to sense her hesitation, Fenton spoke in that brisk, yet reassuring voice. "There's an invisible force field around the bridge. You won't fall."

She smiled weakly. "I'm not a fan of heights."

He moved closer and pointed up. "Meteor shower. Focus on that."

"Oh." Her breath caught as she watched the blazes of light

streak across the blackened sky. For a moment she shed her misery, dismissed all her worry, and just watched the glorious display. "It's beautiful."

Rough hands caressed her cheek, and she turned her attention to him as his mouth feathered lightly over hers. The kiss he gave her was sweet and soft, not the kind of thing she was used to at all. Instead of an eager, messy mating, his lips brushed over hers with a sweet reverence. He tasted of liquor and potent male spices. She was so stunned she didn't have a chance to respond before he pulled back abruptly.

"Sorry." He didn't say anything else as they'd crossed from the main tourist area into the military compound on the other side of the bridge. She wondered if he was taking her to some sort of barracks, if he intended to pass her around like a party favor. Military rarely showed up at The Nebula, unless there was some kind of disturbance. Hearing that Fenton was a soldier of some sort had been just one more shock to her already overloaded mind.

If she stopped to think about everything, she was sure she'd go insane. Better to just keep moving.

Fenton bypassed the main area of the compound and the barracks, instead aiming toward a small house. Actually it was more of a metal hut, still a palatial space compared to where she'd been sleeping and probably a grand concession for a military man. Pressing his palm flat against the door, Fenton waited a beat before reaching for the doorknob. He pulled her in behind him, then shut and secured the door before doffing his black utility vest and disappearing into the other room.

Obviously, he wasn't one for small talk. Alison took in the small space, which was comprised of two rooms: the kitchen/dining room, where she stood, and what she guessed was the bedroom. She couldn't sit comfortably without her metallic skirt panels cutting into her legs so she stood still and waited.

Fenton returned quickly, carrying a small case. "We need to see to that wound."

As he spread the contents of his case out on the sturdy metal table, Alison saw that it was a first-aid kit. "Just give me some gauze and I'll wrap it."

"It could get infected." Leveling his frosty gaze on her, he practically dared her to argue with him.

She rose to his challenge. "Not with this." Pressing on the small node beneath the crook of her elbow, she activated her health guard. The snap and sizzle told her the shield was busy gobbling up any DNA not her own.

Fenton's lips parted and he reached forward, taking her hand. "I forgot your species was equipped with those."

His words nearly stopped her heart. "You know what I am? Where I'm from?" No one this far out had ever heard of humans or Earth any more than people back home knew of Pental.

But Fenton did, she saw the knowledge there in his eyes even as he sought to reassure her. "I told you, I mean you no harm. I don't know what you're running from, but it's none of my concern."

Alison didn't trust him that far; she couldn't afford to. "Then why did you save me?"

Reaching for her still-shielded arm, he took a small gel pack and placed it over the wound. She braced herself for the sting of antiseptic, but instead shivered as the cool plasma-like substance adhered to her skin. "Because you remind me of someone I loved. She didn't have any real choice either, was forced to pick between one pile of shit and another. I've seen how you have to make the best with nothing but nerve and determination and the hope that someday it will get better. There, that should help you heal faster."

Alison swallowed when he released her. "Thank you."

He nodded and repacked the kit. "You can stay the night. I'm leaving before dawn and you'll need to be out by then."

She needed to step up her game, stop allowing him to throw her so far off balance. Take the bull by his protruding body part. But first things first. "You mind if I get cleaned up?"

He didn't respond, just turned back toward the bedroom. She eyed the sink and sighed. He had real running water, but she decided to follow him. Maybe he had an actual bathtub, a rarity on Pental, where every luxury had to be imported. And if he wanted to just toss her down on the mattress and fuck her blind, then who was she to say no?

Instead of the small bedroom she'd expected, she found a spiral staircase leading downward, opening into a spacious, below-level apartment. The walls were pure stone but the space was open and warm. More bioluminescent lighting was rigged along the ceiling, the small blue-green creatures casting a cheery glow across the vast room.

"I never would have guessed this was here." Alison marveled at the luxurious accommodations. "You're quite the enigma, aren't you, Fenton?"

The left corner of his mouth kicked up in what she guessed was as close as he came to a smile. "Facilities are this way."

Alison's mouth dropped open when she saw the natural hot spring and pool that acted as his bathtub. With a happy cry she dropped his coat on the floor and started yanking panels off her hideous skirt.

Fenton turned abruptly away, so he wasn't looking at her. "I'll leave you to it," he croaked before striding from the room.

Alison was too excited to puzzle over his bizarre behavior. Shedding her clothes, she hurried to the side of the pool and sat her bare backside down on the cool rock before dipping her toes into the water. The temperature was perfect and she pushed off, letting her entire body sink beneath the surface, reveling in the pure joy of swimming herself clean. Oil floated on the surface, the nasty stuff dispersing in the massive pool. Never again would she coat her body with that hideous gunk.

Pental no longer had water on its surface, but these underground hot springs made life sustainable. Alison only had ever heard of them from a few of the tourist selectmen who frequented the casino. A place like this was beyond astronomical in price. Clearly tonight's winnings were not Fenton's first.

Why would a man with that kind of money serve in the military? A sense of patriotism, perhaps? Or possibly as a kind of penance. Clearly he'd loved a whore at one time. She'd picked up on his use of the past tense. Whether the woman died or left him, she'd obviously broken his heart. Stupid slag. Alison wouldn't be anywhere near that foolish. A kind, scarred, yet good-looking man with money was definitely a keeper.

Yes, Fenton was a prize, one she had every intention of winning.

She's perfect.

Despite his resolve not to touch her, Fenton couldn't help his physical reaction to the display of Alison's body. Her pale skin glowed in the bioluminescent lighting, and he'd enjoyed the soft bounce of her tits beneath the thin fabric of her top. A little too much. An erection wasn't something he needed to deal with right now.

He had much to accomplish. Taking time to fully enjoy a woman, the way his kind craved, was not a quick or simple task. And it was dangerous too. Letting his guard down for any amount of time was a risk he couldn't afford to take.

But her sweet form stirred him as no other had ever done. He'd never had difficulty stifling his attraction before. What was it about her that sought out the cracks in his protective shielding and seeped into the man underneath?

The man who'd made so many mistakes, who'd lost so much.

Moving to his secret chamber, Fenton pressed his hand to the scanner and didn't flinch when the needle snagged a sample of his DNA. When he'd first arrived on Pental, he'd taken over the overlord's private suite, part of his reward for faithful service to Xander. Throw the dog a bone. Now that Xander had left the Hosta System, the rebel leaders would come for him. The overlord had escaped punishment, but his minions would pay the price in his stead.

A few had already touched down and were hunting him even now. The price on his head was obscenely high, considering he was nothing but a grunt. It took triple that amount to secure safe passage on a luxury cruiser, a fee Fenton didn't have until he won tonight. Going to the casino had been a hell of a risk, but his back was to the wall. Eventually the hunters would find him and put him down like a rabid dog.

So bedding Alison was a bad idea, no matter what his body craved. As his DNA was confirmed and the door opened, he glanced over his shoulder to make sure she was still preoccupied with her bath, before stepping inside the chamber.

The sole content of the room was only a meter long and two deep. The low humming sound assured him that the stasis pod was active and it had not been disturbed. The sleek outer casing was opaque but turned clear when he pressed his palm to it. This was the only thing that mattered, the only thing he would take with him when he departed, other than the clothes on his back and the credits in his pocket.

Staring at the outside of the pod, he remembered the last time he'd seen Gili. She'd been pale from the wasting sickness that ate her from the inside out. The pod had been beside her deathbed, looking the same two cycles ago as it did now. At first he couldn't believe what she'd done, what she asked of him.

Her voice had rasped like crumbling leaves. "Promise me."

He'd gripped her small, pale hand in his, as he'd done countless times. A gesture of connection between brother and sister, to reassure her and let her know he would always be there for her. This time, the contact was for his sake. "Don't do this to me. Don't leave me alone with this responsibility."

Her blue eyes, the same color as his, had clouded over. "Brother, I have no choice. There is no one else I trust. Promise me."

"I promise," he'd whispered, though he had no idea how to keep such an oath.

Looking back at the pod, he realized exactly how far he had to come to keep his word. How much he'd sacrificed for the love of his dead sister, whom he had ultimately failed.

He couldn't fail her again, no matter what his body demanded or how much he wished he was free to lose himself in Alison's sweet, supple body for a few hours.

After checking the readings on the pod's control panel, he exited the room. With his resolve firmly in place, he headed toward the kitchen to prepare sustenance. His food storage unit was empty of everything but a protein-rich paste he'd confiscated from a gambler who'd snuck it on world. The stuff was addictive and practical, and he'd be sorry when he ran out.

"Whatcha got there?"

He hadn't heard her approach. Some protector. His mental chastising cut off when he turned and saw she'd donned one of his thin shirts and it hit her just above the knee. She'd braided her long hair loosely until it looked like a thick length of rope hanging down her back. His palms itched to grab hold of it and yank her to him.

The corner of her mouth kicked up when she saw him staring. "Sorry to help myself like that, but I couldn't bear the thought of wearing that skirt again." Her tone implied she wasn't sorry at all.

Dragging his gaze away from the expanse of creamy skin, he offered her the jar. "Are you hungry?"

She moved closer until he scented her unique fragrance. "On Earth we have a saying: Please don't feed the whores because they won't want to eat out later."

"But you need to eat, correct?"

Alison waited expectantly. "Of course I eat. It was a joke."

"Oh." And he didn't catch on quickly enough. She must think he was a humorless drone.

She wouldn't be the first.

Moving even closer, she examined the container in his hands. Inhaling deeply, she closed her eyes and moaned. His cock stiffened and he had to brace himself against the onslaught of lust at the sensual sound. When her eyes opened, they brimmed with emotion as they locked on him.

"Where did you get this?"

"It came in illegally and I confiscated it. I've never tasted anything like it. Do you know what it is?"

"It's from Earth. We call it peanut butter. Just smelling it makes me homesick."

Though it was his last jar, Fenton extended it to her. "Then you can have it all."

He expected some sort of protest but she took it, murmuring a simple "thank you."

Of course he was left with nothing to do but watch her eat it. Fenton only had one sharp knife, which he used for everything from shaving, to opening cans, to gutting enemies. He debated offering it to her, but he didn't trust her enough to hand her a weapon while he was unarmed. Women could be more deadly than their male counterparts.

It was a moot point. Alison had already inserted her finger into the jar and slowly scraped a glob of the sweet, gooey paste onto two of her fingers, which she sucked between her lips. His throat went dry as he watched her pink tongue trace between the digits, chasing the flavor across her own skin.

He imagined her doing the same, not for sustenance but for

hedonistic delight, tasting her own juices while keeping her gaze locked on his.

"This is so good, you have no idea. It reminds me of summer picnics at my Aunt Lola's house. She had this lake in back, with a dock. My mom would take me and my sister, Sally, to her house. The four of us would picnic there with peanut butter and strawberry jam sandwiches. When we were all hot and sticky, we'd jump in the water to cool off."

He didn't know what to say in response, her memory too pure and innocent to be tainted by anything he could possibly utter. Luckily, she didn't seem to mind.

"Aren't you going to have any?"

"I'm not hungry." His stomach growled, belying his words.

Dipping her fingers in the jar again, she scooped it up and held her fingers to his lips. Her eyes were heavy lidded as she whispered, "Share with me. I promise you won't regret it."

3

Did he want her or didn't he? Alison felt like an idiot trying to entice him with peanut butter, but he was so damn difficult to read. Her hand was poised at his lips, and she half-expected him to rebuff her. Her heart pounded as she waited for him to make a decision. When his lips parted, she smiled and fed him from her own fingers.

Those glacial blue eyes flared with heat. She remembered reading that stars that appeared blue were actually much hotter than red or yellow ones. That was what his eyes reminded her of: hot blue stars glittering in the dark of space. Fire and ice, hot and cold, all packaged into one intriguing man.

His tongue twirled over her digits for an achingly long time, cleaning her fingers in the most sensuous way. Her sex grew damp, craving that sort of thorough attention between her legs. She had him on the hook; it was time to reel him in.

Setting the jar aside, she moved even closer to him, pressing her body toward his heat. He stiffened and released her fingers from his mouth. "I don't think—"

Gripping his hair, she stood on her toes and pressed her lips to his in a greedy kiss. He tasted of peanut butter and male spice, a potent and heady combination. She wanted this so badly, wanted him with a compulsion she didn't understand. He was just a man, no different from any other. And men were her specialty.

Nipping his lips playfully, she pulled back, trailing her fingers lightly over his scar and whispered, "Don't think."

Those intense blue eyes went heavy lidded when she brought his hands up to the curves of her breasts. Even as he fondled her through the material, he whispered, "You don't have to do this. You don't owe me anything."

"I know." His willpower impressed the hell out of her. Most men would have had her naked by then, cock poised at one orifice or another. "Maybe I want you. Did you ever think of that?"

Another flash of heat crossed his face when she arched her back, grinding her barely covered mound against the bulge in his pants. He held her, touched her, but the tightness of his jaw belied his struggle to retain control. She needed to tip the scales in her favor.

With a final lick across his firm lips, Alison pulled away and turned her back on him. He sighed audibly, the relief he felt clear. She allowed herself a small smirk as she reached for the hem of the shirt she'd pilfered, drawing it up over her head in one fluid motion, letting the fabric fall to the floor.

He made a strangled sound and she glanced over her shoulder, gratified at his obvious appreciation. Her body might not be as stunning as it once was, but Fenton didn't know that. Though he made no grand gestures, the way he scrutinized her naked form gave her the confidence to saunter back to the bedroom. Feminine power spurred her to put an extra swish in her hips.

Climbing onto the bed, she reclined against the mountain of pillows, keeping her legs together and her hands at her sides. Nervously, she licked her lips. Every erogenous zone tingled with genuine arousal, her nipples formed stiff little points, and the lips of her sex were coated in wetness. She wanted to perform for him, but if he didn't follow her in here, the show would still go on.

He took so long that she almost caved in and started without him. She'd been on autopilot for so long she'd forgotten how sharply arousal could sink its teeth in, blotting out all other thought. Closing her eyes, she suppressed her need to be stroked and petted, instead imagining him watching her touch herself. Men were visual creatures, and Alison loved being watched. It would be worth it when she met his eyes and saw his body respond. His control might be formidable, but she wanted to prove it wasn't infinite.

Sensing she was no longer alone, she opened her eyes and smiled up at him. The thought of teasing him tempted her, but she sensed he wouldn't take it well, that he hadn't made the decision to follow her lightly. The stakes were high, and she wanted a bigger payday than a one-night seduction. She needed to stoke his banked fire, to make it burn hotter for her, to rage out of his tightly leashed control. Desire made even the most cautious lover impatient.

With that thought in mind, she activated her health guard, reached for her belt pouch to retrieve the small bottle of personal lubricant, and spread a small dollop on her hands. Fenton had no way of knowing what it meant for her to use part of her dwindling stash for him. Unlike the thickly scented oils from the brothels, the lube combined with her natural scent would enhance her pheromones as well as ease any penetration. She wouldn't use the precious liquid on any old john, or even for her own pleasure. Once it was gone, her last tie to her former life would be cut. It was her trump card, one it was finally time to play.

Setting the bottle aside, she rubbed her palms together slowly, spreading the slickness over her skin. Starting at her breasts, she massaged the swells, deliberately working her way in to the nipples, holding his gaze the entire time. Her breasts were heavy with arousal, and the reclined position displayed them to her best advantage.

By the time she scraped her thumbnails over her taut peaks, Fenton's eyes blazed, his passionate heat overtaking the cold restraint. Flicking the tips aggressively, she wondered how long it would take to break him down into a rutting beast.

She couldn't wait to find out.

Sliding her right hand down over her belly, she spread her knees to give him a glimpse of her sex. With two fingers, she drew a line down, grazing lightly over her clit and between the puffy lips of her vulva, allowing the lube to mingle and enhance her woman's scent.

His chest rose and fell as he took deep breaths, but still he didn't move. She was dying from a desire so strong the word need didn't begin to describe it. Every erogenous zone ached and throbbed and yearned for his body. Fingers, tongue, cock, she wasn't picky. Her hands were too soft, her fingers too slim where they dipped inside her. Her clit pulsed in time with her rapid heartbeats. Grinding the heel of her hand down on it, she gasped. His eyes glittered in the dim lighting as she started fucking two fingers into her opening, the slickness running down her crease. Her nipples grew tighter still, and she pinched them forcefully—and *still* he didn't break.

Her breathing was completely out of control, the desire to make herself come so strong she had to wrestle her hand out from between her legs. Some instinct told her he'd never bend if she gave in to temptation. This man respected strength, and she had to show him she was more than a needy female body, desperate for release.

He needed to want her more than she wanted him.

Though it pained her to break eye contact, she rolled over, turning her head so one cheek was pressed into the mattress. Raising her ass in the air, she presented him with an open and unobstructed view of her backside. A small groan issued from his position, closer than where he'd stood by the door moments before.

Her lube- and desire-soaked hands roved over her ass, caressing the expanse of skin in smooth, sensual movements. The cool air on her hot flesh made her shiver. Was it her imagination, or could she feel his body heat looming above her?

Deliberately parting her knees as wide as she could, she spread her cheeks apart. Starting from her slit, she trailed the middle finger of her right hand through her moisture and up to the tightly puckered ring. Pressing inward with the pad of her finger, she forced her body to relax and accept the invasion. Anal penetration had never been her favorite sexual activity, but she knew men went wild for it. If fingering her own ass was what it took to make Del Fenton break, she'd do it for hours.

It wasn't working. He hadn't fallen on her, raving with need. Desperation made her movements frantic, not with the need to come, but for him to come to her. His restraint was beyond anything she'd ever encountered. Maybe he'd picked up on her desperation. What more could she possibly do?

Ignore him.

Using her left hand, she played over her sex again, caressing her folds and fucking her channel in time to the penetration of her snug backside. Wet, slick sounds filled the room, and her pheromones practically crackled. She let her mind float, let her imagination take over. In her mind's eye, she saw Del climbing on the bed behind her, using his mouth on her inner thighs and licking slowly inward toward her juicy cunt. Initially she thought she wanted him to fall on her, take her in a vicious fucking that would leave her sore but sated. Now, though, she wanted his slow, methodical deliberation. Wanted to experience the growing anticipation of his tongue tracing her labia in long swipes, his lips surrounding her clit, sucking the bud into his mouth in deep, drawn-out pulls.

Would he use his fingers in her sheath, preparing her body for his massive cock? Or would he spear her with his tongue, over and over until she gushed on his face?

The thought alone had her teetering on the edge.

So lost was she in the fantasy that she hardly noticed when the bed dipped behind her. Hands clamped down on her wrists, drawing them away from the erogenous zones where she'd dabbled. Breath exploded from her lungs as his lips feathered over her spine even as a second set of lips pressed against her mouth. Her shield sizzled, erasing any traces of his DNA from her skin.

The slow, drugging kiss had her so off balance that she didn't notice the blindfold until it covered her eyes.

It was then she realized someone else was in the room, touching her.

"What's going on?"

Fenton knew the second Alison had fought her way free of the heavy fog of lust she'd been mired in. He couldn't fight his desire for her any longer. His body had undergone the phase split as she filled both her openings, so sensual in her abandon. It had started in his cells until he'd replicated into an exact copy of himself, down to the last hair follicle.

Neatly divided in half, he could feel everything, taste every bit of her. One tongue continued following the neat bumps of her spine, while the other flicked over the sweet spot just behind her ear.

"Who else is with you?" Alison shook her head, attempting to dislodge the blindfold.

"No one," he answered honestly. Only a few people knew about the phase split, and he wanted to keep it that way. "Let's take you up on your generous offer."

If she said no he'd stop and secure both versions of himself in the room with the pod until morning. But though she struggled, the scent of her arousal increased. "Have you ever taken more than one man at a time?"

She swallowed, nodded once. "I like to know who I'm fucking, though."

He traced an index finger over her plump lips. "You're fucking me. That's all you need to know." Though both versions of himself could operate independently of one another, he shucked both pairs of pants at the same time and reached for his cocks.

The first time the phase split had happened, he'd been masturbating. His father had warned him of the dangers of getting himself too worked up in any way. The division of self was a genetic anomaly, one only males of their line inherited. It was the reason they were enslaved by the overlord, who feared an ability he didn't possess.

Self-pleasuring took on new meaning with multiple hands and cocks at his disposal, but Fenton had never shifted with a lover before, never shared himself in quite this way. But Alison was different; he couldn't resist her, couldn't hold back any part of himself from her.

Stroking his erections, Fenton adjusted his grips on her arms and flipped her onto her back. Each head bent over a taut nipple, licking the pink peaks into his mouths.

She gasped and bucked up off the bed, trying to force her breasts deeper into his wet heat. The version holding her hands guided them between his legs, urging her to touch his sex. She complied eagerly, rolling his balls the way she might fondle dice in her hands, while the other explored the girth of his rod from base to crown and back again. Her palms were still slicked with the lube she'd used, and her skin glided over his as she tightened her grip.

The unattended cock aimed at her parted lips, seeking the divine pleasure of her mouth wrapped around him. Her tongue darted out, the tip swiping precum from the end. Her personal shield sizzled, protecting her body from him.

"I want to put my mouth on you, to lap at your juicy cunt while you suck that hard cock. Do you want that?"

She couldn't respond, not with her mouth full of him, but the eager way she squeezed his shaft encouraged him. Parting her legs, he ran his fingertips over the silky skin of her inner thighs. "I hope I'll be able to taste you through your shield. I want your flavor on my tongue."

She moaned and his other cock slipped deeper. Dragging her to the edge of the mattress, he let her head hang off the end, making more room for himself between her spread legs. Her tongue swirled around the flange like she was savoring a particularly decadent treat. With the changed angle, he could force his shaft deeper into her throat, but he held back, focusing his attention on his first taste of her juicy sex.

Lying on the mattress, he hooked his arms under her bent-up knees so he could part her legs even wider. Dipping his head, he let his breaths fall directly between her spread thighs, admiring the delicate pink of her labia and the deeper rose hue of her inner folds.

With both sets of eyes fixed on her face, he brought his mouth down to place an open kiss on her sex. She moaned around her mouthful of cock, and he worked the rod in a little deeper even as his tongue penetrated her body.

"Mmmmm," he hummed, enjoying the sweet flavor of her nectar. She creamed for him, more of the delicious syrup spilling into his mouth. He caught as much as he could, but some spilled down into her crease.

He thought about the way she had touched herself and mimicked that attention. Her mouth sucked harder on his length, and he withdrew before gliding it back in.

Moving his focus to her clit, he flicked the nub repeatedly, then suckled the small bundle of nerves between his lips. She arched off the mattress and his cock went all the way down the back of her throat. Though her shield neutralized his saliva, the lube, combined with her own body's response, made her plenty wet.

He could have played with her all day, but the cock in her mouth was ready to explode. With one final lick, he rose up and positioned his other cock at her woman's entrance. "Ready to take me deep into your hot little pussy, beauty?"

She made a noise he took as an assent, and he thrust forward into her welcoming depths.

God, both his cocks were in heaven, coated in her wetness, surrounded by hungry feminine muscles, determined to milk him dry.

He fucked her mouth and her pussy, enjoying the bounce of her tits with each motion. Her small hands dug into the sheets and he sensed her body drawing closer to climax.

Tilting her pelvis up, he braced her legs on his shoulders and fucked her deeper. The version getting the best blow job of his life held her head steady and caressed her cheekbones. The other pressed down on her clit, sending her crashing into release.

Her throat and pussy muscles held him fast, working him relentlessly with every ripple of pleasure. He spurted, hot and thick inside her, shivering at the sound of her shield annihilating his seed.

Slowly, he withdrew both cocks, still semi-hard despite the cataclysmic release. His throat was raw and he could well imagine how hers felt. Shame burned through him as he considered how roughly he'd used her. Whatever her motivation for seducing him, she hadn't deserved to be fucked within an inch of her life until she was limp from exhaustion.

He'd treated her like a whore. No thought to her feelings, just him, using her body however he saw fit. He was no better than those who'd killed Gili.

With a final kiss to her sweet lips, both sets, he recombined himself and left the room.

4

What the hell just happened?

Alison lost track of time as she recovered from her obscenely intense orgasm. Pushing off the blindfold, which she discovered had been fashioned from her whore's half shirt, she looked eagerly around, only to find that Fenton—and whoever his mysterious partner in crime was—had abandoned her.

Unanswered questions swirled through her mind. Who was the stranger she'd taken in her mouth and how had he entered the room without her sensing him? True, her eyes had been closed, but it seemed almost as though one second she'd been alone with Fenton and the next she was being kissed by some unknown man.

Had he been in the apartment with them the whole time? And if so, why hadn't Fenton mentioned him? When she'd asked who was in the room with them, he'd said "no one." If he had a live-in male lover, why deny it?

Even though her body was sated, her mind reeled. If there was another constant lover in Fenton's life, the chances of her persuading him to keep her around were nil. Kinky fuckery aside, two was company but three was a crowd. There would be a constant struggle for power, feelings would be hurt, and eventually someone would be left out in the cold. Damn it, she needed to know who that guy was and how he impacted her plans.

Though her health guard had taken care of any aftereffects from the men, her own desire left her feeling less than fresh. Climbing from the bed, she returned to the hot spring and stared at the pulsing blue and green light from the bioluminescent creatures on the ceiling. She needed an angle, any angle to play, but bluffing without all the information would cost her the game.

Her options were limited. Going back to the brothel now and begging for her job back was not only unappealing, it was risky as hell. That little shark-toothed troll would be hunting for her, and with no idea how close the assassin might be, staying in one place could get her killed. She needed to come clean with Fenton, tell him she was running and ask for his protection, or at least enough money to get her off world.

And he owed her, damn it all, for springing the ménage on her unsuspecting. Though Alison had no moral objections to pleasuring two men at once, she liked to at least have an idea *who* she was pleasuring. Sex with Fenton was meant to be a thank-you for rescuing her, but his pal's BJ put him in her debt.

Decided, she climbed from the water and snagged another of Fenton's clean shirts from the line. A little mouth action might not be enough; they could request another round with both of them inside her to really feel they'd received their money's worth. Her body shivered at the prospect of Fenton working the thick stalk of his erection into her ass while his buddy took his turn with her pussy. *Whatever it takes.*

Padding across the stone floor, she went in search of him. Neither man was in the kitchen, nor did she hear the sound of voices from any of the closed-off rooms. Had he left her alone here?

Weariness overtook her. She was sick of guessing, sick of just scraping by. She eased back into an unusually soft chair that seemed to mold itself to the contours of her body. Curling her legs beneath her, she snagged a worn blanket from the arm of the chair and closed her eyes, letting herself drift.

The screams awoke her, awful, inhuman sounds that ripped through the stillness in the apartment and made her shoot upright in the chair.

The sound came again and she rose to her feet, staggering to the source before she fully thought it through. It sounded almost as though something was being slaughtered, and if she'd been clearheaded she would have run the opposite direction.

Heart pounding in her throat, she moved deeper into the dimness. Several archways led to rooms much like the one she'd already seen, sparsely furnished with a platform bed and hanging rack for clothes. The screams died down and were replaced by a whimpering sound, like that of a small animal with its leg caught in a trap.

A chill gripped her, like icy fingers wrapping around her throat. God, she should run. It could very well be the assassin in there taking out his only real rival. Now was *not* the time for her feet to turn into roots and sink through the stone floor.

"Alison." It was her name that spurred her on, because that was clearly Fenton's voice and he no longer sounded as though he were being tortured. No, now the groan became one she knew well, stemming from a place of desperate need.

Hurrying forward, she stopped when she saw two forms in the bed, both naked with startling erections. Each bucked as his fist clamped down on the massive cock, fucking his own hand in unison.

Her mouth went dry as she watched the spectacle for a moment, but the really startling thing was that both men were ob-viously asleep.

And identical.

Fenton had a twin? One he shared women with and slept next to naked.

"Oh, Alison," they both said again, hands moving in tan-dem.

The bizarreness of the scene did nothing to diminish her arousal at the sight of two gorgeous men pleasuring themselves to thoughts of her. Before she realized it, she moved closer for a better look.

Wait, that was odd, they both had the same scar. She was no geneticist but even if they were identical twins, or had been conjoined twins at some point, the exact same scar at the exact same place didn't seem possible.

Reaching toward the nearest man, she touched his shoulder, torn between wanting to witness the culmination of their hard work and the need for answers. But her touch spurred on an unintended reaction. They arched up, both of them bowing off the bed as pearly white jets shot—coated fists, abdomens, and chests. She held her breath, waiting for one or both of them to wake up.

It didn't happen. Instead the man under her hand surged back toward the other one in an unnatural movement. He didn't roll or shift his muscles in any way. It was more like a powerful magnet drawing metal filings to it.

Into it, until only one Fenton remained.

Air turned to wet concrete in her lungs. What the hell had just happened? She'd seen so many weird things since she left Earth, but this one, this one she couldn't accept.

"Alison?"

She started as she realized Fenton's eyes were open and he was looking at her. His face groggy from sleep, he appeared completely unaware his chest was coated in spooge.

"What are you?" She used all her remaining oxygen to force the question out, needing answers.

He frowned and looked down, touched fingertips to his chest, and rubbed them together. The sharp scent of cum hung heavy in the space between them. Understanding swept across his face, and he leaned his head back against the wall with a dull thump. "Fuck. I split again?"

Her mouth dropped open. He asked it so simply like, *I left the seat up again?* What was next, a token *my bad*?

"Alison." Wiping himself clean with the sheet in a smooth swipe, Fenton moved toward her. "Alison, take a breath."

She tried, but she couldn't get her respiratory system working. It was as though a vise compressed her body together until there was no space left for even a shallow breath. Flapping her hands uselessly in the air, she stared at him, thoroughly panicked.

Her vision tunneled and she fell forward, just as Fenton lunged for her.

Fenton cursed under his breath as he stared out the view port in his suite. Taking Alison with him had been his only option. She'd seen him phase split, and anyone who came looking for him might interrogate her until she told them all she knew about him. Torture her. The people on Hosta might not know his name, but finding him squatting in the former overlord's apartment and discovering that he could split was enough to get him killed.

He couldn't let that happen, not until his mission was fulfilled.

She was still fast asleep. When she'd passed out in his chamber earlier, he'd checked her vitals and, assured that it was only exhaustion and shock that had such an impact on her, he'd dressed and summoned his contact at the docks.

Piggens had raised both his bushy eyebrows when he asked for a travel visa for Alison.

"Is she dead?" the gutter rat had asked.

"Would I need a travel visa for her if she were?"

"She's a right nice piece, but there'll be plenty aboard for you to diddle."

Fenton had just stared the other man down until Piggens withdrew a molecular scanner.

"Payment up-front."

Fenton shook his head. "Payment on receipt of the visa. We'll meet you at the docks." He didn't want to give the man time to run to the patrollers and tell them Fenton was making a run for it.

With Alison's system-approved visa ensured, Fenton had deposited her sleeping body in his bed before opening the door. Most of his pocket money went to ensuring his cargo was secured in a private suite abutting his, and keeping word of it on a need-to-know basis. Scum like Piggens would squeal like the small mammal he was named after if he knew of its existence.

He checked the readouts and then locked it up for the night, returning to where Alison still slept.

The enormity of what he'd done crashed down on him. She lay there in nothing but one of his sister's dresses, owning no clothing, having no credits. He'd taken her off Pental without her permission, and he was completely responsible for her.

Another whore bent on self-destruction. Could he endure this again?

She stirred and looked up into his face. She didn't scream or faint again, thank the stars for small favors. Her hand touched her stomach and she glanced down sharply. "What am I wearing?"

"It belonged to my sister. I needed to dress you in something for traveling."

"Traveling?" Her eyebrows drew together, forming a small

crinkle between them. He stared at it, almost mesmerized by the small gesture.

Perhaps because he didn't want to confess. To have her turn on him, scream at him, maybe even throw things. His sister could be a real brat when he made major decisions without her input.

Shifting his weight onto the bed, he moved closer, ready to pin her if she became violent. "I apologize, but you left me no choice after you discovered my identity."

She looked around and her gaze locked on the star port. Kicking her legs over the side, she rushed forward to get a better view. "You took me off Pental. How?"

How, not *why*. Her reaction made him frown. "I already had passage reserved and I secured you an exit visa. It was a simple matter of credits finding the right recipient."

She turned back to face him, her eyes wide. "A simple matter of credits? Do you know how long I've been trying to scrape together enough to get off world?"

Before he knew it, she was wrapped around him in a strangling embrace. "Thank you, thank you so much. You have no idea what this means to me."

He held her to him, and some tight knot loosened in his chest. She'd been whoring to get off Pental. She wouldn't throw a tantrum because he'd unwittingly given her exactly what she wanted. "You worked as a whore to earn money, to get off world? Why didn't you tell me that?"

"Why didn't you tell me you were leaving Pental?" she asked him back.

He frowned. "I did." But even as he spoke, he recalled that all he'd told her was that he was leaving, not his destination.

She pulled away, though she remained seated in his lap. Her eyes glistened with unshed tears, and if she hadn't been smiling so beautifully, he would have worried she'd cry. Crying women made him twitchy. "I guess this is what we get for not asking more questions of each other, huh?"

She didn't seem displeased about it, or about the erection pressed against her. In fact, she rubbed against him suggestively, almost grinding in his lap. "So tell me more about this phase split."

"Nothing to tell," he muttered, staring at her tits through the thin material of her dress. "It's just something I can do."

"Don't be so modest." She ran her fingers through his hair and pulled lightly, tilting his head back until he met her gaze. "Can you do it whenever you want?"

"No."

She sighed prettily. "You know, on my planet we have this saying: It's like squeezing water from a stone. That's what it's like getting information from you, Del."

Del. No one called him by his given name, not since his sister's death. He liked to hear Alison say it now. "I'm not very interesting."

A smile played across her lush lips as she stroked one finger along his scar. "Oh, on the contrary. I find you extremely . . . fascinating."

He wanted to fuck her, desperately. To rip the dress from her body and bury himself balls deep inside her again. But there were a few things they needed to settle first. "You're not here as my whore. I'm not going to trade you sex for money. When we're in public, you are my intended mate, clear?"

Sinking her even white teeth into that lush lower lip, she nodded once.

"That means you will not trade your body for currency to anyone else for the duration of this trip. Whatever you need, I will find a way to provide it. Agreed?"

"Agreed."

This was too simple; she complied too readily. "I don't expect sex in return for the pleasure of your company. If you want, I can secure separate quarters—"

She silenced him by placing her index finger over his lips. "How would it look for your fiancée to be staying in a separate room?"

"Some people wait until they are unified."

She threw her head back and laughed merrily at that. Struck dumb by the sight of her joy and the feel of her quaking on top of him, Fenton waited for her mirth to subside.

She wiped her eyes. "Fenton, take a good look at me. Do you think anyone would really believe I'm the sort of woman who would wait for commitment?"

Though she no longer dressed like a whore, she moved like a seductress, each swish of her hips and tilt of her head a practiced seduction. "I don't want you to feel obligated to share your body with me."

A small, unevolved part of himself wanted her body, regardless of the circumstances. The male part that could only think of the slickness between her thighs and how many ways he could take her until they were both spent. But the thinking portion, who'd watched his sister be used time and time again, had to make himself clear. "You can say no to me without fear of reprisal."

Alison studied his face for a moment, and he forced himself to hold still while she deliberated. "That's very sweet of you to say."

She thought he was sweet. He barely suppressed a grimace.

"But you see, I *do* require sex, and since you're supposed to be my fiancé, I should probably have it with you."

"Thank the stars," he murmured before lifting her dress over her head to bare her smooth skin to his hungry gaze.

5

Mig Larshe was in a foul mood.

What was the universe coming to when a respectably wealthy Hibariate couldn't buy a whore to nosh on for a night? As he paced around his suite—randy as hell—he debated whether he ought to jerk off or go vent his spleen on Madam Brizella for taunting him with that delectable alien girl with her unbitten skin, only to let her escape into the night with that lousy grunt Fenton.

His teeth ached for flesh, his soul for the cries accompanying a good fuck and feast session.

A knock on his suite door made him jump. "Who's there?"

No reply.

Scowling at the interruption, Mig stomped to the door and threw it open. "What do you want?"

The bipedal male looming in the doorway lacked the iridescent eyes belonging to natives of the Hosta System. His gaze was pitch black, devoid of any feeling. "Mig Larshe, I presume?"

The Hibariate shifted his weight. "Who's asking?"

The stranger pushed past him into the suite. "Close the door."

Mig wanted to sputter at the stranger's audacity, but he found himself compelled to shut the door.

"Come here." The man set a flat plastic card down on the nearest table and depressed a button. A three-dimensional image of a blond woman with hazel eyes and a voluptuous form sprang to life. "Do you recognize her?"

The stranger's voice was low and ragged, as though speaking was an effort.

Mig moved closer to the hologram, tilted his head. "She seems familiar. Wait! That's the whore from earlier, though she's meatier now and not so polished."

"Where is she?"

"She went off with one of the military drones from this system."

"His name." It was a demand, not a request.

"Fenton." Mig narrowed his eyes at the stranger, uneasy that he'd complied so readily. Usually he bartered with his information, did his best to turn a tidy profit before spilling his secrets. Something about the stranger compelled him to speak the truth.

"How do I find him?"

"The barracks on the other side of the bridge, most likely." Mig took a deep breath as his curiosity asserted itself. "Who are you?"

The man deactivated the photo and slipped the plastic card into his pocket before turning his attention to Mig. His irises spilled over into the whites of his eyes as he rasped, "Death."

Those lifeless pits sucked him down into a swirling vortex of agony. Mig gasped as the sensation of thousands of teeth sinking into his flesh, ripping chunks off of him until he was nothing but a bleeding carcass, swept through him. Every female he'd ever bitten now exacted her revenge as he was attacked by hundreds of unseen foes at once. Collapsing onto the hard floor, he groaned, writhing to get away. But the sensation was internal, planted in his mind by the man who made no noise as he left the apartment, with the soon-to-be-mad Hibariate locked inside.

My luck's finally changing.

Alison kissed her savior again, truly enjoying his unique flavor and the way his hands skimmed her body in a worshipful caress. The stars were finally aligning in her favor. On the move again, away from Pental and that awful brothel, and this sexy beast of a man insisted on taking care of her every need.

She shivered as he traced her ribs, his kisses growing bolder by the second. Though she still hadn't come to terms with his replication—or split, as he called it—but really, if that was his worst flaw, she'd learn to live with it.

With that thought in mind, Alison tore her mouth from his, intending to work her way down his body. Activating her health guard, she sent him a wicked smile full of dark promise while unbuttoning his shirt.

Fenton's hands gripped her hips, aligning her bared sex with the bulge in his pants. "Your body delights me."

Her breath hitched a little, though she wasn't sure if it was from the emotion his words evoked or the throbbing of her greedy clit. How she wished he could have seen her at her prime! But the heady knowledge that he took pleasure in her form made her forget all the critical changes and delight in being a woman again.

She hungered for him; her body was eager for his, and her soul yearned for the sweetness shown to her by the rough soldier with a gentle heart. The way he'd insisted that she didn't owe him sex made her want to share it with him even more.

Never had she met a man like him. Or craved a lover so desperately.

"Easy," he said when she ripped the shirt apart, buttons pinging on the floor. "I don't have many clothes with me."

"I'll fix it later." She'd turn into Betsy fracking Ross if it meant Fenton was naked and inside her sooner. Scrambling off of him, she did a one-eighty before mounting back up so she could rub her throbbing pussy against his washboard abs while she attacked the fly of his pants.

Fenton bucked up beneath her when she cupped his cock through the rough material of his trousers. The friction of his stomach against her folds only heightened her need, whittling it to a deadly sharp point. Stroking the hard length of him, she clenched, remembering how he felt buried deep inside her. Eager to repeat the experience, she worked the fastening, set on freeing his stiff prick.

His hand traveled along the length of her spine, a delicate stroke of his fingertips from her neck to the small of her back at odds with her frantic struggle to bare his cock. He adored her body while she mauled his.

Finally, the fabric gave way and she wasted no time in scooting forward, lifting her hips and plunging down until she took him all the way to the root.

His hoarse shout was music to her ears, and she remained still, trembling as she clenched and released with her inner muscles, clutching his body with hers. The penetration should have hurt without artificial lube, but she was so drenched with excitement, it eased the friction of their joining. Knowing he would be coated with her cream turned her on all the more. "God, you feel so good."

Fenton sat up, shifting his angle inside her, driving himself impossibly deeper. His rough palms pulled her back against his chest, his calluses scraped over her stiff nipples. Puffs of air stirred her hair as he whispered in her ear, "You're so hot, so wet. I've never felt anything that compares to being inside of you."

Though she usually preferred raw dirty talk, Alison had fallen completely under Fenton's sensual spell. What woman could resist the things he said to her?

Raising her hips, she began to ride him in slow, gliding strokes. His grip on her torso held her close while allowing her the freedom to gyrate in his lap.

"Yes," she gasped when he slammed up into her.

"I need, I'm going to—" His words broke off and she thought for sure he meant come until another Fenton appeared in the space between his spread legs.

"Let me lick you while I fuck you," they both said.

Words died in her throat as the Fenton before her used his thumbs to separate her labia and put his hot, suckling mouth directly over her pulsing sex.

Sensations overloaded her. His hands were everywhere, tweaking her breasts, holding her thighs wide. One mouth pressed to the hollow just behind her ear, the other licking from where they were joined to the hard button of her clit.

Her hands tunneled through his hair when his lips tugged on her throbbing bud. His hands pinched her nipples in time to the action below, and his cock stirred inside her, hitting every hot spot.

Release swamped her senses. She was no longer in command of her body; he was pulling her strings, making her writhe and twist and clench. Her head fell back against his shoulder, and she gave herself over to him completely.

The one tonguing her cunt held her gaze while he licked a trail of her cream down his own shaft. She shuddered again, doubting she'd ever seen anything so erotic in her life.

"My turn," the one fucking her whispered a second before he lifted her up into the arms of the other one, keeping their bodies joined.

Feeling unbalanced, she reached for the Fenton before her, gripping his shoulders while the other held tightly to her hips and rocked into her hard and fast. She met his gaze a second before he claimed her mouth. She tasted them together, their hot merging even while it was happening a second before her shield obliterated him from her body.

The one not buried inside her gripped his own cock and stroked hard and fast, in time to the pounding inside her. They both came with a triumphant roar, one buried deep in her body, the other marking her breasts for a moment before her shield eradicated his seed into oblivion.

Fenton pulled his cock from her body and set her on the bed. Her eyelids felt heavy, as though they'd been weighted down, but she watched as the two men who'd just rocked her world melded back into one.

His eyes closed. "Are you all right?"

"Never better," she replied honestly. His shoulders sagged in obvious relief. "Come here."

He crawled to her and she deactivated her heath guard so he could lay his head on her breast without the annoyance of her shield zapping every molecule of sweat. "You're not going to hurt me with a little rough sex."

Though he didn't answer, she felt him stiffen, as though he didn't believe her. Quickly she added, "I thoroughly enjoyed that, and I plan to continue enjoying that all the way to . . . ?"

Fenton picked up her cue easily, pulling her over until she sprawled atop him. "The Omicron Theta System. I'm headed to the empath homeworld."

Alison's blood turned to ice in her veins.

Fenton didn't know what happened. One second Alison had been snuggled against him, seemingly content after his total loss of control, and then she'd leapt from the bed while babbling incoherently.

He sat up, his body protesting the quick movement so soon after another round of aerobic fucking. The words spewing from her mouth as she yanked her dress back on made no sense. Something about a frying pan and a fire. Since neither of them was preparing food, he didn't have a clue what she was talking about.

"Alison, slow down, you're not making any sense." He reached for her, but she threw her arms up defensively.

Stung, Fenton sat back. Was this some kind of delayed reaction to his rough claiming? The last thing he ever wanted to do was hurt her beautiful body, she gave him so much pleasure. But once the split took over, he had two minds and he was unable to think beyond the need to fuck her hard and fast, to come on her, in her, fill her up, make her his.

Her eyes were wild as she bolted for the door. "I have to get out of here."

"You can't." Not in this state. He couldn't let her out in public when she was ranting. Though it hurt him to deny her, he wouldn't risk his mission to set her free. "I told you I'd secure you separate quarters."

She pounded on the door, which had been sealed with his genetic code. Frustration radiated from her. Screaming wildly, she struck the metal door. Only once before had he seen a person look so much like a trapped animal. Shoving the memory aside, he reached for his pants. "It's soundproofed. No one will hear you. I promise not to touch you again if you settle down. You have nothing to fear."

She didn't seem to hear him. How could she, over the thudding of her relentless siege on the door?

When he saw the smears of blood she left on the pristine metal, he forgot about dressing and scooped her off her feet. "Stop it, you're hurting yourself."

She screeched again and flailed wildly, but he was through with her tantrum. Dropping her back onto the bed where they'd been blissfully content only a few moments earlier, he pinned her arms on either side of her head. His legs trapped hers between them, ceasing most of her movement. To his shame, his cock stiffened from the struggle, but he made sure to keep it from pressing against her. No need to incite her further. "Alison, you must compose yourself. I won't let you go until you do."

Tears filled her hazel eyes and spilled down her pale cheeks. "Please, let me go."

His gut twisted. "I can't. Believe me, if there was another way . . . I'm sorry."

Sobs broke from her, a horrific, defeated sound, and all the fight seemed to drain from her. Releasing her hands, he moved away, and pain ripped through him when she huddled in the fetal position, making herself as small as possible to minimize damage from an attack.

Oh, how well he knew that mind-set.

Fenton wanted to wrap his body around hers, to physically shield her from any external hurt. But he'd caused this response in her; he had no business touching her.

"I vow on the memory of my family, I will let you go as soon as I possibly can. We'll be in the space lanes for a few weeks, but I won't come near you again. You have my word as a warrior on that."

Turning away, he picked up his ruined shirt and slid his arms through before exiting into the adjacent chamber.

Though the suite was soundproofed from the rest of the ship, her sobs chased him. The door barely hissed closed behind him before he moved into his fighting stance, reaching for his calm center.

You're a fuckup, Fenton. From a line of fuckups. It would be a mercy to put you down now.

Sweat beaded his forehead as he concentrated on the movements of his muscles. But his focus was stuck in the past, haunted by ghosts that lingered in the shadows of his mind. How many times had the overlord threatened his life, or that of his sister? Xander was reputed to be cruel, but Fenton knew from firsthand experience it was the truth brandished like a weapon that cut deeper than any blade.

Doubt had been his constant companion from the day he'd watched the overlord annihilate his father, Raz Fenton. His mother had begged him the night before not to compete. "Think of us. Me and the children and what he'll do to us if you lose."

His father had been arrogant, confident that he could outmatch Xander and end his reign of terror for good. "I must do this, for you and for them. Their futures depend on it."

How right he'd been. After his father's defeat, Xander had taken his mother to his bed, a death sentence in itself. Fenton had huddled with Nella and Gili in their dank cell in the bowels of the palace. His sisters had only been five and seven revolutions old, and they'd cried for their mother the entire night.

His concentration splintered, and he sagged against the door. Pressing the heels of his hands against his stinging eyes, Fenton tried to block out the inhuman sounds of Nella's screams when the guards came for her the next morning. He'd fought, but at only nine revolutions, he hadn't the strength to do more than irritate them. "Your sister's been sold, boy. Settle down or the other one will go on the block next."

"No," Xander had called from the shadows, as Nella's cries grew faint. "For three generations, I've had to defeat the males of your family. You, boy, will be mine from the onset, my tool, my weapon."

"Never!" Del had been coated with blood from his broken nose and split lip, chilled from the hours spent in the damp room. This bastard had killed his father, and his mother too. He would never do anything to help him.

"Oh, I think you will." Xander had leaned in close and whispered, "If you value your other sister's life, you will do exactly as I say."

For a third of a generation, Del had been Xander's puppet, until news of the overlord's defeat at the hands of his son spread through the Hosta System like wildfire. Anyone who was perceived to be loyal to the old regime had been tried, most of them executed. By then both the girls were dead and Fenton had his new mission.

Rising to his feet, he moved closer to his precious cargo, felt the steady reassuring thrum of its energy signature pulsing under his hand. Gili had died for this and he would too, if necessary. He would do everything in his power to ensure Alison wouldn't have to pay the same price all of his loved ones did. She would have been better off with Mig, scarred for life, yes, but physical wounds were simpler to heal than the ones on the inside.

He didn't know how to be gentle with her, no matter how much he wished it were so. He'd been born on a violent world, and given into the custody of a madman. Forged in fire and coated in blood, he'd hidden his tender heart away, until even he couldn't find it anymore. Every person he'd ever cared for had met a horrible and untimely end.

With odds like that, Alison didn't stand a chance.

6

In the wake of her panic, Alison admitted she'd handled the news of returning to the Omicron Theta System badly. So badly that she hadn't seen Fenton in almost an entire day, though she knew he had been back while she slept because he'd left a meal comprised of some kind of roasted meat that tasted like chicken and the purple fruit the Hosta natives served with every dish.

He must think I'm crazy. Was it any wonder? She'd witnessed drug addicts on the subway behaving with more decorum. Beating her hands bloody on the door, for God's sake. What was she thinking?

In short, she hadn't been. She'd reacted to a spike of adrenaline at hearing she was returning to the scene of her crime. Because the one thing she feared more than the assassin tracking her was facing the people she'd helped to enslave.

After she'd eaten, Alison milled about while she waited for Fenton to return. She'd lingered in the tub, but couldn't truly enjoy the indulgence provided by the luxury suite. How could she possibly change his mind? She didn't even know why he wanted to go to the empaths' homeworld. What business could he have there?

From what she'd observed, Fenton clearly battled his own internal demons. Perhaps that had something to do with the trip. She needed more information about him if she had any hope at all of changing his mind.

She combed her hair and stared at her reflection in the mirror. Her hands shook as she worked the wet strands into another braid. With no makeup and wearing a plain dress, she looked so innocent, but appearances could be deceiving. He had no idea of her crimes, and she hoped he never learned. Fenton held all the cards, he was the one with currency, with connections. He was her life pod in the cold depths of space. She couldn't afford to alienate him.

Unable to hold her own gaze, Alison admitted the truth to herself. She didn't want to see the look on his face when he discovered what she'd done. How she'd tricked an entire race of people, covered up the actions of her company, all for profit. Fenton was what her aunt Lola called a "stand-up guy." He would never look at her the same way again once he knew what she'd done.

A tapping on the outer door alerted her a moment before it slid open. Fenton no longer wore his uniform. Instead he'd pulled on black slacks and a blue, skintight pullover shirt that complemented his intense eye color. Muscles bulged in his arms and chest, gloriously defined beneath his clothing. His hair appeared freshly trimmed, and his jaw was cleanly shaven. His hands were clasped behind his back in what seemed to be universal military parade rest. He was imposing, commanding, and she felt slightly pathetic standing before him in her ill-fitting borrowed garb. If she only had one day back on Earth with access to her closet and the neighborhood rejuvi-spa, she wouldn't feel so inferior.

"I'm so sorry." Alison rushed forward, but he held up a hand and she froze under his glacial stare.

"It won't happen again." His tone was definitive.

What *it* was he referring to? Her tantrum? Whatever, she needed to play by his rules for a while, gain his trust back. "Of course."

"I thought you might like to explore the ship, maybe enjoy a meal in the public dining room." He was oddly formal, and she desperately missed the heat his every look had branded on her.

"Sounds lovely. Am I dressed appropriately?" She lifted her chin, allowing his cool inspection. Hard to believe this was the same man who'd made such passionate love to her.

His assessment was brief, and he met and held her gaze without a flicker of emotion. "We'll visit the trade shop first, get you whatever you need to be comfortable."

"Okay." Really, what else could she say?

Fenton moved to the door and pressed his thumb to the pad. The doors swished open. Alison had tried that numerous times, but nothing happened. Fenton waited calmly by the door and she fought the urge to fidget as she approached.

He didn't touch her, but he didn't need to. His energy was all-encompassing. She felt protected, safe, as they moved out into the dimly lit corridor. The floor was soft under her bare feet, made from some kind of synthetic spongy material. The curved walls were smooth and glowed softly, exuding a feel of expensive quality. "What kind of ship is this?"

"A luxury liner. We were lucky one happened to be docked at Pental when I wanted to leave."

Though she doubted Fenton left anything to luck, she nodded. He wasn't much of a tour guide, but then again, she didn't require one. Alison hadn't been born to privilege, but she took to it like a duck to water whenever the opportunity arose. She might be barefoot and wearing borrowed clothes, but confidence could pull off any ensemble. Passengers nodded politely as they passed by and she offered the same in return.

Fenton guided her down a long ramp to the level below. The palatial shop that greeted them must have been the trade shop. Colors and fabrics she had no words for bombarded her every which way she turned.

Fenton would have gone in, but Alison gripped his elbow and pulled him to the side. "Do I have a spending limit?"

Something that looked a lot like guilt flashed in his eyes, but he buried it quickly in an icy avalanche. "Get whatever you need."

"You might regret that." She warned him once, but the idea of shopping, truly shopping for the first time in over two years, had her bouncing on her toes.

He didn't repeat himself, just stared her down. He insisted and she wasn't about to refuse. Money clearly wasn't a concern for him. He could probably gamble back whatever she spent in under an hour anyway.

"Don't say I didn't warn you."

How much could one woman possibly need?

Fenton's lips parted as he watched Alison swoop through the shops like a cosmic storm. He'd thought her warning over her potential purchases had been unnecessary but as he watched her pick out another pair of ill-advised footwear, he realized he'd underestimated her. She was incredibly fussy, but when she found something she liked, she paid no heed to the price tag. Fenton doubted the overlord himself could have picked out finer items.

After the first few hours, he leaned against a pillar to wait. A harried-looking clerk asked for his genetic scan, probably hesitant to make any of her demanded alterations before he verified they had enough universal credits to cover the purchase. Fenton prepaid for whatever she would need. Money mattered to him very little, and the genuine pleasure she derived from spending it was worth it.

He owed her this at least.

With half the attendants in tow, Alison stood at the eye of a frenetic hurricane. She made a sharp, slashing motion over a purple bolt of cloth indicating a cut, then turned and *winked* at him. His heart rate sped up with that simple connection and he looked away first.

"Excuse me." The salesgirl moved forward, handheld scanner aimed at him. "Would you mind standing straight so I can verify your measurements?"

"I don't need anything." Fenton scowled.

"Your wife ordered it." The girl waited patiently. "She said one of your shirts had been damaged and she wanted to replace it."

"No need." He sent the girl off with a wave. His body stirred as he recalled exactly how Alison had damaged his shirt, in a frenzy to get him naked. She pouted prettily at him now, but on this, he would not be moved. With a shake of his head he mouthed the word *wife?*

She shrugged and turned back to her minions.

He'd told her she needed to pretend they were involved, but from the little he knew of Earth customs, a wife was a full-fledged life mate. Even pretending that she was his stirred his possessive instincts. He'd never responded to a woman the way he did Alison, not sexually, nor with the unsettling tenderness that softened his actions. He needed to keep his icy reserve in place. Opening up to her was not an option.

She'd already forced him to cross too many lines.

"Ready?" Alison's soft voice broke him from his reverie. He blinked, startled at the transformation. She'd donned a bright blue dress, much more ornate than the simple sheath garment she'd been wearing. It caught the light and shimmered with her every move, sluicing over her formidable curves to just below her knees. Her hair was still tied back in a braid, but a length of fabric that matched the dress had been woven into it, creating a more polished and modern look. Her shoes were silver, with high wedge heels, revealing freshly painted toenails and a small silver bracelet around one ankle.

"This isn't going to work." The words escaped before he could call them back, and her face fell.

"You don't like it?"

He took his time, considering her from head to toe. How could he explain that he liked it too much? That she drew too much attention? Notice he was desperate to avoid?

Perhaps saying something callous, hurting her feelings, would be the smartest move. Yet one glance at her exquisite face and, for the first time in his memory, Fenton didn't want to take the smartest course. Not if the toll was injuring her in any way.

"You look lovely, a beautiful shine on a rare gem."

His reward was her radiant smile. "Thank you. For everything. No one has ever given me so much for so little. I wish you'd let me repay you in some way."

To the curious ears of the post workers, she could have been referring to the shirt he refused, but Fenton was nothing if not cautious. Taking her hand in his, he lifted her knuckles to his lips, in a gesture he remembered his father using on his mother. As the only role models for a genuinely affectionate couple he had to go by, he hoped it was sufficient. "The pleasure of your company is the only payment I crave."

Alison blinked, as though genuinely startled, and he turned to instruct her purchases be delivered to their rooms. Placing a hand on the small of her back, he escorted her from the store to the grandeur of the promenade deck.

He'd been a little worried about Alison's deportment. Needlessly so, because she fell right into the role of a prestigious lady. He'd had his suspicions about her from the beginning, but her ease at transitioning from *demjong* whore to his doting wife, at least publicly, was without reproach.

He requested a private table, and since the hour was early for the last meal, they were seated on the much-coveted balcony overlooking the central view port. Below them the starscape spread out in an endless blanket of glittering possibilities. Two months ago, Fenton had never been off the central planet of Hosta, had never seen anything but oceans of ice or sand. Now he was speeding away from his home via the space lanes, never to see Hosta again. The change unsettled him.

"Are you all right?" Alison asked, staring at his ruined face instead of the view.

He was about to wave off her concern, but hesitated. Maybe it would be better for the two of them to get to know one another, instead of hiding everything. It could only help with the ruse to understand a few basics at least. "This is only my second time with space travel. First leaving the Hosta System."

Her eyebrows drew down. "Really? That's surprising, considering you were part of the military."

"Ground force only." The overlord wanted to keep him close to home. He'd been forced to stage an unspeakable betrayal to be granted his post on Pental. One he hoped to make amends for at some point. "How about you? You seem to have . . . adapted well."

The corner of her bow-shaped mouth kicked up. "Adaptation has always been my specialty."

He wanted to ask more, to know what put that sparkle in her eyes, but the server came over to recite the specials.

Alison listened, then looked to him expectantly. Fenton had no idea what anything was, since he'd grown used to surviving on military rations. If it was edible and would keep him alive, it was fair game. Gourmet dining wasn't part of his training. "Go ahead and order for both of us."

Her shoulders straightened and her chin went up. She rattled off pronunciations for his native dishes he had trouble with, along with two servings of Risgale.

"One. Just water for me," Fenton corrected and dismissed the server with a wave.

"I'm sorry, you don't drink alcohol?"

He shook his head. "Believe me, I'd like nothing better than to load up on mind-numbing substances, but it isn't an option."

She licked her lips, clearly intent on asking another question, but stifled it and turned to face the window. Her delicate profile was beyond compare as she studied the stars.

He cleared his throat. "I've been thinking about our *arranged* marriage."

"Oh?" She looked back at him, tilted her head to the side. He stared at her forehead so he didn't get lost in her eyes, flecked with green and brown and gold, swirling into infinity.

"We've undergone a serious commitment. It would be a good idea for us to get to know one another a little bit."

"You mean, other than in the biblical sense?"

His translator chip didn't pick up her meaning, but her wicked expression conveyed her message. His cock twitched with interest but he shifted, his course set.

"Yes. Tell me about you."

"What do you want to know?"

Everything, Fenton thought. "About your life on Earth. Your family. You mentioned some female relatives. Do you keep in touch?"

She shook her head and waited for the server to drop off their drinks. "No. Even before I left Earth, Sally and I hadn't spoken in some years."

"Sally's your sister, right?" He recalled the name from before.

"Yes. She didn't exactly approve of my life choices."

"What about your mother? And your aunt?"

"You have a very good memory for details."

Since it was part of his training, he shrugged the compliment off and waited while she took a sip of her drink. "Are you sure you want to hear this? It's an ugly story, not really polite dinner conversation."

"I promise, nothing you say will ever be repeated."

Setting her drink aside, Alison took a deep breath. "Well, first off you should know that Lola wasn't really my aunt, at least not by blood. She was my mother's lover."

It took every ounce of his control not to react to that statement. Two women, together? On Hosta it was a crime punishable by death. Men could only seek out the same sex as part of the ranking, but men were different, more sexual. For women to shun men completely . . . Fenton couldn't imagine the sort of freedom Alison had grown up with.

Alison stared out the window, oblivious to him. "They'd been best friends since they were little, and while Lola always knew what she was, my mother was determined to be married to a man, have a traditional family. You see, on Earth, there's this ideal of a happily-ever-after and even though it doesn't really exist, we're all brought up watching movies and television shows where there's a mom, a dad, kids, maybe a dog. They all live together in a house and it's supposed to be perfect, or as close to perfect as real people can get. Mom's family was old-fashioned and she bought in to that. She married my father instead of following her heart, and it cost her everything."

Before he knew what he was doing, Fenton reached across the table and covered her hand with his own. It had been ages since he offered comfort to anyone, but the pain and sorrow in Alison's tone called out to him. He wanted to soothe her hurt, take the pain from her any way he could. "If this upsets you, you don't have to continue."

She offered him a watery smile. "I've never told this to anyone before. It hurts but it's a good hurt, you know?"

He had no idea what she was talking about, but didn't mind.

The feel of her soft skin beneath his calloused hands was addictive. His thumb brushed across her knuckles exploring the delicate structure of her hand while waiting for her to continue.

"So anyhow, my father, though wealthy with a shiny public image, was an abusive drunk. He never went after me or my sister, but Mom was fair game. He was a smart son of a bitch too. Never hit her face or anywhere that wouldn't be covered by clothing. I think he knew that she didn't really want to be with him, and he resented her for that."

Fenton's throat closed up. "A man should always protect the woman in his care. On my world he would have been banished to the Northlands for such actions."

"If only. No one knew, other than Lola. When my mother finally decided to leave him, she had no money, nowhere to go. Lola took us in. We lived with her for years, until he found her. Found them."

She paused in her narrative, her eyes filled with emotion. She wouldn't cry, though. Alison wasn't a crier, especially not in public. She had a warrior's heart, and he couldn't help admiring the hell out of her.

"He killed them, with a laser rifle. I was away at college, and Sally was at a friend's house. I think he planned it that way, planned to make it look like a break-in gone wrong, but Lola had compiled a file against him. I didn't know about it until after the fact. She'd been trying to convince Mom to report him to the authorities. Mom was too scared, though, of his power, his connections. She thought he'd forget about her and leave us alone. It was a mistake that cost her her life."

Fenton closed his eyes, squeezed her hand. He didn't offer her any words of comfort because they were just that—words, empty and meaningless. Tragic loss was heartbreaking and soul-crushing. No doubt the trauma she'd suffered had shaped her entire life. That she'd survived and even flourished afterward impressed the hell out of him.

"So he had to pay for his actions?"

She withdrew her hand, offered him a reassuring smile. "Life sentence, which turned out to be only six months. He died in a prison riot."

"So justice was served."

"I guess." A shadow crossed her face and he wondered what she was thinking.

Their meals were served, an assortment of delicacies from stuffed gourds to spiced meats. Alison picked at the offerings on her plate, but without her usual zest.

"Aren't you hungry?"

She shook her head. "My appetite's gone."

He stood and pressed his thumb to the menu, paying for the meal and ordering the same dishes to her room in three hours. "Let's go."

Extending his arm he waited.

"You haven't eaten anything." Those beautiful multihued eyes scrutinized his face.

His hand went to his scar automatically, wishing it wasn't a part of him, that she wasn't forced to behold such ugliness when her life's cup spilled over with it. "I'm fine. I want to show you the ship."

She took his arm, then stood on her toes to kiss the ruined flesh on his face. "You have nothing to be ashamed of."

If only he could believe that.

7

Guilt was eating Alison alive. Talking about what her father had done made her realize what a monster she'd become. She didn't dwell on the sins of her parents—her father's pride and bloodlust, her mother's weakness—but telling Fenton about them and watching his reactions made her question her past actions.

True, she'd never taken a laser rifle to someone, but she'd been hell-bent on destroying Gen, Rhys, and anyone who stood in her way. Just like her father. Her own personal sin was greed, and it had turned deadly during her tenure at Illustra.

She wondered what sort of justice would be fitting according to Fenton. Alison wished she could leave him, find a new patron. Credits equaled freedom, and being dependent on someone else, especially such an upstanding man, made her twitch.

She wanted to sully him, to knock him off of his holier-than-thou pedestal and drag him down into the muck with her. It was petty, but she'd feel like less of a parasite if he was just as flawed. She might be a weak and disgusting creature, but so was he, and she only needed to get him back into bed to prove it.

Patiently, Alison walked by his side, feigning interest in the ship's various services. Every luxury she'd ever imagined was offered, beauty treatments from old provincial to DNA contouring. She could become someone else entirely, someone taller, thinner, blond, and beautiful.

But for the first time in her vanity-driven life, Alison wasn't worried about her exterior. Because a man she truly wanted, a man capable of incredible generosity and kindness, desired her just as she was. She couldn't even resent him, or his money, because his every word, his every glance, was focused on her. She'd tried to buy him a shirt made from that celestial material, to make up for the one she'd damaged, but he'd refused. Did he *want* her to feel inferior, indebted to him? His lack of demands only doubled her guilt and unease.

Consumed by the need to even their playing field, she pulled him into a private sauna a deck above theirs and stripped off her fabulous dress. One thing that was not universal: undergarments. She sashayed up to his side, wrapped her arms around his neck, her invitation clear.

His hands cupped her shoulders, held her at a distance. "Alison, don't."

"Why not?" She skimmed her hands over her breasts, her nipples puckered with desire. "If this is the only way you'll let me repay you, I've got my work cut out for me."

"No." He shook his head, bent, and picked up her dress. "Not like this."

She glanced around the small steam room in confusion. "You mean here?"

He extended the hand clutching the material, not meeting her eyes. "I mean, not for repayment. I told you, I don't want that."

The fingers that wrapped around the dress were numb. "You mean you don't want me."

He didn't contradict her, and even despite the heat she shivered. Maybe she should have booked an appointment for the DNA contouring after all. Another possibility occurred to her. What if it had nothing to do with her body, but instead with what she'd told him? It had been a calculated risk, opening herself up to him that way, but she thought he'd appreciate her honesty.

It looked like she'd thought wrong.

Pulling her beautiful dress back on, she moved past him out into the common corridor. He fell into step beside her silently, both of them lost in their own thoughts.

She knew without a doubt that she was his captive now. If he refused to take her body in trade, she had no cards left to play. It was one thing to be a whore, another to be a whore no one wanted.

Fighting tears, she strode into her quarters. He hesitated at the threshold. "Thank you for accompanying me."

"Of course." She couldn't look at him, didn't want him to see how much his rejection stung.

"Do you need anything?"

You. The idle thought stuck in her head. He had all the power. She wanted him more than he desired her, he had the money, the connections. She was completely without value, a pet that he locked up when he went off to do whatever it was he did. She had only one option left, the most unpalatable of all.

She had to tell him the truth.

Staring at the starscape she whispered, "Please don't take me to the empaths. They'll kill me."

He didn't reply, but she heard the *hiss* of the door shutting, sensed he was still in the room. Playing games no longer made sense; he was on a winning streak. Better to throw herself on his mercy and hope he had some.

His hand landed on her shoulder, and she fought the flinch. It wasn't a sexual gesture, but one of comfort and connection. One she didn't deserve.

Spinning her to face him, he tilted her chin up and stared into her eyes. "They are a race of pacifists. Why would you think they would hurt you?"

Her throat closed up and she shut her eyes.

He continued to study her, his eyebrows drawn down. "It's crucial to my mission that I contact an alchemist there. From everything I know, they are a welcoming, peaceful people. You don't have to go planetside with me, if you are frightened, but if you have information that might affect me, please, tell me now."

Her teeth sank into her lip and she shook her head.

His knuckles skimmed over her cheek. "You are under my protection, and I vow I will see you safe. Try and get some rest."

The doors hissed again and Alison sagged onto the bed. What the hell was she going to do? Could she really ask him to trust her when she couldn't bring herself to trust him?

Something beeped, breaking her out of her miserable downward spiral. Scowling, she rose to her feet and searched for the source of the noise. Someone tapped on the door.

"Your delivery from the ship's post," a female voice called through the door.

She had no way of opening the door, but perhaps the crew had some kind of override. "Bring it in."

The door hissed open and for a second she considered bolting, but dismissed the idea. Where could she go? She had no weapons, no money, and Fenton was bound to find her. Next time he might chain her to the bed instead of buying her a king's ransom in pretties.

A woman with orange hair and gray skin pushed a hover

cart into the room and smiled at Alison. "Where would you like these?"

"Closet, please." She watched as the attendant stowed her new purchases. On Earth, clothes could be replicated, except for designer copyrighted material, which was wicked expensive. Alison had splurged on an original Orbit cocktail dress when she'd been promoted out of the field. Mark Orbit had designed a stunning sapphire and gold confection that she'd no longer fit in. Her new threads might not be Orbit originals, but she was just as happy to see them.

Another summons at the door made her jump, but luckily gray girl was too entrenched to notice. "Enter."

This time a young man with a more typical skin tone and violet eyes pushed in a cart of food. "Your husband ordered a few savories for you."

"He's too good to me." Alison smiled to hide her surprise. "Don't tell him that, though."

The server, obviously a consummate professional, tipped his head. "Of course not. Where would you like me to set this up?"

She tapped her lips as she examined the tray. Somehow she doubted Fenton would return to her room that night. "The window seat, so I can take in the view, will do nicely."

"Of course." He set the tray down and turned to her. "My name is Evers. If you need anything else, just call for me."

Since he'd offered . . . "Would you mind digging up something for me to read? I'm afraid my bags were lost on the space station, and I'm a little stir-crazy without my news feeds."

Evers dug in his shiny silver pants pockets and pulled out a small round ball. "Sector news feed, updated hourly. Just plug this in to your view screen and punch in your room number."

"You're a lifesaver." She smiled at him and was gratified to see him blush. Knowing she could wrap a young server around her little finger eased the sting of Fenton's rejection. "Charge it to the room, if you would."

He ducked his head in what she supposed passed for a bow and then left with the gray girl.

Lifting the lids of the covered dishes, Alison found the same delicacies she'd ordered at dinner. He'd ordered the same food she had, had it delivered fresh to her. He didn't want sex, yet he still treated her like a queen. Would she ever understand him?

The news sphere was warm to the touch, as though it retained her body heat. She saw the indentation beneath the viewer and settled the round object in it. Immediately the screen flashed to life, displaying what looked like a city in the desert. Alison stepped away. Below the photograph alien words were scrawled. Some looked like hieroglyphs; none made any sense to her. Obviously, English was not an available option.

Irritated, she smacked her palm against the screen, then jumped when a voice-over narrative started to play. It was like a news broadcast, she realized, the calm, cool voice reading of death and destruction on the main planet of the Hosta System. Settling down, Alison began to eat as she watched the alien news.

The overlord's palace has been overrun by the oppressed natives of Hosta. The new government is offering rewards to anyone with information that will help bring the war criminals who'd supported Xander's reign of terror to justice. At the top of the most-wanted list is the former commander of the Northern territories, the overlord's former ward. His identity is still unknown as the hall of records burned in the uprising. Rumor has it he never participated in a ranking ceremony due to his ability to phase split.

Alison choked on the bite of fruit she'd just taken. Spitting it out into her napkin, she moved closer to the screen.

His whereabouts are currently unknown, but the elected representative of the people of Hosta promises that anyone with information leading to this war criminal's capture should contact him directly.

Was it possible?

Alison removed the sphere and rolled it between her palms as she paced. It fit, the fact that Fenton could phase split, as he'd called it, that he never talked about his past, or elaborated on his mission. He'd only brought her with him after she'd seen his ability firsthand. Was it because she knew too much?

She shook her head. He was so noble, so generous in every way, she couldn't believe Del Fenton was the war criminal the news feed made him out to be.

An insidious voice hissed in her ear. *No one is that good. What do you really know about him? Are you willing to bet your life on a few hours of pleasure?*

He'd turned her away the last time she made an advance, for no apparent reason. He'd been so hot for her before, so what had caused the reversal in his behavior? Now that she thought about it, she'd expected him to have a stronger reaction to her telling him the empaths wanted her dead.

What if he'd already known who she was? What she'd done? Alison thought he'd grown tired of her, but perhaps it wasn't about her lack of sex appeal. Instead his own guilt over what he planned to do squelched his physical desires.

Her imagination took over from there, leaping to conclusions she had no proof of, but feared were correct. Perhaps the reason he was so insistent on going to the empaths' homeworld was to get rid of her under the guise of seeing justice served.

If it was true, she had no choice but to beat him at his own game.

Alison restarted the news and settled down to watch and learn all she could about the war criminal. If her suspicions were correct and Fenton planned to betray her, she had to beat him to the punch.

Through the door separating their rooms, Fenton heard the murmur of voices as Alison received her clothing and food. The words were too low for him to make out, but he thought she sounded pleased.

He paced the confines of his secret chamber, restless and turned on. He wanted to go to her in the worst way, to commune with her on a primal level after all she had shared. She was a survivor, a skill he admired and envied. Saying no to her advances was one of the most difficult things he'd ever done. If he were free, he'd take her in his arms, hold her, ease into her pliant body again and again until they both came unraveled.

His gaze automatically slid to the pod, a visual reminder that he wasn't free to do what he wished, to trust her, or even to cede to her demands that they not go to the empaths' homeworld. His course was set; he must find the alchemist who resided on a private island there and hope the intelligence he'd gathered from light-years away was trustworthy.

Though he knew it wasn't rational to be angry at the dead, he couldn't help balling up his fists as he thought of his family, all who had left him alone on this plane, cursed and burdened while they set off on their next adventure. The room seemed to vibrate and he sucked in air sharply, focusing on a spot on the wall. Phase splitting from anger was the last thing he needed to do right now. He knew better than to let himself get so wound up.

If he couldn't fuck, perhaps he could fight off his excess energy. Alison and the pod were as safe as they could be. He'd hacked the passenger manifest to be sure no last-minute additions had come aboard. No one knew who he was, who she was. No one was after either of them.

His mind made up, Fenton departed his quarters and headed down to the combat holo-ring. The ship's promotional material had listed the holo-ring programs to be state-of-the art, uniquely engineered to suit all the passenger's needs, from exercise programs to exotic getaways.

Right now, what Fenton needed more than anything was to beat the hell out of someone, exorcise a few ghosts, and exhaust his backlog of unused energy.

The suite was unoccupied when he strode in, the beige walls looking no more remarkable than the empty closet in his cabin. Pressing his thumb to the credit panel, he waited while his universal credits were deducted and a small box containing six silver disks slid out of the wall.

Attaching the self-adhesive side to his pulse points, he imagined the gambling hell at Madam Brizella's the night he'd met Alison. Too much had been at risk that night for him to lose control the way he'd wanted, but now, with all he protected secured . . .

Closing his eyes, he imagined the room just as it had been before he'd won Alison. Her at the bar, Mig making that stupid bet. The sounds, the smells, the charged and almost desperate air. The murmur of voices, the feel of his uniform against his skin. He held the image there, allowing the ring to absorb his memory and project it into reality.

Someone bumped into him, jolting him from his concentration. Lifting his lids, he smiled in grim satisfaction as he saw the Hibariate perched on his stool, sharp teeth gleaming. Alison, back in her whore's garb, clutched her arm where the fiend had bitten her.

For the first time in his life, Fenton released his control. With a roar of rage, he picked up the Hibariate replica and flung him across the room. The scrape of chairs and the shatter of glass filled the small space. Around him, fights broke out, fists connecting and men grunting. Whores ran for cover—all but Alison, who watched him with a mixture of hope and awe in her beautiful eyes.

Mig recovered quickly and launched himself in a counterattack. The force that knocked Fenton onto his back felt real, and his training kicked in along with a surge of adrenaline. Though the Hibariate was half his size, he fought viciously, keeping Fenton on his toes.

Someone hit him across the back with a solid object, probably a bar stool. Mig took advantage and sank his teeth into Fenton's thigh. The pain was all too real, and dots floated before his eyes.

Tucking down into a roll, he tumbled forward. The sudden move shook the Hibariate free and more blood gushed from his leg. Alison rushed forward, cloth in hand. "Are you all right?"

Her concern sounded genuine, and for a moment, Fenton forgot that this was all just a product of his fantasy. Ignoring the pain, the chaos surrounding them, he clasped his hand around the back of her neck and pulled her lips down to his. The kiss consumed him as her sweet mouth sealed over his, her soft body rubbed against him in an evocative way. As his desires changed, so did the setting. The bar faded away, and between one heartbeat and the next, they were back on board the cruise ship. His leg was healed and her clothes were gone, so there was nothing to stop his questing hands as they explored her luscious form.

Nothing except the clapping. One pair of hands in a slow rhythm that seemed to mock him. The discordant sound, probably some defect in the program, brought reality back to Fenton with collision-course impact. Shame burned through him and he ripped the disks off his pulse points.

The clapping continued. Turning his head, he saw a tall, lanky man leaning against the doorway. His skin was deathly white, his hair cropped to his skull. He wore an ill-fitting ship's uniform, the sleeves too short and the shirt too loose for his lean frame. At first glance he didn't appear to be much of a threat, but one look into his soulless black eyes had every hair on Fenton's arms standing on end. This man was a killer.

"Del Fenton. You are a difficult man to find."

"Who are you?" Fenton scowled at the intruder.

"One who seeks. I believe you have something I've been looking for." His smile was the most unpleasant sight Fenton had ever beheld.

He opened his mouth to respond but pain flooded over him, a tidal wave that made the injuries he'd sustained via the holo-ring seem like mere annoyances. Panting, he fell to his hands and knees, willing the agony away.

Shiny black boots moved into his line of sight as the man stood over him. The agony abated but left every muscle twitching.

The stranger's voice was low and even, as though they were discussing new trade routes over drinks. "Now, tell me. Where is Alison Cartwright?"

"Go fuck yourself." Fenton gasped as the searing blaze consumed him again.

"I was going to make this easy on you." The man crouched down, his dark eyes like gates to the void as he watched Fenton writhe. "A quick death, unlike the Hibariate. I can show compassion when I choose to. Just give me the whore and it'll all end. No more needless suffering."

Again the shock as the torture shut off left him gasping. His eyes watered and his throat had closed up. Death would be a relief for him, not just from the stranger and his abilities but because his burdens were so heavy.

"What are you going to do with her?" Del wheezed.

His torturer actually smirked. "Does it matter? She's just a whore."

Just a whore. Like his sister. Not really a person, just a thing to be used and discarded. Clarity broke through the haze of pain. Fenton suffered because he was the only one who cared. Without him, Alison would be left at the mercy of this evil bastard.

In that moment, he recognized that he'd done his best for

Gili and he could do no less for Alison. If he was to die either way, he would die as her protector.

Distantly he thought of the pod, his mission, his promise, then let it go as he stared into the face of destiny.

"Last chance, Fenton. Be smart. Tell me, where is Alison?"

"Right here, you sick fuck," she said from behind him.

8

Alison's plans to confront Fenton were jettisoned into space as she met the assassin's soulless gaze. She'd been running from him for so long, afraid of what he'd do when he caught her, that witnessing him coercing Fenton to relate her whereabouts was like a dream.

But the blood trickling from Del's ears and nose were all too real. Seeing him bleed, almost ready to die for her, caused something to shift in her mind. Hell, maybe she had snapped because instead of running, she stood her ground and lifted her chin, her eyes trained on her doom.

"Alison? It's been so long, I hardly recognize you." His smirk told her he found her downhill slide into homeliness amusing.

"A lot of things have changed." Fenton lay still behind him, showing no signs of movement. Was she too late?

"Indeed. You've led me on a merry chase, and were much more resourceful than anyone at Illustra ever imagined. And here I always thought you were just a pretty face."

Another dig she let roll off her back. "Leave him alone, he's just a john I've been using. Not his fault his dick got him into trouble."

The assassin actually smiled, an unpleasant twist of cruel lips. "Oh, you poisonous harpy, how you wound the male ego with your sharp barbs. And here the poor fellow was falling in love with you. You should have seen the fantasy I interrupted. That'll teach him."

She'd forgotten how much the assassin loved the game of cat and mouse. How he liked to play with his prey. "Only if you let him live, so much the wiser. Illustra has no gripe with him, and I've told him nothing of value."

Those empty eyes narrowed to snake-like slits. "You told him about *you*. Why is that? You were never the type to share with your coworkers, let alone a mark. What makes this one different?"

She shrugged. "He wasn't. It was just another tactic to keep him interested. He likes to play the hero, rescue the baby bird with the broken wing. I thought my tragic past would help sway him." Fenton stirred, still out of it. If she could only keep the assassin talking long enough, maybe they could figure a way out of this.

"I think you're lying. One way to find out."

Time wasn't on her side as the throbbing started in her skull. Memories she'd suppressed, things she'd buried in the darkest recess of her mind flowed to the forefront in a barrage of images and the feelings attached to them. Summer at the lake with her mom and Sally, her first training session as a pleasure companion, the screams of the empaths as they were contained, the connection when she met Fenton's gaze the very first time.

Her knees hit the deck as sensations bombarded her, every feeling in the range of human emotion churning in a frothing sea of shattered glass, cutting her, making her bleed until she was in danger of drowning in her own blood.

Then it stopped, left her huddled and panting on the floor

with tears tracking down her cheeks. She cried silently, all too aware that she'd reached the end.

The assassin crouched down, so he could meet her gaze once more. "Just as I suspected. Sometimes I hate being right."

His words made no sense, but since her brain had been scrambled like an egg, she wasn't surprised. "Let him go."

One midnight eyebrow rose. "Self-sacrifice even? From you? Will wonders never cease?"

He was a maggot, a disgusting filthy malevolent bottom-feeder who gorged himself on other people's pain. Fenton stirred again and she swallowed hard as she met and held his gaze. "I'll give you whatever you want. Just let him go."

He actually sneered at her, bringing his black-gloved hand to circle her throat. "You're not my type. Good-bye Alison."

All the air seemed to be sucked from her lungs in a rush. She writhed, struggling to breathe, to fight even though she knew it was impossible. Her vision tunneled and filled with little black dots and her mind fuzzed over.

A clang resounded through the room and the pressure on her chest eased. She sucked in air gratefully, coughing, and struggled to sit up.

Even though he still lay on the floor with his back to her, Fenton also stood over her, holding a large metal chair. The assassin had crumpled to the deck in a heap, obviously unconscious.

Tossing the chair aside, Fenton knelt down and ran his hands over her. "Are you all right?"

"Yes," she wheezed and coughed again. "Thank you."

He helped her to her feet just as his other self rolled to a crouch. They circled the assassin, the intention to finish him off clear.

Panic filled her. "Wait! You can't kill him!"

"Watch me," the Fentons growled in unison.

"If you do, it'll release a plague on the entire sector."

The Fentons froze, still poised to attack. "How?"

"His brain has been genetically altered. If he dies, the space where his mind was will act like a vortex, sucking in all the brain waves for a light-year. He's the ultimate killing machine, programmed to take out his targets by any means necessary."

Slowly, Fenton recombined himself, then looked to her. "So how do we beat him?"

She shook her head. "I have no idea. That's why I've been running, hoping to evade him. If not for your gift, he would kill us both. He's telepathic and telekinetic and I've heard he can even take control of other people, like possession."

"Then we are left with only one option." Taking her hand in his, he led her from the room. Once the door closed behind them, he pulled a panel from the wall and yanked the wires out, sealing the room off.

"That won't hold him for long."

"It doesn't have to." Fenton tugged her through the corridors of the ship, heading back to her room.

"I don't think I should bother packing," she argued as he tugged her through the door.

Fenton ignored her, instead going to the window seat. He rattled off a few commands, and the seat itself flipped over into a smooth 3-D command console. "Do you know how to fly?"

"Not well," she admitted, moving to his side. "What is this?"

"The reason I chose this particular suite of rooms. Here's propulsion, docking clamps, navigation, communication." He pointed each system out. "We can't go fast but we can go. And you're flying because I know nothing about space travel."

"The suite is a ship?"

"We don't have much time, Alison."

Taking a deep breath, she released the docking clamps. The entire room listed downward, and a giant shudder rocked them.

"What heading?" she asked.

He rattled off coordinates as if by rote. She had no idea where that course would take them or what he had planned next.

Fenton grabbed her around the waist with one hand and braced them against the bulkhead. Anything not bolted down tumbled forward and he grunted as various objects hit him.

"Sorry," she said, fighting for altitude.

"I knew it was a bad idea to let you purchase so much stuff." His tone was light, teasing almost.

The ship righted itself and she took a deep breath as she set their course. "If I didn't know better, I'd think you were enjoying yourself."

The hand around her waist tightened, and she shivered as he breathed into her ear, "Maybe I am."

His hard body pressed into hers, and there was no mistaking his erection. Unbelievable.

"Seriously? What about that turned you on?" After engaging the autopilot, she turned to face him.

He nuzzled the side of her neck. "It's complicated."

For the first time in her life Alison wanted answers more than she wanted sex. Shoving him back, she whirled on her heel and snapped, "You are a moody pain in the ass, you know that? Before, I'm throwing myself at you and you couldn't get away fast enough. But now you know I have a demon straight from the fires of hell hunting for me, and you're all raring to go?"

His eyes were bright, his lids lowered with lust. "You have someone after you. You need protection."

"And that's your hot button, huh?"

He shook his head and she saw him clench his fists at his side.

"Explain it to me, Del. Explain what's different now from an hour ago."

"Everything," he rasped, moving toward her again. He needed release so badly he could taste it, and with the autopilot engaged and the bed not even a foot away, all he could think about was stripping Alison to her skin and loving her body until they reached their destination. "We almost died."

"I'm well aware of that." Moving to the other side of the room, she started picking up random items. "What I don't understand is why you're all hot for me all of a sudden."

"It's not all of a sudden." The words came out more like a growl. "You have no idea how difficult it was for me to resist you earlier."

"Then why did you? I'm a whore, Fenton. A sure thing and you still refused."

"You're not a whore. You only did that because you had no other choice."

Shoving an armload of clothing into the closet and sealing the door, she turned to face him. His heart nearly stopped when he saw her eyes were wet. "That's all I am. All I've ever been. Back on Earth, it was different. I was a pleasure companion, one of the best in the business. An hour with me cost more than most men earned in a month. And I made sure they got their money's worth."

Shame burned color on her cheeks. "But I fucked up. Epically. I traded more than my body, I traded my soul. So don't sit there and kid yourself that I was only doing what I had to in order to survive. I'm not a good person. I'm not even a good whore anymore."

He couldn't stand to see her cry. Slowly, so as not to startle her, Fenton moved closer until he tugged her into his embrace. She struggled at first, but he persevered until she was wrapped in his arms. Rocking back and forth he offered her silent comfort until she sagged, emotionally spent.

She was so soft and warm in his arms, she fit like she'd been born to mold into him. Hearing her confessions should have cooled his ardor, but he was still hard, still fighting the phase split.

Tilting her chin up he said, "Alison, listen to me. You risked your life to save me back there. I owe you my life. You aren't bad. I know, I've seen evil up close."

"The overlord?" she mumbled.

Fenton wasn't sure how much she knew, but he refused to lie to her. "Yes. He was pure evil. He killed for sport, for pleasure, to alleviate his boredom. The deaths of my entire family are on his head. And to save myself I did some despicable things too. But I'm determined to atone for my sins as best I can."

She sniffled and wiped her eyes. "You ever sleep with someone for money?"

"No. But my sister did."

Raising her watery gaze to his, he watched her shock register. "What happened to her?"

"She died of wasting sickness. Gave of herself until there was nothing left to give. It was horrible to watch the disease consume her a little bit at a time."

"I'm sorry."

He nodded, accepting her softly spoken condolence. Fenton could have told her then about his mission, why he'd been resisting her, but she had that look, the one he'd seen on some of the men under his command, desolate and exhausted and utterly without hope.

"I only told you that because I want you to understand that I will not judge you on what you've done in the past. I see the person you are now, strong, self-sacrificing, a survivor. A beautiful, independent woman."

She snorted, but he saw the pleasure creep over her face so he forged onward. "How did you learn so much about the culture in the Hosta System?"

"Observation mostly. I watched and listened to others to pick up what I needed to know."

"And you've done this before, correct? Mimicked other cultures to help yourself blend in?"

Her teeth sank into her full lower lip but she nodded.

"Do you have any idea how impressive that is for me, someone who has never left his home sector before? Being a soldier, gambling and killing, is all I've ever done. But I hope to do more. I want you to show me how to be more."

For a moment he worried he'd gone too far, because her eyes were once again filled with tears. But then she smiled beautifully. "I'd add sweet-talker to the list."

He shook his head. "I'm only speaking the truth."

His gaze dropped to her lips. Her tongue darted out, wetting them. His cock twitched and slowly, he gave in to the temptation to lower his mouth to hers. A soft puff of air escaped, a surprised and eager sound. The kiss heated and he pressed her up against the wall, tasting her fully, thoroughly, the way he'd been yearning to do. Her pliant body yielded to him with a sensual grace, melding around him, pulling him in deeper.

There was so much left unspoken between them. He still didn't know why that man with the uncanny abilities was after her, or what he could do now. But what he did understand was that Alison's life had been in danger before they'd ever met. Resisting her was pointless, fruitless, and he refused to waste his energy fighting her magnetic pull any longer.

Her fingers tangled in his hair and her legs wrapped around his waist. He rubbed against her, seeking her warmth and wetness. The hum that indicated the phase split was eminent spread through his body but he tamped it down, not wanting to share her right now, even with himself.

Breaking the kiss, he whispered low in her ear, "Share your body with me. For no other reason than because you want me as badly as I crave you."

"Yes." Her reply was breathless but immediate.

"Tell me you want me." Fisting his hand into her hair, he rocked his shaft against her.

"I want you. Only you." Her lids were heavy as though drugged with lust.

Though it pained him, he set her down and backed away. "Take the dress off before I tear it from your body."

She wobbled slightly but her hand went to the side closures. He watched eagerly as she unfastened the pin holding the shimmering fabric in place over her decadent curves. She held it apart, baring herself to his greedy gaze.

Before he knew it, he fell to his knees, nuzzling the plump breasts, the curved waist he'd fantasized about. The honey-colored thatch of hair at the juncture of her thighs glistened. He scented her need, her desire. It was sharp, a flame licking through her bloodstream, but he wanted it to burn like a wildfire, raging out of control until she was desperate for him.

Holding her gaze, he licked over the tip of one breast. Her back arched as she shoved more of the ripe flesh to him, as though eager for him to consume her. Swirling his tongue around the beaded peak, he explored the dip of her waist with his fingers, lightly teasing and caressing all the wonders she'd displayed.

"My shield," she whispered as he switched to the other breast. "I need to activate it."

Plumping the wet breast with one hand, he used his teeth to scrape lightly across the other, tormenting the pretty bit of flesh to a point. "Do you?"

"Yes." Panic flared in her eyes at his suggestion. Clamping his hands down on her hips, he kept her from bolting.

"I vow I harbor no disease. I wouldn't risk you if I did."

Shaking her head she tried to pull away again. "I could still get pregnant." Her words were laced with terror.

He wanted to pleasure her. To cement their new understanding. The need to mark her with his essence clawed at him, but he wouldn't get anywhere with her so apprehensive. Slowly, as though gentling an easily startled creature, he traced her woman's seam back to her puckered opening. "Not if I take you here."

If anything she appeared even more distressed as he massaged the tight ring of muscles with the pad of his finger. "I don't ... that is, I'm not really sure ..." She closed her eyes, swallowed, then tried again. "I don't like that, okay?"

The way her hips rocked back into his touch told him otherwise. "I know how to make it good for you. I've had plenty of practice."

She scowled. "That's not exactly reassuring."

His lips twitched as he caught wind of her jealousy. It thrilled him that she could feel possessive over him. To ease her unnecessary apprehension, he elaborated, "On myself."

Alison blinked, then blinked again. He watched every flicker of her face as she wrestled with his words, groped for comprehension before reaching the correct—and by all appearances, shocking—conclusion.

He couldn't resist teasing her mind the same way he did her flesh. "With my ability, do you really think there's anything I haven't tried?"

For a moment he thought he had gone too far, that she would order him away from her body once and for all. Then a wave of lust washed over her features and she bent down to whisper two words that were his undoing.

"Show me."

9

The look on Del's face was priceless. Stunned definitely, but she also picked up on traces of excitement around the corners of his mouth. He wanted to show off for her, share his intimate secrets almost as badly as she wanted to see them.

Better he demonstrate his skills on himself than on her. She was still floored he wanted to fuck her without her shield. On Earth, there was an amendment to the Constitution, that only legally bound couples who had a permit to spawn could engage in unshielded intercourse. Sure, people still did it, but Alison had never even been tempted, even by her few private lovers who insisted sex was better sans shield.

Fenton wasn't human, though, and he didn't have a shield. As an alien whore, her patrons were usually just relieved that her cool equipment package left her disease- and pregnancy-free so they could have their fun and be off without consequence.

Was that why Fenton so badly wanted to come inside her unshielded body? Did he think he needed to set himself apart from the other alien men she'd been with?

Whatever his motivation, she'd found a simpler solution. Moving away from his touch, she sauntered to the bed, shucked her dress, and crawled onto the mattress. With the autopilot engaged, there was no way to tell that their luxurious cabin was moving on its own. "How far will the ship take us?"

"Not far. It's a short-range cruise ship leased from the parent vessel. A day or two and we'll have to disembark before the homing beacon is activated." He rose from his crouched position and turned to face her, his skin flushed. "Are you sure this is what you want?"

She smiled the triumphant grin of a woman who knew when she'd won. "Better your ass than mine."

He didn't smile back but lowered his eyelids. For a moment she thought he was having second thoughts, but the air shimmered next to him as he replicated himself.

Alison rose up as the two men—who were really one man—began to strip. Her curiosity could no longer be contained. "Which is the real you?"

"Both," they replied in unison. "I feel everything, just as your left hand and right hand can act independently of one another, so can my two forms."

Both of whom revealed delectable eyefuls of hard male flesh. Alison licked her lips as more and more tanned skin was made bare.

There was no slow seduction here, just pure intent. Fenton was a man on a mission, both of his hard cocks ready for action. Her sex creamed just imagining the show in store.

Two sets of celestial blue eyes fell on her. "You're going to help."

"How?" She'd been intent on watching, observing the proceedings like her own private erotic peep show. But Fenton had other plans. Sprawling on his back next to her, he pulled her over to his side. "Lie on top of me, like a blanket."

She moved, activating her shield. His sigh filled her ears, but too bad. The kind of close contact he was looking for, her body flush with his, meant she needed to protect herself.

"One of these days, luscious, you will trust me." The Fenton still standing stroked his fingers down her cheek, her shield snapping and sizzling away all traces of him.

"If it makes you feel any better, I've trusted you more than I've ever trusted anyone." The words slipped out before she thought about them. It wasn't like her to make herself vulnerable in any way. She didn't know who she was anymore; her priorities were skewed, all jumbled up by her need to survive. Pretending she even distantly resembled the same woman who'd left Earth was ridiculous.

His thumb roved across her lip even as arms from the male body beneath her wrapped around her, guiding her into place. "Lie back."

She would have thought it would be uncomfortable, that she would feel unbalanced. But Fenton's big body seemed carved like a sensual piece of furniture, contouring to her form precisely. Her head rested on his shoulder, his hands roved across the expanse of her torso. His cock had somehow managed to nestle itself between the cheeks of her ass. Her thighs were parted by his and when he drew his knees up to rest his heels on the end of the mattress, hers were parted wide, putting her sex on display for the man looming above them.

Exposed, she shifted restlessly and he groaned aloud. Big palms cupped her breasts even as they ran up her legs.

"You have no idea how sexy you are, do you?" It wasn't a question, not really. "To see you like this, spread out before me like a banquet, all sweet and hot and *mine*." His head lowered between their spread legs.

His tongue made a zigzag motion across her parted folds, a light caress that made her ass cheeks clench. Beneath her he arched, pressing his cock against her more fully. Fingers tightened on her nipples, pinching and squeezing the taut buds, adding kindling to the fire raging out of control.

"You taste so good," the one beneath her whispered in her ear even as his counterpart swept deeper into her folds. "I love the way your flesh yields to me, your sweet cream flooding my senses. I want to lose myself in your wet warmth."

Turning her head, she took his mouth even as another set of his lips mated with another set of hers in a primal kiss. He invaded her every sense and she forgot the end goal, forgot everything but his overwhelming presence.

He worked her body hard, urging more and more wetness from her sex until it coated his face, her thighs, his balls drawn up tightly beneath her. Two fingers glided inside her grasping cunt just as he dragged his teeth over her clit. She broke the kiss, her body bowing up off the bed as release slammed into her with meteor-like impact. The cock between her buttocks twitched eagerly and a soft sizzle let her know precum had seeped from his shaft onto her shield. The thought alone made her come again, the next wave cresting before the first broke as she creamed over him, for him, on him.

"Beautiful," Fenton whispered in her ear, his breath stirring her hair. "Time for the next stage?"

"Hmm?" Alison was a little dizzy, and very sticky. The question made no sense in her post-orgasmic blissed-out state.

Squeezing her tightly, Fenton rolled her off him and to the side. "That was for lubrication purposes, though I've never enjoyed the preparation quite so much."

She blinked as he shifted his attention from her to himself. A blush crept up her face when she saw how wet she'd made him, but he didn't seem to mind.

Her breath hitched when the Fenton on the bed lowered his mouth to the other's cock and swallowed him whole. Her clit actually twitched as she watched him suck himself deeply.

The one on the receiving end of the blow job watched her, his whiskers glistening with her essence as his cock disappeared into his own mouth.

"How does that feel?" she whispered. "Do you feel both at once?"

"You mean, can I taste my cock even as I feel it being sucked?" He grinned at her, his hips lunged forward, fucking deeply into his own face. "Yeah. It's perfectly choreographed too, because I know instinctively what I need, can be as rough or as gentle as I want with a second's thought."

"Have you ever come like that? In your own mouth?" She wondered how that worked, if they both came at the same time from one version sucking 2.0 off.

"Lots of times. But that's not what you wanted to see, was it?" Gripping his own hair, Fenton withdrew his now-glistening cock and ordered his other self to lie back.

Alison couldn't have torn her gaze away if her life depended on it as one Fenton lay flat on his back on the mattress, holding his legs behind the knee. The other bent low, following the trail of her lube with his tongue. He licked and sucked his balls into his mouth and up under the sack before continuing down to his perineum. From her angle, she could see every intimate detail of a man pleasuring himself. Even her most erotic training had never prepared her for this moment. Almost absently her hand slipped into her drenched pussy as she watched Fenton rim his own ass.

"Let me see you," the version on his back murmured. She shifted so he had a view of her fingers massaging her greedy flesh.

"This turns you on?" he asked as he accepted a finger into his body.

"God, yes," she groaned, stuffing her wet channel with her own digits. Feminine walls clamped down on the hardness, just as she imagined his channel squeezed the invading extremity.

She had more questions, so many more questions, but her gaze locked on his as they each pleasured themselves, him in preparation, her in response.

He took his time, stretching the opening, licking and wetting it for easier penetration. She pinched her clit, the bite of pain pushing her higher, but not quite over the edge. The scent of sex permeated the air as Fenton rose and dragged his wet shaft up the cleft of his ass, positioning himself at his own opening. Her lube trickled from her clenching core.

They gasped together as the thick head pressed against the puckered ring, pushing instantly until the aperture relented, expanding around the invading flesh. He pressed relentlessly onward, sweat beading his brow, teeth digging into his lower lip in both incarnations.

They paused, both gasping for breath, then turned to face her. "Alison." Her name was like a benediction, or perhaps a summons because she moved closer to grip the unattended cock, needing to be part of this.

Alison didn't recognize herself anymore, but she still knew how to enjoy herself.

Fenton threw his head back and grit his teeth as her soft palm wrapped around his neglected shaft. The pressure in his ass, the feel of his own channel being stretched, his own cock being hugged so tightly and then her touch . . . it was too much.

The ridge of his staff pressed against his prostate and his balls ached with the need to come. The entire experience had been incredible, from having his staff nestled between her luscious cheeks, to seeing her pleasure herself, drugged with lust from watching him.

Color rode high in her cheeks as she stroked over his engorged rod. Her breasts swayed with her gentle rhythm. Fenton held perfectly still, feeling worshiped and fortunate to behold her.

"Does it hurt?" She paused, right when he was about to pass the point of no return. "Why did you stop?"

"Feels great." He bucked a little, wedging his shaft in deeper at both junctures. "Keep going."

"I didn't mean to interrupt." She pulled her hand away.

Closing his hand over hers he kept her in place. "You didn't. You feel better."

She raised an eyebrow. "A hand job feels better than sex?"

His eyes burned into hers. "I'd rather feel your touch than my own."

Something flickered over her face, an emotion so poignant and beautiful it stole his breath. It was gone so fast he wondered if he'd imagined it. Lust for her muddied his thinking.

"Alison, make me come."

"Together." Her other hand slipped back between her legs and he was gone.

Thrusting hard and fast, his cock penetrated deep, scraping over the hot spot inside him. His channel squeezed his prick in thankful return, a maneuver he'd done more times than he could count. Combined with her soft palm engulfing him, still wet from her juices and his tonguing, squeezing tightly, and one look into those hazel eyes, and he knew he wouldn't last much longer.

Sweat coated his body as he worked himself hard, slamming his hips home roughly, burying his dick as deep as possible. A little pain made the pleasure sharper, sweeter, but Alison's touch made him immune to any discomfort.

A final lunge sent him into orgasm. Semen jetted hotly from both shafts, sizzling where it made contact with her shield. Her cry of ecstasy added to his own as she came with him, for him.

He went limp on the mattress as his essence recombined and he was made whole again. She collapsed next to him, her skin flushed from excitement, body practically boneless. He dragged her on top of him, arranging her soft form to blanket his once more. They were both a mess and he'd never felt happier.

On the run for his life from an unstoppable assassin with an alien woman in his arms. Life was just funny sometimes.

The server twitched in final death spasms on the deck as the assassin took her previously occupied chair. He hadn't needed to kill her, but after being bested by a whore and her lover he wasn't in a forgiving mood.

Another person's finger would drum impatiently on the desk or shift while waiting for information on the shuttle suite's location. His prey was resourceful and his blood actually quickened as the thrill of the hunt sang in his veins, resounded in his mind. The fact that Alison's lover had a few tricks of his own had taken him by surprise once. The assassin couldn't wait for his next encounter with Del Fenton.

His mind skim of the soldier had been his downfall. He'd focused exclusively on the man's thoughts of Alison and hadn't come across the knowledge that Fenton could divide himself, manifest into two beings. Perhaps even more. His handheld computer was busy compiling information on the man, which he would peruse later, once his course had been set.

The tracker on their shuttle suite blinked steadily. It was a safety measure installed by the cruise line to ensure that any richer-than-fuck star troller who rented the thing, wouldn't get hopelessly lost, costing the cruise line both the price of the expensive suite and the bad press associated with such an incident.

The screen blinked several times in rapid succession. The shuttle was well away from the parent ship's current course, heading deeper into the Taylith Sector. Did Alison or her beau have a plan in mind? Dozens of worlds were populated in this system, possibly hundreds of moons. It wasn't exactly a tourist hot spot, though, and regardless of her personal changes, Alison would undoubtedly fall back into the same patterns as always. He simply had to wait for news of the whore with the health guard to reach him and he'd peg her location.

Unless she was exclusive with her man. The assassin dismissed it almost as soon as the thought came to him. Alison was predictable, even if she'd proved herself to be elusive. Sooner or later she'd want something her man couldn't provide, and then the next man with a full wallet would appear in her sights. Not many things were truly universal, but he'd learned to trust people to be who they were.

It was always their downfall.

After downloading the coordinates and the code for the shuttle's beacon, he headed to the aft of the ship, striding purposefully forward. His comm unit beeped, signaling someone was trying to get in touch with him. Only four beings had his personal comm code, three of whom had mysteriously vanished.

Ducking into an unoccupied alcove, he opened the device. "Yes?"

"Status." The woman on the other end sat with her fingers folded neatly, the picture of innocence.

Pictures could be deceiving.

"I found her, but she wasn't alone."

"She escaped?" Full lips thinned.

"A minor setback."

"Alison knows too much. What's in her head could destroy our entire operation. She has the power to expose Illustra, the empaths, everything."

The assassin thought the woman overstated Alison's importance, but he wasn't paid to correct her foolish notions. "I have her signal and am in pursuit."

"You're sure she knows what you are?"

He nodded once, unwilling to repeat himself, regardless of her high rank or position.

"Still no contact from the board?"

Shortly before he'd been dispatched after Alison, the assassin had been recalled from a mission by the Illustra board members. He'd been irritated to be pulled off that assignment when he'd been so close. Just a few crossed wires on their transport and the stinger pilot and her space pirate would have been nothing more than cosmic dust. "No, ma'am."

"Then proceed with fulfilling your objective. And contact me the moment you hear from them."

The screen went blank and the assassin stowed his device. He had the sneaking suspicion that the Illustra board members were gone for good. Without the reigning figureheads, the company would begin to crumble. Killing Alison would only delay the inevitable.

But he'd do as ordered, because it was who he was.

He moved with purpose until he stood outside the suite the ships schematics indicated and chimed the door.

A middle-aged woman with orange skin holding some sort of small, fluffy creature answered. "Yes?"

The assassin stared down into her eyes until her jaw went slack and she sagged under his influence. "You and I are going to take a little trip together."

10

"Del?" Alison reclined against him on the bed. They'd each showered, separately, to listen for any alarms, but now they snuggled together under the shimmering bed coverings. Her head rested on his chest and she listened to the steady beating of his heart.

"No one has called me that since my sister died." He stroked her hair, pausing to work some strands between his thumb and forefinger. She'd noticed that he liked touching her hair even if it wasn't captivating or attention grabbing.

"I'm sorry. If you want, I can just call you Fenton."

He squeezed her to him. "No, I like hearing you use my given name."

She turned her head and smiled up at him. "Good, because I like using it."

Those luminescent blue eyes seemed to glow in the dim light. The cabin was dark, as he'd transferred all power other than emergency systems to navigation. The man might have no background with space travel, but he was an electrical genius. He shifted beneath her, and she felt his hardness against her leg.

He didn't make a move for her, though, seemingly content to simply hold her close and talk.

One dark eyebrow went up. "You were going to ask me something?"

She was, but looking at him, lying there so content, had blanked her mind. The sight of him alone erased all intentions, all thought between one heartbeat and the next, and she simply existed, basking in his glow. Shaking her head as though she could rattle her senses loose, she composed her wayward musings. "Do you know where we are going? I know you've never been there, but I was wondering if you had a plan?"

"Not a plan, just a few things I set up in case my primary objective failed. Which it did."

Because of her. This sensation of wanting to apologize for her actions was still new, but she went with it anyway. "I'm sorry."

He pulled her closer, brushed a kiss on her lips, one designed to comfort, calm things down not rile them up. "Don't be. I'm not."

"What were you going to do?" Perhaps she was a glutton for punishment for even asking but Alison wondered if he would come to regret her interference.

He stared at the ceiling. "There's an alchemist on the empath home world. He used to work for the overlord, before Xander banished him. I heard them talking once and he said he might be able to annul my phase split."

She frowned. "Annul?"

"He would kill half of me."

"But why would you want to do that?" Sure, his ability had surprised her at first, but she'd accepted that it was just something he could do. And it was magnificent, especially when he used it to save her life. Or pleasure her. And the way he phrased it, killing half of himself . . . she shuddered.

Tucking her into his side, he drew in a deep breath. "Imagine that anytime your equilibrium is upset for any reason, you have to fight not to react, to show no emotion at all, because if you did it would cause your body to split in two."

"Any strong feelings?" She hadn't realized how affected he was.

Del nodded. "Fear, lust, anger, anything that affects my adrenaline levels causes the split. I've learned to control it well, but during combat, sleep, or sex, it's almost impossible. The only way the bounty hunters can track me is through the phase split. I thought ridding myself of it would help us hide."

She shivered again at the way he said *us*, as though it was a natural assumption that anything they'd take on would be a joint effort. "But your ability saved me from the assassin. Saved us both."

He nodded. "Right. And if he has access to the ship's passenger manifest he'll know exactly where I'm heading, which means we can't go there anytime soon."

Relief coursed through her and shame nipped on its heels. "I'm sorry, but I like you exactly the way you are."

The kiss lasted longer, was slower, more sensual but still full of tenderness. Fenton rolled her to her back. She reached to activate her shield, but he stopped her.

"Not now. We need to make a new plan. Tell me all you know about the man hunting you."

Her ardor cooled instantly as she recalled their pursuer. "He's called the assassin. I don't know his real name or anything about his background." He'd cloaked himself in shadows, rarely speaking but always drawing notice. She shivered.

Fenton rubbed her arm as though trying to warm her. "What about his abilities?"

"He's a mind warrior. One of the strongest my planet has ever produced. The Cerebral Advancement Institute, or CRA, was founded in the beginning of the last century by the United States government. It was a specialized program designed to encourage the development of underused portions of the human brain. Sometimes drug experiments were used to advance people's natural abilities, but mostly it was training and conditioning. Some people were telepathic, able to read minds. Others were telekinetic, could move objects with only their thoughts. Mind warriors are both."

"So he read our minds earlier." Fenton didn't look pleased by this information. "I've never experienced anything like it, such an invasion of self."

"It doesn't have to be painful. He delights in making it hurt. He can also command a mind, take over, like in a possession, or embed images that will drive his victim insane."

"What's his range like?" Fenton's face looked grim, understandable after hearing news like that.

"I'm not sure. Relatively close, a few meters or so."

"Do you know why he's after you?"

Alison nodded, but didn't say anything else.

He tilted her chin so she couldn't avoid his gaze. "You say you trust me, but you don't, do you?"

She jerked her chin away. "It's not that I don't trust you, more that I don't want to tell you about all the mistakes I've made."

"Alison"—he laid back and folded his hands behind his head—"we're being hunted. The sooner you trust me with the truth, the better our chances of survival."

Anger welled up and she threw the covers back, needing to put some distance between them. "You think I don't know that? Really, Del, I'm not some fluff-brained idiot. If you don't want to help me, that's fine. Just let me off at the next habitable world and I'll make my own way."

His face closed down to the expressionless mask she was beginning to detest. "You know I can't do that."

Stepping into her dress, she yanked the fabric up. It was wrinkled but she didn't care, needing some sort of covering between them. "Now who's the untrusting one? You expect me to bare myself to you completely, yet you're still hiding things from me, aren't you?"

"We just met," he protested, reaching for her. "It'll take time to learn everything about each other. A lifetime perhaps."

The last three words, spoken almost hesitantly in his rough bass, chilled her to the bone. Through the darkness, she made her way to the bathroom door. "I'm going to take a bath."

"You just had one. Our resources are finite. We should conserve the water."

Pausing at the door she called over her shoulder, "Get a clue, Del. I need some space from you." Without waiting for an answer, she locked herself in the pitch-black bathroom.

Fantastic. With nothing else to do, Fenton redressed and moved into the other room to check on the pod. The glow from the bioluminescent stasis chamber lit the suite in a soft pulsing blue light. He touched the smooth surface, checked the readouts, anything to stall the miasma of thoughts swirling in his head.

Alison was upset with him. Again. He was beginning to see a pattern to her behavior. They didn't communicate well, their species or perhaps even their genders too different to reach a compromise. She hid things; he'd ask for the truth, she'd distract him with sex. Not that it was difficult, since he wanted her endlessly. Their carnal relations would escalate, but just when he thought she'd lowered her guard, she resurrected the walls at light speed. Almost as if she was afraid to let him in.

She'd risked her life for him. That had to count for something. Perhaps he just hoped it did, hoped that he was getting through to her and she was as affected by him as he was by her.

The ship's proximity alarm let out a warning blare. Fenton rushed back to the controls, just as Alison emerged from the bathroom.

"What is it?" she asked. "An asteroid?"

He checked the readouts. "It looks like a ship. How do I disengage the autopilot?"

She moved to his side, showed him the sequence. "Should we hail them?"

The shuttle shook violently. Fenton threw his arms out to brace himself against either side of the wall, with Alison wedged between the console and his body. "What's happening?"

Her fingers flew over the controls. "They've locked onto us with a magnetic web. They're pulling us aboard."

His heart beat against his rib cage. "Do you have any idea who they are?"

She turned to look up at him just as a bright light emanated from the docking bay, casting her features into shadow. "This isn't my sector of space. I don't know the rules any more than you do."

His throat had gone dry. "Pirates, perhaps. Or military patrollers. Regardless, don't use my name or mention Hosta or the assassin. If they ask, we're just a couple out for a pleasure cruise who got lost."

"What if they try to return us to the pleasure cruiser? The assassin might still be there." She cracked her knuckles and he noticed her hands were shaking, the only sign of fear she allowed herself to show.

He took her hands in his, brought them to his lips. "Trust me?"

Her head bobbed just as the ship scraped along the metal decking and ground to an earsplitting halt. The doors were pried open in a shower of sparks, rendering their craft useless for further space travel.

Sure to keep Alison safely behind him, Fenton blocked her body with his own as the door became nothing but a gaping hole. At the last minute he realized the chamber containing the pod was still unsealed. He shifted, ready to bolt for it, but a hooded figure appeared in the doorway, weapon aimed at his center mass.

The phase split took hold but Fenton fought the urge. Alison needed him to keep himself together in every sense of the word. "We appreciate the rescue."

The armed invader moved closer. "Name, cargo, destination."

"My name is Axe and this is my mate, Lorna. This is a passenger shuttle from the cruise ship docking code 4587. We were out for a recreational star voyage and got turned around. Thank you for the rescue."

Alison nodded mutely, her eyes wide and trained on the sharp-bladed staff the newcomer carried.

The hooded figure didn't move and Fenton waited patiently. He'd played enough *demjong* to know that half of selling a bluff was outwaiting the other players. Alison's breathing was shaky, but her response could easily be construed as a distraught woman having a weapon pointed at her for the first time in her life.

"I wasn't addressing you, breeder. Lie facedown on the floor." The voice was soft but rang with command.

Fenton wondered if he'd overpaid for his translation chip because the words made no sense. "Could you repeat that?"

An energy beam leapt from the muzzle of the stranger's weapon. Fenton dove to protect Alison, knocking her to the floor, but the beam curled like the lash from a whip and connected with his back. He hissed in pain as an acid-like substance burned through the fabric of his shirt and seared the flesh below.

"Stay down, breeder." A small booted foot pressed down on the back of his neck, even as a hand reached out for Alison. "Are you injured, mistress?"

Her eyes filled with confusion as she looked from the hand to him and back. "Release my companion."

"He didn't show the proper deference to a patroller." The foot on his neck didn't budge.

"We didn't know who you were," Alison replied, though she was careful to keep her tone soft and undemanding. "Please, he's hurt."

The patroller pushed the cowl back, displaying a feminine face shaded orange. Her hair was a deeper hue of the same color and her eyes were emerald green. "He'll heal. This breeder is insolent and ignorant of our customs. Pain will teach him his place."

Fenton closed his eyes, trying to will away the burning on his back and holding himself together. Obviously they'd stumbled into a matriarchal society of some sort. Though it chafed, he'd have to rely on Alison to get them out of this. Any move he made would only result in further lessons and his flesh had been marred enough for one lifetime.

"Where is the third life form we detected?" the patroller asked.

Alison frowned. "It's just the two of us."

"Our scans clearly identified three unique life forms."

No. This was not how Fenton wanted her to find out about his cargo. He should have told her earlier, prepared her so she didn't end up blindsided. Ignorance would get them killed.

Risking the patroller's ire, he made a sound of pain to attract Alison's notice. When she looked to his face he cut his gaze to the door to the other chamber, hoping her human eyes could see the small movement. Her lips parted and he could see the question written on her face.

"Through there," she mumbled.

The patroller gestured with her head. "Open it."

Alison swallowed and backed toward the door. Removing what looked to be a master override key from the pocket of her dress, she held it over the scanner. Of course, he'd wondered how she'd escaped the room earlier. She must have lifted the override from the server. Clever minx. It wouldn't have worked if he'd remembered to seal the chamber with his personal passcode, but his oversight worked in their favor.

The doorway opened and he heard the steady thrumming from the stasis chamber. Though the pain slowed him up, he phase split around the corner of the door, so the patroller couldn't see.

"You go first." The patroller bent down and set a restraining field over his body. The version on the floor couldn't twitch so much as an eyelash. "He is undamaged and will remain so as long as there aren't any surprises."

Quickly, Fenton skirted the areas visible from the doorway and moved to the pod. His hands shook as he tapped in the master code to start the regeneration process. The circumstances were less than ideal, but if someone attempted to open the pod without starting the resurrect sequence Ari could die.

He was her protector, her only living relative. Fenton just hoped he would prove to be enough.

11

Alison crept into Fenton's secret room, wondering what she would find. Life signs could mean anything from bacteria to a giant, genetically mutated monster. The bold woman with the chemical whip followed a few yards back. Obviously if there was something large and hungry in here, she was supposed to be its main course. She swallowed, recognizing that she had no choice.

Why hadn't Fenton told her about his cargo?

Because he doesn't trust me any more than I trust him, that insidiously snarky inner voice hissed. She couldn't ignore the truth behind that statement. They both kept secrets, just as she'd suspected. Sure, they'd collided in bed a few times, but that didn't mean the universe would suddenly revolve around them, or that stars would align into a happy picture of forever. They'd been brought together by circumstances, not choice. She couldn't lose sight of that.

"Move," the patroller woman ordered, her tone impatient.

"With the power out, I can't see where I'm going." Alison

spoke softly, not wanting to wake whatever creature lay dormant in the shadows.

"The way is clear up to the pod. Remove the covering and stand aside."

Her teeth sank into her lower lip as she shuffled forward. Reaching for the pod, she ignored the tremors in her hands as she followed orders. Whatever Fenton had been hiding, it couldn't be worse than a lash from that awful weapon.

At first the cover didn't want to budge. The smooth surface pulsated with a blue-green glow, similar to Fenton's underground lair on Pental. Bioluminescent organism. Perhaps those were the life signs? As far as she knew, the small glowing creatures from the Hosta System were harmless.

But why would he want to bring them all this way? Now more curious than afraid, Alison put her back into it and shoved the lid up. A slow hiss, like steam being released from a pot, sounded, but the air inside was cold, not hot. Waving her hand to clear the icy fog away, Alison peered down into the covering. And nearly fainted.

A baby sprawled on a soft cushion, a little girl. She was alive, her chest rose and fell as she took deep, steady breaths. Her hands were positioned up by her head, her fingers curled, and her knees were bent up. With her eyes closed, she looked human, though Alison was sure she was not. What the hell was Fenton doing with this infant?

A million horrific possibilities came to mind and she felt sick as she considered the fate of this tiny, defenseless child. Ignoring the inner voice that told her he was a decent man who would never harm a child, she sucked in a deep breath. This was her worst nightmare come to life. Powerless and burdened by a child and on the run from a killer with no friends to help her. No resources, only a lover who hid things from her.

Like mother, like daughter.

The baby sighed and Alison knew she couldn't walk away from the helpless infant. She was invested now. Whatever he'd intended, she'd stop him. This girl needed an advocate, someone who looked after her, put her first. And the poor mite was stuck with her selfish ass.

The patroller moved next to her, weapon trained on the pod. Alison knocked it aside and blocked the child with her body. "Put that thing away, she's just a baby."

She expected retaliation, but was stunned when the patroller stowed her weapon.

"Apologies. Had I known you and your breeder had a child in stasis I never would have asked you to open the pod. You should have told me."

I didn't know! Alison's mind screamed. She couldn't believe the woman's matter-of-fact attitude. Was this a normal way for people to transport their young? Keeping her outward composure, Alison lifted her chin, falling back on her old fake-it-'til-you-make-it. Or 'til you can find a way out.

Behind her a soft mewling sound came from the pod. Alison's heart thundered in her chest as she watched the little being wake up from her interminably long hibernation. Bright blue eyes, so much like Fenton's, fixed on hers. The baby stretched languidly, and kicked her legs.

"Aren't you going to pick her up?" the patroller asked with a raised eyebrow. "I'm sure she's hungry."

"And I have nothing to feed her," Alison whispered. Panic settled on her shoulders, the weight of responsibility pinning her down. This little one needed everything and was looking at her to provide it.

"Bring her to my ship. We are well stocked. How old is she?"

Having had no experience with children other than a few hours with her nephew, Jonah, Alison was far from a baby expert. Especially alien babies. "Um...five months?"

"You don't know?" The patroller eyeballed her suspiciously.

"She's not mine, biologically. He acquired her." The baby made a grunting-type noise and a foul stench filled the room.

The patroller covered her mouth and nose. "Looks like she's regaining her equilibrium, and all life functions appear normal. I'll release the breeder to tend to her."

"I'd appreciate that," Alison said faintly, gagging from the smell. The little one flailed happily, grinning her toothless smile, obviously proud of her handiwork.

A groan from the other room told her Fenton was still alive. Good, she might want to kill him herself. Rage the likes of which she'd never known unfurled inside her as she watched the little one flail her arms.

"What's your name, little beauty?" Breathing through her mouth, Alison moved closer to touch the perfect, poreless skin. Even the finest silk wasn't that smooth.

"Her name is Ari." Fenton's voice was tight and laced with pain.

Alison glanced at the doorway, checking to make sure they were alone. The baby—Ari apparently—started to fuss, her mood changing in an instant. "Are we alone?"

"Yes." Moving forward, Fenton removed the soiled linens from the pod. "Over there by the wall, there's a bag with her things and a medical kit."

Alison didn't move. "What were you going to do with her?"

He met her gaze head-on. "Raise her. She's my sister's child, my last living relative."

She wanted to believe him, but she had so many questions.

"Alison, please. The patroller will be back soon, probably with reinforcements. We need to be ready to move her."

"Why did you have her in stasis? It seems so cold to transport her like she's a specimen."

His jaw clenched. "Gili, her mother, was the one who put

her in stasis, right before she died. She thought it was the best way for me to get her off world. I gave her my word that I would protect her daughter from the overlord and anyone else who might harm her. Now please, help me get her ready."

Alison could accept his explanations. Retrieving the bag, she watched him tend to Ari with the devotion of a loving parent. Even though she should be relieved that he meant the child no harm, her chest ached. Forgiving him for his deceit and for roping her into this mess might be more than she could handle. He hadn't trusted her, and now she was partly responsible for Ari's well-being. The thought sickened her.

Next opportunity, she was leaving him in her cosmic dust.

With Ari's pack strapped to his back and his niece in his arms, Fenton was sure to walk several steps behind Alison, who was escorted by two patrollers off of their busted-up shuttle suite and onto the carrier, showing his supposed subservience. He was her stud and Ari's nursemaid, and nothing more. It took effort for him to move a little clumsily, hiding his warrior's gait. Their survival might depend on whether or not he could fool their captors into thinking him harmless.

Alison, of course, knew better. Her concern for Ari warmed him, gave him hope that she would be willing to stay with him, with them. Watching her walk along as stately as a queen, he smiled to himself, knowing her confidence was just a façade, an act she put on for those around her.

He'd seen her at her most vulnerable. And it only served to fuel his lust for her. His craving to know her better grew stronger with every passing second, served to distract him from their surroundings, which was both foolish and dangerous. Crooking his arm, he shifted Ari into a more reclined position as he took in their surroundings.

The ship was older technology, at least three generations removed from the cruise vessel, although here and there he saw signs of patched-in advance tech, possibly stolen or traded from another culture. The job had either been done in a hurry or by someone who just didn't care if the vessel exploded. Perhaps he could lend a hand with his technical expertise, gain their trust slowly while he and Alison plotted their next move.

Their. As he watched her shapely backside sway with every step, he smiled to himself. He liked the sound of that. His niece fussed and he shifted her back to his shoulder, knowing from experience that she wouldn't hesitate to let him know if she was displeased with an irate bellow.

One of the patrollers pressed a door. "These are your temporary quarters. It is stocked with provisions for you and your child and breeder. Her highness will be with you directly."

Alison nodded regally, a queen taking her due from a minion, and stepped inside the open doors. Fenton followed with a now squawking Ari. The doors whizzed shut behind them.

There was no furniture to speak of, just mounds of fluffy jewel-toned pillows piled around the room. Alison sank into one nearby. "From one locked bedroom to another. This see-the-universe spiel is so overrated."

Fenton knelt down on one knee next to her and made a slicing motion with his free hand. Her brows drew down and her lips parted. He kissed her, hard and fast to silence her. Pulling back he looked to the corners of the room then back to her. She nodded once, understanding his message. Someone might be watching.

Ari started to cry in earnest, her face scrunching in displeasure.

Fenton attempted to shift her into Alison's arms. "Please take her while I prepare her food." And searched for listening devices.

Panic flared in Alison's eyes and she whispered, "I don't know how."

Fenton hid his surprise. After seeing her defend his helpless niece so vehemently, he thought for sure that she had experience with young ones. "Hold your arms like mine."

She mimicked his pose, her hands overlapping, arms forming a circle.

Tenderly, he transferred Ari's slight weight, blankets and all, into Alison's arms. The smooth fabric of her clothing helped ease her transition, despite the tantrum she threw. Not knowing how any foreign food would impact her freshly reawakened system, Fenton yanked her pack off his back and popped a specially formulated restorative cube into her rosebud mouth.

"Won't she choke?" Alison watched him warily.

"No, it's almost like powder, see?" He crumbled another cube easily in his hand. "I have some liquid restorative too, but let's make sure she doesn't have any adverse reactions to it."

The squalling stopped as the crystals instantly dissolved in her saliva, nourishing her empty stomach. Her blue eyes fixed on Alison's face as she sucked on it.

"She likes it," Alison murmured.

Fenton smiled at the picture they made, so beautiful together. "She just likes food."

"We have that in common." Alison watched Ari as raptly as the little one watched her.

"Isn't this cozy?" a female voice said from the doorway.

He turned and took in a tall female clad in diaphanous bloodred robes that flowed over her lush curves. Her hair was done up in a series of coils across her head. Her skin, hair, and eyes were dark, as though she spent a great deal of time on the surface of a planet. Some of the Hosta natives had coloring like that, especially the ones who spent generations in the desert city. His family had been from the northern territories and colored to match the prevailing snow.

Fenton took Ari back. She let out a squeak of protest, and he popped another cube into her mouth, eyes trained on the door.

Alison stood up and shook out her own skirts. "Are you in charge here?"

"Indeed. I am Gwella, Empress of Daton Five. And you have trespassed into our space."

"I apologize for that, your highness." Alison did some complicated dip, a sign of respect, he thought. Clever wench. Fenton stayed where he was, showing deference to the women as he guessed a good breeder should.

"Under the laws established in the last space lane summit, any ship that enters our borders without authorization may be confiscated, the passengers relocated to the nearest habitable planet."

"As you see fit, your highness. Might I ask your indulgence in keeping our personal effects? We are far from home and there is a man hunting for us."

The empress made a sound of disgust. "Men, their usefulness is overstated and virtually nonexistent. No offense to your breeder."

Alison stroked his head like she might a pet. "None taken."

Fenton swallowed his pride. Ego had no place in a game of survival. Having Alison touch him so sweetly took the sting out of her patronizing words.

"I have to say, yours is more . . . sturdy than most. Would you mind if I borrowed him?"

"Not at all." Fenton's heart nearly stopped at Alison's breezy answer. "Mind if I watch?"

The empress actually threw her head back and laughed. "Oh, I like you. Perhaps we would be better served to leave him here to tend to your young ones while you and I get to know each other better."

"Sounds divine."

She would go and be with someone else? Share her body, just like that? Fenton reached out, gripped her arm, holding her wrist tightly. "No."

Both women looked at him as he rose to his full height and stared them down. Ari sighed contently, taking away from the imposing image he'd intended to cast but there was nothing for it.

"You dare object, breeder?" The queen raised an eyebrow as though challenging him to continue on this course. He could feel the confident authority rolling off her in waves. She could have him whipped again; his back still burned, though the pain had lessened somewhat. He was sore, exhausted, and losing his composure by the second.

"She is with me. Only with me." He leveled his stare at Alison. "As were the terms of an earlier agreement."

"Is this true?" The queen assessed Alison, who still held his gaze.

She swallowed visibly. He clenched his jaw and waited for her to make her choice.

A millennium seemed to pass as they stared at each other. Fenton refused to blink or shift or back down in any other visible way. She'd promised him, damn it, and that was before the assassin, before she knew about Ari. He waited, watching her, willing her to understand what weighed on this decision.

Their future. *I need you. Ari needs you. Please.*

She closed her eyes and he couldn't contain his sigh of sheer relief. They communicated better without words; he could read the meaning behind her every response.

"Yes, I'm afraid I did." Turning back to the empress, Alison plastered a smile on her face, though he could see the strain around her eyes. She didn't like saying no, closing that avenue of escape. "Any of our meetings will have to be strictly . . . platonic."

The woman studied them. "Understood. Keeping your word is the most important consideration, second only to your offspring. Shall we sit?" She didn't wait for an answer, simply chose a large purple cushion and lowered herself gracefully onto it.

It had been a test, he was sure of it. And they must have passed because no one was ordering the skin flayed from their hides.

Alison blinked as though stunned. Moving his grip down, he clasped her hand in his.

With the tense moment behind them, the women settled into the cushions. Fenton handed Ari back to Alison and moved toward the food unit in search of refreshment.

"Where will you take us?" he heard her ask.

"The nearest habitable planet is mine. I fear it is not an ideal place to raise your offspring, though."

"Why not?" Returning with a purple decanter he'd found in the cooling unit, Fenton poured their drinks.

Gwella frowned. "Is he always so forceful?"

"You have no idea." Alison grinned with mock sweetness as she accepted her drink.

When he got her alone later, he would turn her over his knee. "I'm from a different culture, one where men make the decisions."

The empress mock-shuddered with obvious distaste. "I can only imagine the chaos."

"It's not so bad," he responded, then grimaced at his own lie.

"And you are no longer there . . . why?" She smirked at him as though she knew she'd won.

Fenton could admit defeat. "Because it is being ripped apart by war."

The empress's amusement vanished. "I'm sorry to hear that. Unfortunately my society is on the verge of collapse itself."

"Because of the men?" Alison asked.

"Because of greed and an experiment gone wrong. It is a

long, troubling story, one I shall save for another night. I'm sorry to do this to you, but know I take my responsibilities seriously and I will do everything in my power to keep you safe."

Fenton watched her rise smoothly to her feet. She nodded to them and strode out at a brisk, purposeful pace.

"Why do I have the feeling our situation hasn't improved?" Alison mused.

Fenton took Ari from her. "It hasn't, not in the least."

She sighed. "We have a phrase for this kind of thing on Earth. SNAFU. It's an acronym, stands for Situation Normal: All Fucked Up."

Ari chewed on her fist and stared up at him as he shifted his weight back and forth rhythmically. "What choice do we have?"

"Same as usual, bad or worse." She rose, moved behind him. "How's your back?"

It hurt like the fires of hell. Just what he needed: another scar. "It will heal."

"Let me wrap it up for you." Without waiting for his answer, she dug into Ari's pack.

"That's for emergencies," he protested when she withdrew sealant and a bandage.

"What do you call this?" Taking Ari from him, she propped the baby on a low pillow and then gestured for him to lie down next to her. "Don't make me get rough with you."

He reached out, stroked her jaw with the back of his fingers. "You almost left us. I could see it in your eyes."

She knocked his hand away and pointed to the cushion. "Yeah, well, that's my gut reaction when guys lie to me."

"I never lied, Alison. I had to protect her."

She shook her head. "I never would have agreed to this crazy deal if I'd known about her."

Direct hit, center mass. To keep her from seeing his pain, he eased down onto the pillows and pulled off his shirt. It hurt more to force the words out through his tight throat. "If that's how you feel, perhaps the empress will still take you on."

Her cool hands touched the relatively undamaged skin of his shoulder. "I'm here, aren't I? Doesn't that count for something?"

Sprawling prone, Fenton concentrated on his niece, who stared merrily at nothing he could determine, waving her fists as though in greeting.

"I'm going to wash this out first, make sure there aren't any chemicals in the wound before we close it up."

He heard her rummage around on the other side of the room, muttering to herself as she searched. Fatigue swamped him and he closed his eyes, not even opening them when the cool water slid through his wound like molten lava.

Her hands were sure and steady as she knit his flesh back together, then coated the wound with the sealant and covered it with the bandage.

"All done." She stroked his hair.

He wanted to shrug her off, but couldn't. Instead he turned to face her. "She doesn't want you. Not like I do."

Alison nodded. "I know. That's why she's safer."

He wanted to respond but found his eyelids were too heavy to keep up any longer. Sleep, that demanding mistress, dragged him under her seductive spell.

12

The assassin prowled the seedy corridors of the space station where he'd docked the suite shuttle. The tracking beacon had burnt out hours earlier, and this station was the most likely place for her and her manmeat protector to have headed. Though there had been no sign of them, he felt certain they would wind up here eventually. The waiting grated on his nerves and the buzz of conversation from the distant travelers, both those voiced aloud and the ones reverberating in his head, made him edgy.

Luckily there was a fix for his restless distraction. He just needed to select the right specimen. Pivoting on his heel he stalked down to the lower deck, where the hopeless refugees congregated to pool their pitiful resources. A universal standard credit would go a long way with this sort.

The smell of unwashed bodies made him curl his lips in disgust. Either the station attendant was an idiot or just didn't care to fix the broken sani-facilities for those who couldn't pay for a room. Still, better to select his sample here than to choose someone with connections.

Someone who might be missed.

A group of users huddled around a small space heater, too strung out to talk. He dismissed them immediately because G-dust addicts were unpredictable, their mind patterns too unfocused to read, too easy to control.

Two elderly women, one distinctly humanoid and one more reptilian, sorted through a trash receptacle looking for useful tidbits. They burbled something at him as he strode by. He ignored them, as the pitiful creatures were beneath his contempt.

He found what he was looking for beneath the crossover walkway, huddled in a filthy blanket.

"You." The assassin nudged the unshod foot of the young man huddled against the metal supports. He was thin, almost gaunt, but his eyes were clear of the purple streaks G-dust users developed. "How would you like to make some credits?"

The man turned hollow eyes up to him. A surface skim revealed he was a runaway from an abusive family several sectors away. The money and supplies he'd packed for his journey had been stolen and he was here, without resources, alone and afraid.

Perfect.

"What do I have to do?" His tone held a rough edge from disuse. It had been a while since he'd talked to anyone. He eyed the assassin skeptically even as he imagined pulling out the bigger man's cock and sucking it for the currency. The idea aroused his subject.

"Does it matter?" Flashing a handful of universal credit strips, the assassin waited.

"My name's Marv." The man stayed where he was.

"I've procured a room, Marv. Number 617. It's unlocked. Go inside, eat, and clean yourself. Then wait for me to come to you."

"You leave your room unlocked?" Marv frowned.

The assassin moved closer, studied the beaten-down figure. "No one would dare steal from me. Go now and be ready."

Turning on his heel, he headed up to the commons, a small, satisfied smile firmly in place.

His dick grew hard just thinking about what would come next.

Who knew taking care of a baby was so much fracking work? After spending months in stasis, Ari was wound up and looking to Alison for entertainment. She couldn't crawl yet, but she sat up and squealed and managed to slither between the cushions every time Alison put her down.

Fenton slept deeply, a healing rest, hopefully recovering from the effects of the chemical whip. Alison left him to it as she carried the infant around the room, murmuring out loud whatever thoughts came into her head. Talking to Ari was only slightly better than talking to herself. Or dwelling on Fenton.

She had mixed feelings about what had happened earlier. Part of her still wanted to go find Gwella and ingratiate herself with the other woman, secure her position. But Fenton had been right. While the empress seemed amused, maybe even intrigued by her, Del wanted her more. He craved her endlessly, and not just her body. Heavens help her, but being desired so strongly was addictive.

He'd been hurt by her offering herself up for the other woman's use. She'd heard his indrawn breath, felt those crystalline eyes boring holes into her. And she'd caved, weak-willed sap that she was.

"Let this be a lesson to you," she murmured to Ari, who gripped her hair in a tight fist. "Men are manipulators. Better to use them than let them use you."

"How is she?"

Alison jumped at the sound of his voice. Crap, she hadn't intended for him to hear that.

"Heavy." She shifted the baby from one arm to the other. "And how can something so small make such a gawd-awful mess so often?"

"One of the mysteries of the universe." The words were carefully spoken, utterly neutral. Cold and detached, the way he was with everyone else. She hated it.

"Are you punishing me for trying to look out for myself? Because it won't work."

"I know." He was so calm and Zen-like and it pissed her right the hell off.

"Come on, Del, cut me some slack. I'm here, aren't I?"

He didn't say anything, just rose and took Ari from her. Her arms felt like overcooked spaghetti but she missed the little girl's warm weight.

"I've got her from here. Why don't you get some rest?"

"I'm not tired."

"Alison." Her name was a heavy sigh, as though it burdened him to speak it. "I don't want to do this in front of my niece. She's been through enough, and I don't want any more of her memories warped by our arrangement."

The baby cooed affectionately at him even as Alison laser-drilled him with her eyes. "Warped?" Was that really how he saw the two of them together? Or was it just her?

He ignored her and carried Ari over to her pack and trundled through it, clearly searching for something. She didn't know which stung worse, that he ignored her or his last shot that hit her head-on.

"Just be aware that keeping secrets from people you love always fucks you in the end."

He rose, holding a brilliantly colored set of shapes hooked together like a belt for his niece. She gurgled and reached for the toy even as he scowled at Alison. "You've kept secrets from the moment I met you."

Putting her hands on her hips, she said, "That's because I don't love you. Right now, I don't even like you very much."

No reaction, her words bounced off him as though he had some kind of deflector shield. The lack of impact hurt her more than anything else he said or did.

"I'm going to take a long, hot bath," she announced, though she didn't know why.

"Good luck with that." He didn't lift his gaze from Ari, who swung at the shape chain. When her meaty little fist connected, the shapes shimmered from neon to pastel and back.

Alison strode into the bathroom, where she stopped dead in her tracks. His parting shot hadn't sounded sarcastic, but given that there was nothing even resembling a tub in the small space, his words took on new meaning.

The space was about six meters in length and width, a perfect square. The toilet stood in one corner with a sink that folded from the wall above. Both were made from nondescript gray metal. A sprinkler type showerhead loomed above with knobs on the wall. The drain in the floor reminded her of some ancient horror movies where the victim was strung up and tortured so the blood wouldn't muss the space. It was a horrible room.

Alison stared at the utilitarian chamber with loathing. True, the other room had been simple in design, but the rich fabrics on the pillows had somehow blinded her to the shabbiness of it. She'd gotten used to the accommodations on the suite shuttle, but it hadn't been all that long ago she'd had nothing but a bucket of water to wash herself with. Fenton had changed that, had given her a taste of decadence again. Hating him for that more than everything else, she grimly hung up her dress and set about the task of cleaning herself.

A small niche held a towel but no soap. Rolling her eyes, she made a mental note to request some and turned on the lever. Her hair clumped together where Ari had gripped it with her grubby hand, coated in what had looked like baby oatmeal. She'd have given a kidney for a bottle of decent-smelling shampoo.

"Fracking great," she mumbled when nothing happened. The temperature in the room had goose bumps breaking out all over her naked body. Staring up at the spigot, she shouted, "Would it be too much to ask for a shower?"

Some white, soapy-tasting chemical spewed down on her. She shrieked as it landed in her mouth and burned her eyes. To compound her misery, it was cold and she hopped from foot to foot as the deluge continued, searching frantically for the control panel.

Male laughter filled the small space. She whirled on her heel and would have gone down on her ass if strong hands hadn't caught her. Fenton tugged her into his bare chest that shook with amusement.

"Shut it off!" she shrieked.

"Already done. Quit panicking and hold still. It's already evaporating."

True enough, the suds seemed to be dissolving, slithering down that horrible drain. The bubbles on her skin popped, leaving a tingly sensation behind.

She spit, the lingering taste of soap still on her tongue. "That's just foul."

"I should have warned you. Water is heavy, and transporting on a space vessel is a costly endeavor. Most don't bother with keeping more than enough to sustain those aboard, instead choosing a chemical composite for cleaning. To conserve fuel and space."

Her eyes still stung as she glared up at him. "You enjoyed that," she accused.

Fenton dragged the towel over her face, clearing away the rest of the foam. "Maybe a little."

His smile was infectious and she found she couldn't hold on

to her anger. "My mom always threatened to clean out my mouth with soap. I never reckoned it would taste quite so vile."

His eyelids lowered, "Come here. I've got something you could put in your mouth to help speed your recovery."

Fenton watched as Alison licked her lips. His cock shot hard as steel at the miniscule gesture. She was glorious, covered in the cleansing foam, the color high in her cheeks from anger. Her question took him by surprise, though. "Where's Ari?"

"With me." At her raised eyebrow he elaborated, "The other me."

"So you . . . ?"

"Split."

"Why?"

He wasn't sure how to answer that one. His gut told him it was a trap he'd verbally stumble into if he wasn't careful. Add to that the fact his dick throbbed like an ion engine and she definitely had the advantage. "I thought you might . . . need me."

Her face closed up. "For sex?"

"Not necessarily, although now that we're on the topic you missed a few spots." Before she could react, he turned the foam back on, albeit on a lower setting so it misted gently down on her instead of the floodgate she'd opened earlier.

Alison ducked her face, and the foam drifted down on her back like snow falling in the Northern Territories where he'd spent much of his adult life. When she wasn't buried in the chemical the way she'd been before, her features softened and she actually turned her face into the spray.

After shutting it off, Fenton moved to her side and ran his hands over her shoulders and back, coating her skin thoroughly. She arched like a cat into his touch, always so beautifully responsive. The chemical tingled where it touched his skin and he could only imagine what it felt like to her, with so much of it evaporating all over her body. The heat that sparked between them intensified as he gripped her thighs in either hand, forcing her to spread her legs.

The motion sent her off balance, and she leaned forward, bracing herself on the wall.

Caressing her plump backside, he spread her cheeks apart, baring all of her secret places. Scooping up a handful of foam, he cupped his hand over her sex and let the cleansing solution have its way with her pussy.

"Right there." Fenton watched as she shivered and shook all over as the tiny bubbles popped and dispersed. He worked some around his index finger and then pushed into her tight channel. Slickness greeted his invasion, telling him that between the sensations and his hunger for her he was getting to her. "You like that, sexy?"

"God, yes!" She clenched around him, her inner muscles gripping his fingers, trying to draw them even deeper.

Slowly the cleansing chemical broke down into its base components, leaving her flesh clean and pink from the unusual sensation. Unable to help himself, he lowered his head and tasted her juicy folds. She gasped and leaned forward until her forearms were braced against the walls. Her sweet lube coated his tongue with every swipe over her luscious nether lips.

"Del," she gasped in that husky voice of hers. "I'm so close."

He knew, could feel her body yielding, softening and preparing itself for his. His fingers and mouth and chin were all coated with her sweetness and still he wanted more of her, wanted every luscious secret she withheld, every last bit of her soul that she kept hidden away like a treasure.

Standing behind her he withdrew her fingers, and though it pained him, he spoke the words she needed him to. "Activate your shield."

"What?" Her body shook with need and he saw the confusion masking her features.

The fact that she was so far gone, so out of her head with desire, soothed his pride at not being able to stake his claim. "I'm going to fuck you now."

He wanted to say so much more to her, to tell her why burying himself inside her was so important. Their physical relationship was their only connection, and with Ari awake, he didn't want to lose his only tether to Alison. It was his only outlet to show her how he felt.

Her health guard activated and he didn't waste a second shoving his hard prong into her hot sheath. They moaned in unison, reveling in the base thrill of their union. Fisting her wet hair, he tipped her head to the side as he withdrew slightly before thrusting forward. His free hand wrapped around her hips and delved between her labia until he pressed into the stiff little bud. She rocked up onto her toes and he felt the ripples as she came around him, milking his cock, urging him to follow her over the edge. Gritting his teeth, he ignored the weight in his balls and held on to his control for everything he was worth.

Moments passed while Alison shivered through her release. He gentled his touch, left his cock in her wet heat while he kissed along the curve of her neck and played with her breasts. Her eyelids fluttered up and she stared at him over her shoulder. "What's the matter?"

"Nothing." His hands cupped her breasts, hefting the heavy globes, memorizing the feel.

"Aren't you going to come?"

Slowly he shook his head. "No."

She scowled. "Why not?"

Running one knuckle along the curve of her cheek, he spoke softly. "This wasn't for me, at least not physically. I want you to understand, Alison. I will go to any lengths for you. It's not a bad thing."

Astonishment scrawled across her face. "You don't even know me. Why would you go out of your way for me at all?"

"Because we're the same, and I know how much it means for someone to fight for me with everything they possess. It's a gift I want to give to you." Before she could ask any more questions, he pulled himself back together, leaving her alone in the bathroom.

13

Marv had done exactly as he'd requested. The tray from his dinner still sat on the small table, the only piece of furniture in the room other than the huge bed. This was not a room someone lingered in for longer than a meal and a rest.

Or, in this case, a punishing fuck.

The younger man stood when the assassin entered the room. He had re-donned his ragged clothing, but the flesh beneath was clean.

"Take your clothes off. I've brought you something else to wear."

He read the hesitation but his tone left no room for argument. Marv stripped down to his skin and lowered his gaze. "Whadya want me to wear?"

"This." He offered the sleek black cloth.

Puzzlement flitted over Marv's face. He fingered the single hole in the fabric, ran his hand along the silky cords. "I'm not sure—"

"I'll show you." Without waiting for a response, the assassin took the bag back and placed it over the other man's head. Marv gasped but the assassin spun him around and wove the cord around the wrists he trapped at the small of his new toy's back.

Excitement and desire bubbled up in Marv and his cock lengthened and distended. His darkness excited him, the choice being taken from him fueled his lust and made it burn hotter even while it frightened him. His physiological response didn't stop him from making the token protest. "Hey, man, I didn't sign up for any of this kinky weird shit."

"You ate the food I provided for you, washed your body in my shower without a problem. I know earlier you were ready to suck my dick until I shot my load down your throat. Does it really matter that I can't see you while you do it?"

"I guess not." Marv sank to his knees slowly. "We gonna do this?"

"Patience. Anticipation can heighten the experience." The assassin gripped the other cord, the one attached to the hood that held the wearer in place. "Take me out."

"I can't, not with my hands tied."

"Imagine yourself doing it." Reaching into Marv's mind, the assassin pressed against the telekinetic cluster of nerves, adding to the gift he'd seen, the spark that, in another time, in another place, would be nurtured and cultivated to a full-fledged ability.

The thick muscles in his shoulders tightened as though straining physically with something that took physical exertion. "You have to want it, to want my thickness free to slide into your mouth. I know you like to suck cock, like the taste of cum spurting on your tongue. Own it, revel in it, like the filthy little whore we both know you are."

Precum beaded on Marv's shaft at his words but with his hands bound he couldn't do a thing about it. He grunted and the assassin pushed harder on the cluster, almost *too* hard. Jerking his hold on the hood, he took out his frustration on the bound man. "Maybe I'll just flip you over and fuck that ass. Ride you raw. One way or the other I'm going to use your body to come."

Fear slithered into the hired whore's mind. Marv didn't like that idea, he'd been ridden cruelly by an abusive stepfather. Which was precisely why the assassin said it; a spike of adrenaline brought forth the ability in some people.

Slowly, as though it was held by a trembling hand, his zipper slid down, one tooth at a time. He could imagine the look of concentration on the other man's face, another reason for the hood. Nothing would ruin this perfect moment of achievement, passing his gift off to another. In his more fanciful musings, he thought this must be what siring progeny was like.

He wore no underwear and his stiff prick was bared. When Marv would have slumped in exhaustion, the rope attached to the hood held him in line with his next meal.

"Very good. Now suck as though your next breath depends on it. Because it does."

The tongue darted out, searching for its reward and connected with the head. The gentle swipe was pleasing, as was the way his subject honed in on his length and swallowed him whole. Warmth and wetness welcomed him eagerly, sucking with greed and purpose. He let Marv work him at first with wet licks and deep, drawn-out pulls, enjoying the pressure, but as his balls tightened he drew up on the string again, holding the other man steady so he could fuck his mouth.

The first drive rammed his rod deep into the other man's throat, until he started to gag. Using his mind the assassin implanted the sensations he experienced in Marv's head, until he could feel wetness coating his own dick. Conversely he relaxed his gag reflex and the assassin rammed him again, fucking the face beneath the hood.

It didn't take long before he was shooting down the gulping throat, his body easing into release. It was pleasant, but nothing to write home about, as the old aphorism said. Marv didn't glom on to his new ability, didn't turn it back on the man he sucked off. Pity.

Stepping back, he distanced himself before Marv's own release forced jets of cum out from his engorged staff. The assassin despised mess and sneered at the streaks across the floor. Marv still shuddered and cursed in his native tongue, phrases the translator chip couldn't begin to interpret.

As he watched the other man struggle to recompose himself, the assassin considered the void inside him. Usually these little encounters served to clear his mind from the murkiness shrouding his path. The encounter with Marv left him just as muddied as he'd been before, his path as unclear as ever. There was no epiphany, only a hollowness that was growing more uncomfortable by the day.

Unbinding the ties with his mind the assassin growled, "Be gone."

"What the hell was that?" Marv yanked the hood off with a shaking hand.

Breaking his own rule of contact, he gripped the younger man's hair and leaned in until their faces were inches apart. The sharp scent of cum and the slick of perspiration drifted to him. "I said, be gone. Do not force me to say it again."

Marv's eyes widened and he scrambled to collect his clothing. Not stopping to redress he bolted from the room.

Bending at the waist, the assassin picked up the hood and worked it between his fingers. Mutual wasn't working for him anymore. The sickness was spreading. He had been many things, but never a rapist. He didn't know why, but that was a bridge too far.

Lying back on the bed, he thought about Alison's companion. She had no idea what a warrior she traveled with, the great violence he was capable of, or the lengths Fenton would go to protect her. Perhaps having a man like that in his hood, a powerful man who would fight him every step of the way, would lift his ennui.

His cock twitched with interest, imaging Fenton on his knees, taking his cock between his lips. He had no doubt Fenton would do it voluntarily, if he thought the action would save his woman's life. The assassin would make him come, would make him enjoy it while Alison cried. He'd never comingled business and pleasure before, but the seed, once planted, unfurled to take over his mind.

He smiled to himself. The mess would be worth it.

Daton Five was a beautiful world, at least in Alison's opinion. The forest surrounding Gwella's village was lush and green, with the merest hint of autumn colors tipping the leaves. She stood beside the empress as the shuttle landed on the raised platform high above the main city, taking in the dense expanse of greenery. Fenton knelt behind them, as was fitting for breeders when in the presence of their women. Ari was slung in a pack strapped to his chest, her head resting against his heart. Though they hadn't spoken since the encounter in the bathroom, Alison felt his eyes fixed on her every move.

"You are the first visitor we've had here in almost a century." Gwella's remark was casual. "I'm curious as to what you think."

"It's glorious," Alison murmured. "The region on my planet where I was born has trees and mountains very similar to this. I feel right at home."

"Looks can be deceptive," Gwella said. The cryptic statement, combined with her earlier inference that there was some kind of problem here, stuck like a splinter in Alison's mind. She desperately wanted to talk to Fenton about what they had gotten themselves into, but he wasn't receptive. His behavior vacillated from sulking to sexy and back in a heartbeat. If Ari ever slept again—and Alison was beginning to doubt she would—

she and Del would have it out. They were on the same side, just the way he'd wanted it. Why was he being so difficult?

"You seem distracted," Gwella murmured.

Alison cast a look over her shoulder until her gaze met Del's. "It's nothing," she said to him, to both of them.

"I see." The empress's lips twitched. "Men are troublesome creatures at times."

The last thing she wanted to talk with the empress about was her relationship. She got the feeling that the other woman looked down her nose at her. Or perhaps it was simply her own insecurities rearing their ugly heads. "Thank you for bringing us here. I can't wait to sightsee."

"I'm afraid your exploration will be very limited. Though the planet looks peaceful from this vantage, only the main cities are safe. We are at war, one I'm afraid we have very little hope of winning."

"With whom?"

Gwella cut her eyes to Alison before turning to the window. "Now is not the time. Come to dinner tonight, bring your breeder and the babe. You will meet my daughter and together we will answer your questions."

The shuttle set down with a thump, and the empress turned to her. "Do exactly as the group leader commands."

"Is there direct danger?" Though Fenton was on his knees, his posture stiffened and he became instantly alert. "If you grant me loan of a weapon, I can protect my woman better."

"Breeders are not allowed weapons. You might hurt yourself." One of the patrollers sneered.

"Del was a soldier," Alison offered, careful to phrase her words diplomatically. "He knows how to fight."

"It's forbidden." Gwella's voice was terse, her decree final.

Fenton rose gracefully and for a moment she thought he was about to challenge the edict. But he put his hand on Alison's shoulder. She looked into his clear blue eyes, even brighter than the cloudless sky. He didn't speak a word, he didn't have to, she got the message as though he'd whispered it in her ear. *Stay close to me.*

She would have offered to carry Ari, but she didn't think the empress and her minions would take that well, and the last thing she could afford to do was piss them off when they had no way off world.

One of the patrollers, a massive redhead who looked like she bench-pressed shuttles for fun, stepped forward. "We move as a unit in a starburst pattern with the empress and the hostages in the center. If you see a helcat do not stop, try to hide, or separate yourself from the group in any way. They like easy prey."

What was going on out there? Whatever a helcat was, she sure as shit didn't want to meet one if they considered people like the Amazon group leader easy prey.

Slowly the shuttle door opened and two of the patrollers moved out into the open. One turned back and made some sort of signal that must have been an all clear, because Gwella stepped forward.

Fenton was practically breathing down her neck and Ari fussed in her little carrier. The child had a scream like a sonic train whistle and just as piercing. Alison would have bet her heart had swollen to epic proportions as she descended the ramp to the world of trees and moss, because it seemed to throb in her throat and cut off her air supply.

"All clear, my lady." The lead patroller waved them forward. The air was rich with the scent of wet leaves and tree bark, the ground soft, almost spongy beneath her feet. Above them the main ship hovered as though standing sentinel on the small party.

Though she had a million questions, the atmosphere of the small group didn't invite idle chatter. Beside her, Gwella moved at a purposeful clip, like her ship cutting through space, knowing she owned it and cowering to none. If empress of Daton Five was a profession, Alison wanted to be Gwella in her next life.

Ahead of them, what looked like leafless trees sharpened to spear-like points surrounded the village, with the whittled tips crossing like entwined fingers in the center. An iron doorway was the only entrance she could see.

Fenton dogged her heels, so at first she thought the sensation of being stalked was from him. The empress's brisk pace kept her from really taking in the scenery, but she caught movement out of the corner of her eye. "What the frack?"

The group leader's head whipped in the direction she'd indicated, and her chemical whip lashed out just as what looked like a giant mountain lion with wings charged from the trees.

"Run!" Gwella barked out the command as the patrollers whipped at the humongous beast with their chemical whips. It roared in fury, rearing up on its hind legs to lash out with its massive claws. Alison gaped in horror as the group leader was cut in half with a single swipe.

More patrollers spilled from gates, chemical whips at the ready. The helcat took down two more patrollers, one with its teeth and another with the sharp barb on its tail.

"Don't look anywhere but forward." Fenton gripped her hand in his as the patrollers surrounded their empress and her hostages and ushered them through the gates. Alison protested when the heavy iron doors slammed shut behind them. At least ten women were still out there.

Fenton too seemed annoyed. "Aren't you going to send help?"

Gwella shook her head, still winded from the mad dash to safety. "They are already dead. The helcat is probably feeding on them even now. Anyone I sent would just die beside them."

"That's a helcat?" The name fit; that huge creature looked as though it had been forged in the deepest pit of the inferno. "Why would anyone settle on a planet inhabited by such awful creatures?"

Gwella didn't answer and Fenton squeezed her shoulder as though warning her to watch her tone. But the screams of the dying carried through the gaps in the roof, and she didn't understand why the empress didn't just evacuate all her people to safety.

A patroller, the one who had led the rescue from the village, moved toward Gwella, who shockingly, hugged the other woman fiercely. "Well done, Dani. If it had replicated or brought others we would have been done for."

Dani pulled back and Alison saw worry on the young woman's face. "They are prowling closer to the village at every pass."

"Despite the sonic disrupters we planted. Damnation." Gwella shook her head. "We can't withstand many more attacks like this."

The sounds accompanying the helcat's latest meal added a sickening validity to the dire prediction.

Alison met Fenton's gaze and saw her own worry reflected there.

From the people of Hosta, to the assassin, and now giant, monstrous predators with a penchant for humanoid flesh. Would they ever catch a break?

14

_____

Fenton had never truly appreciated his sister's life as a whore until he came to Daton Five. Playing the role of Alison's breeder, he had no power and his opinion mattered not at all. He watched the men of the small village go about their daily business, drawing water from the lake, tending children and taking orders from the women, even though the male inhabitants of the planet outnumbered the women by at least three to one.

As he and Alison were escorted to their small hut, he grit his teeth when a patroller remarked to Alison at the audacity of her breeder to walk by her side as though he were her equal.

"He is," Alison murmured.

He was appreciative for that, even if the gratitude galled him. What was wrong with these men that they'd continue with mundane tasks while valiant women died just outside the gates? Why didn't they rise up, protect their females, whether the women wanted it or not? They had both the strength and the numbers, yet they all lived as second-class citizens with their fates not of their own making.

One thing Fenton had learned as the overlord's ward: Sometimes the smartest move was to keep his observations to himself, no matter how much he resented it. Especially if his input would only end in punishment. He shuddered remembering the burn from the chemical whip. Not an experience he wanted to repeat.

The village was actually more of a colony, with private rooms built along the perimeter one on top of the other in a hive-like fashion and a large lake in the center. Sunlight filtered through the fallen limbs that protected the community. The lake, he'd noticed, was well stocked with fish, and crops grew up on either side of the lake. Fruit trees surrounded a common eating area. The villagers under Gwella's protection clearly functioned as a collective. Given the horror that existed just beyond their walls, they had no other choice.

"These are your assigned chambers. Our numbers are few and none will bother you. Do not try to leave without an escort." The patroller had hard, piggy eyes as she stared at Fenton with disdain.

"Thank you." Alison smiled, breaking the tension by pulling him inside and shutting the door with a groan.

The rustic interior surprised him. Fenton saw no modern amenities, no running water, no electricity like on the ship. Still, he intended to search for listening devices. Unfortunately, Ari was throwing an angry fit.

"Let me take her." Alison unfastened the sling he'd rigged to keep his niece secure. Hiding his surprise, he helped her free the irate little girl and handed her over.

She quieted instantly, fat teardrops clinging to her thick lashes.

"She likes you."

Alison cast him a withering glance. "Don't sound so surprised."

He hadn't meant to insult her. "You said before you didn't want to have children."

"I don't." She rocked back and forth with Ari on her hip, a small smile tugging up the corners of her mouth as the baby stared at her in wonder.

"Why?"

She made an irritated sound. "Del, I'm tired and she's hungry. Could you please make yourself useful before you grill me like a fracking steak?"

He moved closer to her, invading her personal space. "Lovely, don't think for one heartbeat that I will put up with that derogatory shit in private. You want something from me, you ask. Nicely. Are we clear?"

White teeth sank into her lower lip, but she nodded. "Please, would you get Ari something to eat?"

"Of course." Fighting a smile, he shrugged out of the pack.

"She's a little bit ripe. You think they'd give us some water to bathe her?" Alison set Ari down on the nearest pillow and the spell was broken. The little one shrieked like Alison was sticking pins in her.

"You can ask. I doubt they'll whip *you* for it."

"Does it still hurt?" she asked softly.

He rehydrated some baby formula with water from his canteen. The skin still ached dully but he shook his head. "I'm fine."

Conversation was cut short after that, as Ari wound herself up to wailing. The sound irritated him, but Alison seemed deeply disturbed by the piercing shrieks. Her hands shook as she changed the little one's diaper.

Picking up his niece, he plopped the bottle in her mouth. Her rosebud mouth closed around on it and she sucked greedily. The quiet was sheer bliss.

"Are you all right?" He frowned at Alison.

She sank onto a cushion, rubbing some chemical cleanser between her palms. "Those creatures. God, Del, it was awful. The women just didn't stand a chance."

"I know." He wasn't sure what to do about it, though.

"You know how something looks fantastic on the surface and then turns out to be awful?"

"You mean this planet?"

She nodded. "I like Gwella, I like the scenery, like the culture."

He scowled. "Don't you believe men and women should be equals?"

"Of course. But there's something about seeing the women take charge here that really speaks to me. They've made their own society and are determined to protect it. I can't say I'd make the same choice, but it's admirable."

"Admirable? They whip their lovers for disobedience." The words came out like a snarl. "Do you really aspire to that?"

She put her head in her hands. "I'm not explaining this right. I'm so tired and I don't want to fight with you anymore."

He backed off immediately. "Try and get some rest if you can. I'll work on getting Ari to sleep." A nasty side effect of the stasis pod was that the one who'd spent time in it had a hard time establishing a decent sleep cycle. Ari had been awake for more than thirty-six hours without rest. So had Alison.

She nodded slowly. "I just need a nap."

Stretching out on the pillows, she pulled the blanket over herself.

Del rocked Ari for several moments and watched Alison sleep. The men of this backwater planet might not feel a need to protect their women, but Fenton sure as hell did. Even if he had no idea how to go about that.

Ari drifted to sleep and he wrapped her in a blanket and placed her on a low cushion next to Alison. Though he craved nothing more than cuddling up next to them and getting a little shut-eye, he instead turned toward the door.

The sour-faced patroller was still there. "What do you want, breeder?"

"My women require water for both drinking and bathing." Alison would be ecstatic to have the stone tub he'd spied by the fire pit filled with hot water to wash herself in when she awoke.

The patroller pointed to the lake, which was visible from where they stood. "Buckets are down there. You have to haul it up yourself, unless you find another breeder to help you."

"Has the water been purified?" Alison had her shielding, but Ari was susceptible to all sorts of alien microbes.

The patroller nodded. "We take care of our own."

He thanked her and under her sharp gaze headed down to the water. Buckets lined the shore, leading him to believe this was the normal way of doing things.

On his fifth trip, he paused to catch his breath when a noise across the lake caught his attention. Men had been piling logs in the freshly dug hole, most likely for the cooking fire. But work had ceased as the shouts grew louder. "Explain yourself, you frigid bitch!"

Patrollers pushed through the gathering crowd. "Breeder, control yourself or we will put you in chains."

The irate speaker ignored them. "You took her from me, and for what? How many more will die for your pride?"

A chemical whip struck him on the back. He grunted on impact but remained standing. Fenton winced in sympathy, having experienced the lash firsthand.

"Answer me, you heartless harpy!"

Again the lash struck him and even from this distance, Fenton could see the welt on the other man's back. He fell to his knees, his voice too low to hear. The patroller drew the handle back, but a hand gripped her wrist before she let it fly again.

"The breeder is grieving for his woman. No pain you give him will trump the loss he's endured." It was Gwella's daughter, Dani, who spoke with authority.

"He disrespected our empress. The law says—"

"The law be damned. He is not a helcat, you cannot punish him as though he were one when his only crime is love." Dani moved to the injured man's side.

Before Fenton knew what he was doing, he moved closer to the spectacle. The lure of obtaining information had him hooked and Dani seemed reasonable.

Creeping through the trees, he moved aside the common area and watched as the empress's daughter cleaned the grieving man's wound.

"I want to fight," he said, but with no conviction behind his words. It was clear to Fenton that they'd had this conversation on more than one occasion. "I could have saved her, gotten her back inside before the gates closed."

"She died a hero, protecting her empress and the lives of innocents. Did you see the little one with the strangers? She wouldn't have stood a chance if not for Jori's sacrifice."

He didn't respond, didn't so much as twitch as the young woman patched him up. "Go home, Har, you have little ones who need you."

"I don't want another one. You can't just replace what Jori and I had, slide someone else into her slot."

"I'll try to put it off a few days. But your offspring need a protector. It's what Jori would have wanted."

"I won't fuck her."

"Then you'll be replaced." Dani didn't say it cruelly, just as though she was stating a fact. "A breeder who won't breed is useless."

The man turned to look at her, his face lined with misery. "It's not right. None of this is."

She watched him walk away. "I know." Dani's shoulders slumped.

Another man, taller, broader, almost Fenton's size with a thatch of jet hair threaded through with gray moved away from the crowd. "Are you all right?"

He didn't touch Dani, but Fenton could see he wanted to.

She shook her head. "Kel, how can I chastise him when I agree with him? The men *should* be fighting alongside us, we need every able-bodied person out there helping us hunt the helcats. The rules are archaic."

"Love, don't. Don't do this to yourself. You're only follow-ing orders." This time he did reach for her and tugged her into his embrace. "If I'd lost you today . . ." He let the statement hang.

"Ssshhh." Dani pulled out of his hold and cast furtive glances around the green. "You can't say things like that out here. What if someone knew? They'd never let you come to me again."

Fenton had heard enough. Not wanting to eavesdrop on what was clearly a private moment, he snuck back around the lake, considering what to do with all he'd learned.

Alison woke when Fenton shook her shoulder. "You need to get up if you want to bathe before dinner." Groaning, she rolled to her side and slung an arm over her eyes. "Don't tease me with that. It's below the belt."

He frowned at her midsection. "You're not wearing a belt."

"It's an Earth slang term for a low blow, hitting outside the marked areas." Some things just didn't translate well.

He still appeared mystified but nodded. "I wasn't teasing you. The water is warming in front of the fire. I thought you could go first and then I'll bathe Ari."

She sat up and saw steam rising from the stone tub before the roaring fire. "But there's no running water. How . . . ?" Her gaze slid to him.

Fenton shrugged. "A bucket at a time from the lake. It's clean, I checked."

Her jaw dropped. "But why?" She could have dealt with the chemical foam. Hauling enough water for her to bathe in went above and beyond.

Fenton shifted his weight, his gaze landing anywhere but on her, as though the question made him uncomfortable. "I knew it would make you happy."

Her heart clenched so hard her hand actually went to her chest. Just when she thought he was ready to be done with her, he went and did something amazing just to make her smile.

"You are so good to me." The words tumbled out and she followed up by wrapping her arms around his neck. Strong arms snaked around her, molding her body into his. There was nothing sexual in the hug, it was pure affection and it scared her a little, but she refused to let go.

Any woman who let go of this man was an idiot.

He pulled away first. "Come on, we're expected at dinner."

"As long as we're not *for* dinner." She shuddered when she thought of the helcats. "Have you checked everything out?"

"Yes, no listening devices. The technology these people employ is limited. Their lifestyle is primitive, which is odd for a space-faring society."

"Why don't they just leave?" Alison asked as she unfastened her dress.

Fenton's eyes turned hot as they skimmed her body and his tone was a little rougher as he replied, "Where would they go? Every planet has problems."

"Not of the man-eating cat variety." She stepped over the lip of the tub and sank into the warm water. Closing her eyes she let the water soothe her aches and pains. "Mmm, that's nice."

Fenton crouched to tuck Ari's blanket more tightly around her. "So, you don't want to stay here?"

Though he posed the question casually, she heard something else in his voice. "Why would I?"

"You are very well protected from the assassin here. I doubt even he could best the helcats or sneak past Daton Five's front gate. And you said you liked the culture."

Lifting one leg from the water she studied it, enjoying the warmth from the flickering fire. "Admired is a better word, especially for Gwella. She's so strong and in command of herself and those around her."

"Not as much as you might think. There is dissension among the men. They want to fight, and some of the women agree with them." He briefly related what he'd witnessed by the lake. As he spoke he moved closer to the tub.

She loved the way he looked at her. Even at her peak, no man had ever stared at her the way Fenton did. Almost as though he didn't see her flaws, or more accurately, that he didn't think she had any. "Why do you want me so much?"

Reaching forward, he traced her collarbone with one finger as if he had to touch her. "Do I need a reason to desire you?"

Slowly, Alison nodded. "I come with an entire space freighter of baggage, and you have your own to contend with. Why take on mine too? I'm not all that unique in the galaxy."

He didn't answer right away. She appreciated that about him, that he was so deliberate, not running his mouth to hear the sound of his own voice. So many men just told a woman what she wanted to hear.

"You accept me as I am." His fingers sought out his scar as he spoke. "I haven't always had that."

"I know what you mean." She shifted in the water, feeling a sudden chill of foreboding. She covered the hand he had on his face with her own. "You're a beautiful man, Del. Inside and out."

The blue in his eyes turned molten, hot with the searing lust that was never far away. Instead of falling back on old patterns and enticing him sexually, she continued to stroke his face with tender care. "What happened here?"

"One of the overlord's lessons." His words were shaded with bitterness. "He'd failed to bring his own son to heel and he was determined to mold me, the child of his enemy, into a weapon. I was about thirteen and he summoned me to his chambers. I didn't know why."

His lids closed as he lost himself in the memory. "There was a young woman there. A slave. It was obvious he had used her, the sheets were stained with blood. I was old enough to know what that meant, even without the scent of sex. Inflicting pain aroused him.

"She was huddled in a corner shaking in terror. I just stood there. I knew if he saw any sign of weakness he'd punish me for it. So I just stared at her. He said, and this I remember clearly, 'You're a man now, so it's time you prove it.'"

His eyes opened and Alison saw the horror he'd endured, etched on his face. "He ordered me to rape her."

"Oh, God," Alison shivered at the scene his words painted in her mind. "What did you do?"

His expression closed up. "Do you mean, did I go through with it?"

Slowly, Alison shook her head. "I know you didn't. You don't have that in you."

His shoulders relaxed. "You're right. As I looked at her, this pitiful creature who'd so obviously suffered, I couldn't see a way out of it but one. I refused. And he laughed and called me weak. He was so fast, so damn strong. It was the blessing from the infinity pool. I thought that was it, that he would kill me for my defiance. But instead he took the knife, still coated with her blood, and he started cutting. He was meticulous, twisting the knife to deaden the nerves and taking enough flesh so it would never heal right."

Taking her hand in his, he helped her trace the length of his scar. "I passed out from the pain of it at one point. And when I woke up I couldn't see, my face was so covered in blood. But I could hear her screaming as he forced himself on her again. When it was finally over, he slit her throat and then spit on me. He told me that I was disfigured for life, so I'd better get used to taking what I wanted from women because I was so hideous one would never accept me."

"Del." She reached for him, her heart aching at what he'd endured, but he rose and moved away.

"We need to wake Ari. Gwella is expecting you at dinner."

Alison rose from the water, realizing his change of subject was really about the shame of his confession. Stepping out of the tub, she wrung the excess water from her hair and reached for a towel. "He was wrong. I want you. I have from the moment I first saw you."

He didn't respond, just turned his attention to his niece. Alison watched him fuss with the little girl so gently and knew that she had lost a part of her heart to this man.

God help her if he ever found out.

15

Full dark had fallen by the time the scowling patroller led them to the bonfire. Despite the dangers lurking just beyond the fallen trees, the people of Daton Five laughed and danced and ate. Or maybe, Fenton mused, they celebrated *because* they knew firsthand how quickly it could all end and were determined to enjoy every breath as though they might not get another.

Gwella directed Alison to sit on her left at the stone table, which was hardly more than a flat-topped boulder. She raised an eyebrow when Fenton lowered himself beside Alison, but didn't comment. Ari perched in the crook of his arm, full and clean. His niece grinned toothlessly, charming everyone around her.

A young man deposited a bowl in front of him. It appeared to be constructed from half a petrified gourd and filled with some pale orange mush. Fenton tilted his head and wondered how he could eat while holding Ari and whether it would offend anyone if he asked Alison to hold her for the two minutes it would take to slurp down the bowl's contents. His stomach rumbled.

The man who'd brought his food held out his hands. "I'll take her while you eat."

Fenton was about to refuse, unwilling to let the little one out of his sight, when he felt Alison's fingers on his thigh. She squeezed once before removing her hand, never turning from her conversation with Gwella. Gritting his teeth in what he hoped passed for a smile, he handed the baby to the young man.

Turning, he saw Gwella stare at him, her gaze cool and assessing. She nodded once and turned to her own meal. Alison had been right, he had to demonstrate trust or the empress would have taken offense.

"Very good." She leaned back, observing them. "I'd like to extend a measure of trust. The patroller guarding you is needed elsewhere. Will you give me your word that you and your breeder will not cause trouble?"

Alison looked at him and he nodded once. Getting rid of their sour-faced guard would allow him even more mobility.

"Excellent." Gwella turned back to her bowl, a pleased expression on her face.

"This is delicious." Alison scraped the remaining soup into her bowl.

"My personal breeder's recipe." Gwella smiled at one of the men still ladling out food to the gathered congregation. "We grow most of our food in the green here. Mostly root vegetables or fruit that grows on vines. It can grow tiresome after a while, but luckily, he's an excellent cook."

Fenton tried to imagine taking pride in preparing a meal and failed. To him, food was simply fuel for his body. Sure, some things tasted better than others but if a protein cube kept him going as long as a gourmet dinner, why waste time fixing the latter?

Setting her spoon aside, Alison reached for her water glass. "Personal breeder? Do you have committed relationships?"

Gwella nodded. "Women are only allowed to enter in monogamous unions after yielding a female heir with another breeder, to keep the gene pool as varied as possible. It seems harsh at times, especially to the young and hot-blooded who assume love can conquer all, but we've had to take some drastic measures to survive. Many times our patrollers don't make it to a second birthing."

His gaze cut to Dani, who sat on Gwella's other side. Her eyes were focused on her untouched dinner, her jaw clenched.

Alison nodded, her expression thoughtful. "So women are required to procreate here?"

Fenton couldn't be sure, but he thought he saw her shudder.

Gwella gestured to a breeder to refill her cup. "Only if they wish to become patrollers. No woman can fight unless she has contributed to the next generation, preferably with a female to take her place in case she dies in combat."

"Forgive my curiosity, but I'm wondering why you don't just leave when you have the means? Your ship was impressive and could probably hold this entire settlement."

Fenton's chest swelled with pride. She was a skilled diplomat, fishing for information in a noninvasive way. Her probing was so gentle that the empress couldn't possibly take offense. Not for the first time, he was glad he'd rescued her from Mig Larshe because he'd be lost without her.

Pushing her bowl aside, Gwella turned to face them. "The situation is . . . complex. Daton Five wasn't always ruled by an empress. A millennia ago, this was an industrial world, brimming with scientific creation. We were open to trade, to exploration and advancement in every way. Our people were completely dependent on it, almost addicted to it, especially the men in power. For them, developments in technology meant greater control. The people lost touch with their heritage, all the unique traditions and knowledge forgotten in the need to acquire more."

Gwella paused and drained her cup, her unfocused gaze on the roaring fire. Fenton suspected that the cup wasn't filled with water like his and Alison's.

"That unquenchable thirst was exploited by a man, a foreigner. He claimed to be a scientist from another world. We know little of his origins, only that he had a unique ability that the ruling faction wanted."

"Oh?" Alison tilted her head to the sight, her hair gleaming in the firelight. "What was so valuable?"

"He could replicate himself."

Every curse in every language Fenton had ever heard went through his mind. The phase split was a family trait, something encoded at birth. It only passed down on the Y chromosome. This man that had ruined Daton Five had been a relative of his.

"What happened?" Alison's voice was soft.

"The stranger and the ruling faction experimented on animals, trying to reproduce what the man could do. Of course word got out, but instead of stopping them, other men joined in the game, racing each other to the end goal. Temporary cloning, how useful! Better to fight, to work, the ability to be in two places at once, who wouldn't want that?"

Me, Fenton thought, more regretful than ever that he hadn't gone to the apothecary and purged himself of the phase-splitting curse.

"Your scientists created the helcats by accident, trying to mimic the alien?" Alison whispered. Fenton wished he could see her face.

"Our *men* did." Gwella spat the word as though it tasted bad. "Greedy, power hungry, thoughtless, careless men spliced animal DNA together, trying to create a breed strong enough to survive being pulled in two. The helcats were strong all right. Fast, vicious, and deadly. They were scheduled for termination when the power grid failed. They escaped into the wild, ten males and fourteen females. If the men in charge had reacted differently, we might have stood a chance. Instead, they hid the truth, covered up the escape, and tried to solve the problem quietly. It didn't work. The beasts gestated so quickly, within a year they'd decimated our population to a fragment of what it had been, increasing their numbers by feeding on ours. By that time it was too late. We burned our own cities trying to kill them. With nowhere else to go we fled to the wild. Our reliance on technology, our inability to survive without it, nearly destroyed us all."

"But you survived," Alison said.

"Only because of my ancestor, Frieda. She gathered a small group here, mostly women, and taught them how to survive. It was tough at first, with no medicine for those who fell ill, not enough blankets when the snows came. But we persevered and vowed never to trust men to save us again. We leave when we have to, searching for things we need, something that might help us destroy the helcats and let us reclaim our home and rebuild."

"But why not start over?" Alison asked. There was no chastisement in her tone, just mystification.

Gwella lifted her chin to a stubborn angle. "Where? We haven't left our own solar system in more than a century. With no destination, no ability to replicate food and water, we can only take so much. We would die of starvation before we found a suitable place. It was decided we would rather die here, fighting for our home."

Decided by whom? Fenton wondered, tucking into his mushy squash, though he wouldn't voice it aloud. Dani turned to him, looking past her mother to him. She held his gaze for a long moment, long enough for him to read the defeat on her face. She didn't want to die any more than she wanted to go on living the way she was, turning away from the man she loved.

He felt for her, but could do nothing to help her. He already had two females to save and a mountain of doubt that he could pull it off.

Excusing himself quietly, he went in search of Ari.

After the meal was cleared away, the dancing broke out in earnest. Alison had never seen anything like it. Everyone moved on his or her own, yet the group seemed to move in sync, almost like they had practiced it. But as the tempo altered from one song to the next, the fluidity continued. The natives of this world obviously had a better sense of rhythm than she did. Gwella and her breeder joined the throng, moving with the easy grace of a couple who recognized one another's bodies and adjust their own to fit.

The dance seemed to be telling a story, perhaps the same one Gwella had related earlier about the history of Daton Five. But here the men towered over the women, strong from lives of demanding physical labor. They didn't look cowed, didn't hide behind their women, they appeared just as capable, fierce, and protective as any patroller.

And the women responded to it. In the corner she saw the sour-faced patroller that had been assigned to guard her and Fenton shed her armor until she wore only a thin camisole and loose pants. Two men ground against her, one from the front, the other from behind. She ignored them both as she loosened her hair and swung her hips with purpose as though the movement alone would erase the horrors she'd witnessed that day. Alison had thought her to be ugly before and desperately in need of a makeover and a decent haircut. Seeing her with her eyes closed and her face relaxed she appeared more sensual and enticing. No cosmetics or sexy lingerie were required to transform her into an alluring specimen. The men obviously thought so, as their hands skimmed over her supple body, moving in time with it. Alison wondered if she'd fuck them both, the way she did with both Fentons when he phase split.

Just thinking about him made her squirm, her eyes scanning for his familiar scarred visage. The things he'd told her about the way he'd grown up made her heart melt for him, and seeing such a robust man comply to the limitations that Gwella imposed on men here helped her see him for what he was.

A survivor, like her.

But unlike her he was selfless and had integrity. He cared about Ari and about her, even when doing so put him at risk. No amount of structure or derogatory remarks would bow that man.

When she didn't see him she rose from the table and wove through the crowd. A few of the breeders rubbed up against her enticingly and while her body responded to their attentions, it was only a surface reaction, like blinking against harsh sunlight. Almost involuntary.

She was turned on, but only one man could quench the powerful need bubbling up inside her. Not just his magnificent body, but the look in his eyes when he saw her, the way his lips curled up into that half smile, his satisfied groans of pleasure when they engaged in something particularly filthy. Desire stronger than any she'd ever known propelled her onward, seeking him, needing him. Craving him.

If she didn't know he wanted her just as badly, it would have been intolerable. But he did want her, need her, well past the point of sanity.

After completing her second circuit of the green, she looked back toward the honeycomb, to the room they'd been given. Had he taken Ari back there?

A lone figure perched on a rock beside the water. The familiar expanse of his broad shoulders filled her with relief, which was ridiculous. She was as safe as she could be on a planet filled with winged people-eating monsters. So why did she want to break into a run at the sight of him?

Because I missed him.

Closing her eyes, she accepted the truth. Del Fenton meant more to her than incredible sex. He didn't possess the wealth she'd thought he did, had lost what he did have because of her. He fought the assassin for her, saved her, and she'd risked herself to save him too.

That meant something, even if she didn't want to accept it. And after everything he'd done for her, he deserved to know that much at least.

"Del?" Her voice actually wobbled as she called out to him.

Those massive shoulders stiffened and he turned to face her. "Be careful, the rocks are slippery."

"Where's Ari?" she asked when she saw he was alone. She expected him to stand, offer her his hand to steady her, but he remained seated.

"Being doted on by the entire planet it seems. She's a glutton for the attention."

"You give her plenty." She meant it as a compliment, but he scowled at her.

"You mean because of my ability?"

"No." Confused and hurt by his standoffishness, Alison stopped. "What's the matter?"

"It's nothing." Fenton looked back up the way he'd been doing before she called out to him. She followed his stare and could see a small gap in the roof, revealing a small sliver of the night sky beyond.

Moving closer, she placed her arm on his. "Tell me. Are you worried about the helcats?"

He withdrew from her touch. "Leave it alone, Alison."

"What the hell's the matter with you?" Here she'd been hunting for him for over an hour, and instead of throwing up her skirt and having at her he decided to throw a big fat mantrum instead. Didn't it figure?

He turned to her then, seething with anger. She'd never seen him so livid, didn't know he was capable of such an all-consuming rage. He wasn't loud, but quiet, every word like a slap. "Did you tell her?"

"Tell who? What?"

"Gwella. Did you tell her about me, about my phase splitting?"

Her lips parted in surprise. At the time she'd been so caught up in Gwella's story that she hadn't thought the empress was describing Fenton's ability, almost exactly. She felt like an idiot for not making the connection sooner, but she'd honestly forgotten. Was that what had him so riled? "No. It didn't even occur to me."

"So that's the only reason you didn't say anything to her." His tone was flat and coated in disgust.

"Of course not. I know you don't want that to get out."

"So you're saying you wouldn't ever use it as a bargaining chip. My life and my niece's life depend on you."

"What do you mean, your life? You don't really think Gwella would have you executed because of something not your fault."

"Why not? The message in her story was pretty specific. Men are not to be trusted, especially alien men. I have the power that her ancestors killed each other for. Why *wouldn't* she get rid of me the second she found out?"

"Well then, we can't let her find out." Alison lifted her chin and put her hands on her hips.

"All of a sudden you're on *my* side? When only twenty-four hours ago you were ready to fuck your way into her good graces?"

Alison winced. *The truth hurts.* "I told you, that was a mistake, like a reflex."

"A reflex?" He laughed without humor. "Like an automatic response? Forgive me if that doesn't make me feel any more secure. All it'll take is one slipup, Alison. I can't always control it and if someone walked in at the wrong moment..." The words trailed off.

His worry was palpable, thickly filling the space between them. She wanted to reach for him but couldn't stomach the thought of another rebuff.

"I would never do anything to hurt you, Del. Or Ari."

He let out a tired sigh. "I'm sorry, Alison. I want to trust you, but I just can't. Not with Ari's life. They might kill her just for being related to me even though the females in my family were only carriers. The risk isn't mine to take."

Tears blinded her. She couldn't even argue when what he said made so much sense. In his position, she wouldn't trust her either. "So where does that leave us?"

He shook his head, his shoulders slumping in defeat. "Stuck here until we can get off this rock and go our separate ways." Sliding off the rock, he moved back toward the celebration, leaving her alone with her shame.

16

Fenton had just put Ari to bed for the night when Alison came in. She looked to him and then her gaze fell on the sleeping infant. "Out again, huh?" Her voice sounded strained.

"She's falling back into her normal routine," he responded woodenly.

A gorge of things unsaid seemed to open up in the space between them. He knew he'd hurt her with his confession earlier, but she had to understand Ari came first with him. No matter how much he wanted to believe in Alison, life was not a game of *demjong* where a bad hand could be folded and his niece a credit he could lose.

After a few moments of yawning silence, she looked away. "I'm turning in."

She unfastened her dress, but paused before pulling it off. His eyes locked on to the creamy mounds of flesh at her bodice. She closed her eyes, exhaled, and climbed onto the pillow fully dressed. The exquisite gown that contoured to every lush curve was dingy from wear, yet she'd rather sleep in it than let him see her bare body. That hurt.

He wanted nothing more than to climb onto that oversized pillow with her and hold her close. It didn't need to be about sex; just breathing her in would be enough. But he'd already taken his stand. Even if she would let him touch her intimately, it would only lead to deeper pain later on.

"I'm going for a walk," he announced. Even if the patrollers gave him a hard time about it, anything was better than sitting here imagining all the ways he would like to take her supple body.

She rolled to her side and he felt her eyes on him as he ducked through the door. Closing it quickly behind him so the cool night air wouldn't seep into the room, Fenton stared up at the wooden ceiling of the habitat. The giant redwood trees were really a flimsy protection from the monsters waiting beyond.

A soft sniffle carried to him through the door. Closing his eyes, he punished himself by listening to Alison's soft sobs. She deserved so much better than to be holed up in a dinky room alone after the things he'd said to her. He should have let her go to the empress when he had the chance. Selfish bastard that he was, he'd wanted to keep her to himself.

And now I'm going to lose her anyway.

Scooping up the buckets in case a patroller questioned what he was doing, he headed toward the lake. Lustful moans and hoarse cries emanated from behind many of the doors he passed. The breeders were hard at work, pleasing their women warriors.

The bonfire still blazed, though the flames weren't as high as they had been. The music had faded and he detected the soft murmurs of elderly people huddled around the dying warmth. All the younger denizens had retreated in pairs, and sometimes more than that, to burn off the rest of their frenetic energy in private.

With nowhere else to go, Fenton returned to the flat rock

where he'd sat earlier. Stretching out on his back, he stared at the sliver of night sky visible through the gap between the trees. A full grown man could easily slip through that, but the inhabitants of Daton Five weren't hiding from men. Only he and Alison were.

Would the assassin find them? And if he did, could he get past the helcats? Undoubtedly he was powerful, but would he stand a chance against one of those genetically engineered beasts?

He was so lost in thought that a blade was pressed against his throat before he realized he was no longer alone.

"Why were you watching me?"

Even in the darkness, he could make out Dani's features. Denying that he had been watching her was pointless. Obviously she'd noticed him earlier. "I was trying to learn more about your people. I didn't mean to spy."

Her fist tightened in his hair, holding him immobile. If he moved, she'd cut his throat. "Did you tell my mother you saw me with Kel?"

Weighing his words carefully, he murmured, "It's not my place."

"And at dinner? Why were you looking at me? Are you dissatisfied with your own woman? Is that why you skulk about in the darkness?"

"No. Alison and I fought, but I am not in any way dissatisfied with her. I told you, I am trying to understand what's going on here and how I can protect those under my care."

"I believe you." The blade disappeared and she released his hair. "I saw the way you looked at her and I knew you fought."

He sat up and frowned. "Then why . . . ?"

She shrugged and sat beside him on the rock. "I wanted to see if you would lie to me or try to seduce me. You didn't and you kept my secret. For that I thank you."

Fenton nodded. "I understand what it is like to live with secrets."

"I wish I didn't have to. My mother is unbending in her decrees. I've already borne a son, yet she won't let me choose Kel as my own until I have a daughter. I'm afraid I'll die before that happens, that we all will."

"How bad is it?" Fenton asked quietly.

"Bad. The helcats are starving. Used to be the noise from the ship's engine kept them away, but now they chance it. The one that attacked yesterday was badly wounded. If any others were nearby, he became their latest meal."

"How many are there?"

"It's difficult to get a precise count, but as our numbers dwindle, so do theirs. Nothing to eat, you know."

"So if you did evacuate the planet long enough, they would all die off?"

"Eventually, yes. The creation of the hellcats destroyed the food chain. It's why we no longer have meat, other than fish. No game to hunt."

"So why doesn't your mother evacuate everyone? Once the helcats are gone, you could rebuild, have a real civilization again and no one would have to die."

"It's not so simple. There are too many of us and we only have one working ship anymore. In order to evacuate, we'd have to either make several trips or ask someone else for help."

"And she's too stubborn to ask." Fenton recalled the scorn in the empress's words when she talked about alien men.

"Exactly." Dani nodded. "I don't understand her sometimes. She'll capture the three of you and bring you here to our home, confiscate your ship and belongings for being in our space, but she won't deal with another race long enough to ask for help. It makes no sense."

From what Gwella had said, his shuttle suite had been broken down into useable parts. Even Alison's wardrobe would fill needs all across the community, cut down into clean bandages or sewn up and stuffed for extra bedding. He'd expected her to balk at that, but she'd nodded and said she hoped everything would be put to good use.

They sat there quietly for a time, listening to the fish jumping out of the water. "Are there any other options for defeating the helcats?" Fenton asked.

Dani paused and he could tell she was assessing him again. "If the men fought, it would double our numbers, increase our chances of taking them out once and for all. But they are untrained in combat and my mother wants them to stay that way. I have my hands full leading expeditions beyond the wall."

Fenton blew out a breath. "So either way, you are up against the empress's iron will. If you could convince her that training the men was in everyone's best interest, I could bring them up to speed."

"You'd train the men?"

"I'm a soldier. I'll do whatever I'm ordered to do. And like your Kel, I'd rather die defending those I love than sit safely on the sidelines watching it all come apart around me."

"Then let's do it," a male voice said from the darkness.

Dani was up off the rock in an instant. "Kel, how long have you been there?"

"Long enough." The big man hugged her to his side even as he moved closer to Fenton. His deep voice rumbled low as he spoke. "You mean it? You can train us for combat?"

"Yes. I was a commander until a few months ago. I spent my life making men combat ready. It will be difficult, the training intensive. Are you sure you want this?"

"More than anything."

"My mother will kill you both if she finds out," Dani whispered.

Fenton was losing count of the things he was hiding from the empress. "Then she best not find out."

Alison woke to searing agony in her midsection. At first she thought it was some sort of reaction to the foreign food, perhaps even microbes in the water. But the cramping took on an all-too-familiar pattern. *Frack.* It was that time of the month and her period arrived with a vengeance.

Groaning, she curled into a ball on her side, trying to breathe through the worst of it.

"What is it?" Fenton was by her side in an instant.

Talking to him about her flipping menstrual cycle was the absolute last thing she wanted to do. She'd rather the assassin got her. "Nothing."

"Alison, you're deathly pale. Are you sick?"

"No, just cursed," she groaned as another sharp flame stabbed her. Her cycle had always been wonky, skip a month, even two and then have the red sea knock her on her ass for days. Like so many other things, she'd grown dependent on regular medical treatment to see her through the worst of it. Pain pills and heating patches, plus a lot of wine and chocolate. Medication too, to keep her hormones regulated.

But here she had nothing, not even the *basics.* And with Fenton breathing down her neck, compounding her embarrassment, her misery was complete. "Go away." She tried to shove at him, but he hovered like a damn transport pod.

"Not until you tell me what's wrong. Do I need to get a doctor?"

"You need to get a clue." Sniping at him wasn't helping her though, and he was tenacious enough to wheedle it out of her. He'd had a sister; this wouldn't be his first rodeo with the great red beast. "It's my period."

"Your what?" His brows drew down in confusion.

Fracking translator chip. Of course he didn't know what that was, just to compound her humiliation. "My female fertility cycle."

He blinked and the light dawned. "It pains you?"

Closing her eyes, she nodded. "Not always, but right now it's unbearable."

"What do you need?" His warm palm slid over her throbbing abdomen, applying gentle heat and pressure. She should push him away again, but his touch felt too good, a sweet connection to distract her from the discomfort.

"Whatever they have here to deal with this." She could only begin to imagine her beautiful dresses, torn up and used for absorption purposes. Pillows and bandages were one thing but for *that*? Yuck, yuck, yuck. Gave the phrase "on the rag" a whole new meaning.

He didn't bat an eyelash. "I'll go ask a patroller."

"I'll be here." She watched him move through the room with catlike grace, open the door, and look back at her.

Alison's lips parted as the truth dawned. He didn't want to leave her, alone and in pain. Perhaps he was simply worried about her not being able to take care of Ari should she wake up but his concern touched her. "I'll be fine. The sooner you go, the sooner you get back, right?"

He went.

Shoving herself upright, Alison shuffled toward the small alcove with the sanitary facilities. The waste reducer and sterilizer was the only modern technology in the hut, which made sense. If people were going to have to live together in such a confined space, it stood to reason that they'd need a way to eliminate all the unwanted byproducts of life.

Hanging her dress over the door, she stepped into the chamber and activated the foam. She'd barely begun to clean between her legs when a wave of dizziness hit her, sending her to her hands and knees. The foam evaporated, leaving her chilled to the bone and shaking. *Not my brightest idea ever.* Rolling onto her side, she closed her eyes as exhaustion swamped her. *I'll get up in a minute.*

"What the fuck, Alison?" Fenton had returned and he was clearly pissed to find her huddled on the floor. She couldn't recall hearing him curse out loud before, and definitely not at her. The patroller stood behind him, taking in the scene with a concerned glance.

"Sorry," she said weakly.

His thunderous expression clearly stated that he wasn't falling for it, but he just grit his teeth and turned to the patroller. "Would you please watch over the baby while I tend her?"

The woman handed him something and nodded. "Worry not, breeder. Help your female."

The door closed and Alison actually flinched as he crouched beside her.

"What were you thinking?" The words were harsh, even whispered.

"That I can take care of myself." Her point would have been stronger if she wasn't naked and shivering.

"You could have fallen, cracked your skull open. What if had taken me longer to find a patroller? Someone came in and took Ari while you were passed out in here? I could have lost you both." An edge of fear laced through his words.

She hadn't thought of that. "I'm sorry. I didn't mean to worry you."

"Come on, let me help you up. Grab on to my shoulders."

She did, but muttered, "I hate being helpless."

"I know, lovely. You're not, you just need help sometimes. That's not a crime, or even a weakness. We all do." As he spoke, he ran the towel down the length of her body, wiping away the last traces of the foam.

"Spread your legs so I can insert this." He held up the tiny thing the patroller had given him.

She eyed it skeptically. It was metallic and about the size of her thumb. "What is it?"

"It's what they use to collect what your body discharges. It breaks everything down into basic elements, like oxygen, hydrogen, sodium, and chloride. It's similar to what the women used on Hosta. Safe and efficient."

"I can do it." She reached for it but he snatched it away.

"Damn you, why do you have to be so stubborn about every little thing?"

Heat scaled her cheeks and tears threatened. "I'm humiliated enough as it is."

"Humiliated?" He scowled. "Why?"

"Because this is something I deal with on my own. It's my body, my problem, and I'd like to at least hold on to the illusion that I'm desirable, okay?"

He rose slowly, until he towered over her, his eyes transforming to blue fire. "So it's acceptable that I can kiss and touch your sex, that I can shove my cock in it, come inside you there, but for this you refuse my help? I've never treated you like a whore, Alison. So I'd appreciate not being just another john to you."

"You're not," she pushed the words out through her clogged throat. "Dear God, Del, you're not."

"Then let me help you." He knelt down again and waited.

Gritting her teeth, she inched her legs apart. Though she wanted to turn her head away, she forced herself to meet his gaze, to hold it while he pushed the small device into her body with his long fingers. It went up farther than she would have thought, farther than she would have been able to situate it on her own. She saw the confirmation in his eyes as he removed his fingers from her channel and wiped them on the towel. He brought the fabric up to her sex lips and cleaned her meticulously. She let him, her heart pounding in her chest. No one had ever treated her this way.

"Thank you," she whispered.

Placing his lips on her mound, he gave her a soft kiss there, a sweet, intimate gesture that had nothing to do with sex. "You're welcome."

He rose and retrieved a fresh towel to wrap around her. "Are you still in pain? The patroller gave me some kind of tea that is supposed to help if you need it."

"It's not so bad now." Gripping his arm, she steadied herself and took a hesitant step forward. She couldn't feel the metal thing pressed against her womb, thank God. That would be a little too cyborg weird for her to handle. "How long before I take it out?"

"When your cycle is complete."

"Seriously?" She had some pretty heavy periods and that little thing didn't seem up for such a task.

But Fenton nodded as he opened the bathroom door. "That's what the patroller said."

The patroller had Ari in her arms and was cooing softly to the little one. "I just changed her diaper and her bottle is heating."

"Thank you," Fenton said.

Alison echoed his sentiment. Although the yawn she emitted halfway through didn't exactly underscore her point. After helping her ease down onto the pillow, Fenton covered her up and stoked the fire. He turned and took his niece from the patroller.

"You've got a good breeder here, miss. Knows how to treat his womenfolk." With that sage bit of wisdom imparted, the patroller left.

"I know," Alison whispered.

"Warm enough?" Del asked as he settled on the floor next to her with Ari.

She wasn't but he had his hands full. "I will be in a minute."

Strong arms circled around her from behind pulling her snugly against a solid chest that radiated the blessed heat she craved. She gasped when she realized Del had phase split so he could tend her and Ari at once.

"Del—" She turned to face the version holding the baby. What if the patroller came back? He would be putting himself and Ari at risk.

"Ssshhh." He held a finger to her lips. "It's our secret."

17

___

Fenton didn't sleep. Once Ari was fed and drifting happily back off, he recombined himself with the version holding Alison.

Seeing her in pain, so vulnerable, had twisted something inside him until he suffered too. Everything he'd told her earlier still stood; he couldn't trust her. But neither could he pretend he didn't have feelings for her, feelings that had nothing to do with his sister's death. He hadn't taken her with him out of fear, but out of desire for more of her, more time to know everything about her. He'd kept her like a trapped animal, completely dependent on him. Of course she'd resent the leash and the hand holding it.

It wasn't her fault he'd seen things about her he didn't like. He wasn't above reproach either. If she could get past his flaws, he owed her the same consideration.

So in the dark, snuggled next to her soft form, he plotted out a new course of action. There were so many missteps along a winding and treacherous path, but doing nothing wasn't an option, not for him. Fate didn't treat him kindly if he gave it half a chance. So he wouldn't, instead devising a strategy and seeing it through to the end.

Alison let out a soft moan and shifted against him, pushing the blanket down past her lush breasts. Her brow furrowed as though she were in pain. His hand settled on the soft curve of her belly. She sighed and snuggled deeper against him, as though his touch had slain her imaginary monsters. And his niece needed them both. She'd bonded with Alison instantly, and though she might complain about diaper changes and feedings, he'd seen the protectiveness in Alison's eyes, the way she assessed if they posed a threat to Ari. She needed him and as he looked down on her soft, sleeping face he accepted that he needed her too.

Ari stirred restlessly, just as soft light spilled through the windows. Brushing Alison's hair away from her face, he pressed a gentle kiss on her forehead and murmured, "Rest, lovely."

After using the facilities, he packed enough supplies for the day and fed Ari. His own stomach rumbled, but he was anxious to get out of the hut for the day. His convictions were too new, too raw, and he wasn't up to discussing them just yet.

Better to move forward.

With Ari strapped into the carrier, he moved in the direction Dani had said her chamber could be found. Though it was early, many men moved about, several with infants or small children, going about their morning routines. From what he'd gleaned, the women fought, gave birth, and the ruling empress made decisions. Everything else fell to the breeders.

Fenton smiled to himself. No wonder Alison liked it here. To be treated like a warrior goddess, pampered and spoiled, it was in her demanding nature. Indulging her gave him such pleasure, knowing he alone could fill all her needs. There was something primal and sexually enticing in that.

Ari fussed against his chest, but the hard-backed carrier gave her little wiggle room. He murmured softly to her, mentally counting off doorways as he walked. At the sixty-seventh one, he found the staircase, winding upward. He began to climb, his thighs burning from hauling Ari's extra weight on top of his own. The training would do him good. He'd been aboard ships too long and was growing soft.

Knocking on Dani's door, he stepped aside when Kel opened the door.

"We'd hoped you'd show up," the other man said. "Come in."

The door was small and he had to duck to get through it. The space behind it surprised him as it was four times the size of the space he shared with Alison. Separate rooms for the kitchen and living space as well as what he guessed was a bedroom in back.

Dani approached and saw the question in his eyes. "Not many wish to live this high up. We'll be the first picked off if the helcats break through. Have a seat."

Unstrapping Ari, Fenton sat with her on his lap, stretching the little one's arms and legs to ease her stiffness. "You said there is a place large enough for our purposes where the empress won't notice us. Where?"

Dani and Kel exchanged looks. "The old tunnels. They were dug beneath the settlement and lead into the mountain several clicks to the west. As an escape route in case the helcats ever got through."

"An escape route?"

But Kel shook his head. "There was a rockslide years ago. The mountain itself is inaccessible and our colony is too short on manpower as it is to try and dig a new exit."

"But there are chambers large enough to hold maybe a hundred men. It's the perfect place to train."

"When, though? Won't the breeders' absence be noted?"

Kel and Dani exchanged a glance. "Not at night. By day they need to fetch and carry and are seen throughout the colony. Chores, meals, and child rearing will keep them busy.

But at night after the patrollers are asleep . . ." She let the statement hang.

"You want them to slip out of their lovers' beds, sneak down into abandoned tunnels to learn how to fight?" Fenton shook his head. "That will take some serious commitment."

"It's the only way, unless your woman can convince the empress of the need, and allow us to train in the open," Kel said.

"She could. My mother respects her," Dani put in.

"No." Fenton rose, cradling his niece in his arms. "Alison can't know about this. If anything happens to me, I need her to take care of Ari for me."

"Then the tunnels it is. When should we start?"

"Tonight, an hour after full dark. Tell all who are interested to meet us down there. And to trust none of the women, not even their lovers, or daughters. We can't arouse suspicion with the patrollers."

"I'll show you the caves." Kel stood too.

Fenton turned away as the big man embraced his woman, but though the space was impressive; he heard every word.

"I can't come back here tonight." Kel's voice was filled with regret. "If your mother thinks we are exclusive she'll banish me. You should call for another."

"I don't want another. Not another lover or even another child that I never get to see. The rules are ridiculous, you know they are. If it's between living like this and the helcats, I'll take on the beasts single-handedly."

"How I love you, my fierce warrior. Be safe."

Fenton followed Kel down the stairs and around the lake in silence, content to give the other man his privacy. Though he and Alison had their shares of troubles, at least they didn't have an entire civilization opposed to their union.

"Sometimes," he whispered to Ari, "life just plain sucks."

* * *

Alison rolled over, searching for Del's heat. All her hands found were cool sheets. Opening her eyes, she searched, but the one-room hut was quiet, the door to the sani-facilities wide open.

Had it all been a dream? The cramping in her midsection told her that part at least was real and not some dream. Good, because if she started dreaming about her menstrual cycle, she'd need to go hunting for a life.

A wooden crate caught her eye. The large box hadn't been there last night. Curious, Alison went to inspect it and found a data pad with a blinking message.

They were too beautiful to cut up. Join me for breakfast, directions on the pad. ~G

Grinning, Alison lifted the lid and found a few of her dresses, still intact, inside. The woman had taste; the four outfits left were the choicest material, the perfect cut. Slipping into a pair of black silk pants and a royal purple top, Alison pinned her hair up and, clutching the pad, went out to greet the day.

She was surprised to see that Gwella's domicile wasn't part of the main hive of housing. Instead it sat amongst a copse of trees, much smaller than the giant redwoods and pines with heavy boughs of the outer forest. These were spaced evenly enough that Alison guessed they were being farmed, either for firewood or furniture. Perhaps both.

Gwella sat on her front porch, wrapped in a shawl, a steaming mug of something in her hand. Patrollers stood as unobtrusively as possible around the porch, obviously there to protect the empress.

"Good morning," Alison greeted her with a wave. "And thank you for the lovely gift."

"No need to thank me." Gwella rose and gestured toward the door. "You look stunning. I thought about keeping one or two for myself, but that would just be too selfish."

"You are the least selfish person I have ever encountered." Alison looked around the small but tidy space. A long, wooden table took up the majority of the front room. Data pads were strewn about, along with stacks of paper, giving the space an unbalanced, harried feel.

"Welcome to my insanity." Gwella nodded at the mess. "If I'd known there was so much documentation involved with this job, I never would have taken it on in the first place."

"Don't you have anyone else to do it for you?" Alison asked as she followed the empress into a spacious kitchen.

"Technically, the next in line is supposed to take care of this, but asking Dani to do paperwork would be like asking the hel-cats to adapt a vegetarian diet. Goes against nature."

"Maybe I can help?" Alison surveyed the mess. "You'd have to show me what to do, but I could give it a shot."

"I confess, that's precisely why I asked you over this morn-ing." Gwella smiled. "And why I sent you a peace offering. I truly am sorry I confiscated your vessel and your belongings and put you and your breeder and child in danger, but I am glad to have you here."

"Believe it or not, I'm glad you came along when you did." Alison smiled back. "I like your world and respect your deft handling of it against such odds."

"I'd say I'm immune to flattery, but I'd be lying. Unfortu-nately most who offer it are doing so in an attempt to manipu-late me."

"Gwella?" A deep voice resounded from the back room.

"Speak the beast's name . . ." Gwella turned as a giant of a man made his way through the kitchen. His biceps, which were revealed in the thin vest he wore over tight breeches, were thicker than Alison's considerably hefty thighs. There didn't seem to be an ounce of excess fat on him.

"Apologies, Empress, I wasn't aware you had company."

The massive man bowed, though he still towered over both the women. His dark skin glistened with sweat as though he'd been exerting himself.

"Alison, meet Link, my personal breeder."

Unsure of the protocol, Alison nodded her head in respect. "It's nice to meet you, Link."

He didn't touch her but deep, chocolate eyes warmed as they scanned her face. "Welcome to Daton Five, my lady. If there's anything I can do to make your stay more pleasant, please don't hesitate to call on me."

Alison bit her lip and shot Gwella a nervous glance. The empress rolled her own eyes and shoved at her lover playfully. "Pay him no mind. He's an incorrigible flirt."

"I may be bound to you, but I am still a man." He winked at both women. "I have finished chopping wood, Empress, we have enough for several weeks. What else do you require?"

"Send a messenger to Dani. I need to confer with her after second meal."

"I could go in person if you wish it."

"No, she threw something at you last time you went to her place. The messenger shall suffice."

"As you wish, Empress." Another bow and Link lumbered from the room.

Gwella poured more of the hot beverage into her own cup, along with a second one for Alison. "Sorry, family drama. Link and Dani don't exactly get along."

"I'm not judging." Taking a cautious sip from the proffered cup, Alison smiled as the strong flavor coated her taste buds. "Not exactly coffee, but still delicious."

"Thank you. It's from Link's private garden. He grows the fruit and mulls it himself. Come, we'll sit on the porch and ignore the paperwork awhile longer."

"The two of you seem very content together." Alison observed as she lowered herself into the second wooden seat. The patrollers stood in the exact same position and didn't bat an eyelash at their conversation.

"Link was the first breeder I was ever with," Gwella stated. "He was so gentle with me, so loving. I knew from the moment he first touched me that I wanted him for my own. But he was sterile, unable to father children. A shame, you've seen his size and strength. He would be an ideal man to pair with, but it was not to be. And I was destined to be empress. So I used others, until Dani was conceived. It broke Link's heart, watching other men give me what he could not and knowing I wanted him by my side. Once Dani was born, I gave her to her father to raise until she came of age."

"A very efficient system." Alison shuddered to think what would have happened to her or her sister if they'd been given exclusively to their father to rear.

Gwella frowned and stared out at the trees. "It's heartbreaking for all involved. But necessary, something my daughter has failed to accept. She was born to fight and her father trained her well. When he died and Link and I decided she was old enough to come live with us, she fought us as though we were the enemy. Only when she procreated her first child did she settle down, but she still resents Link. I think she believes if he wasn't in the picture, I would have selected her father as my exclusive breeder."

"In my culture, children want their parents to be together. Even if that isn't for the best." Alison compressed her lips, determined not to reveal her own father's history of violence. Gwella didn't need any more fuel added to her "men are untrustworthy" fire.

Gwella rose, her gaze fixed in the distance as though she could see the lives she was responsible for beyond the trees. "Our system is not designed to nurture, but to breed warriors.

We do what we must in order to survive. And right now, that means paperwork."

"Lead the way." Alison followed the empress, wondering if she would have made the same sacrifices as Gwella had, for the good of her people.

The assassin studied his instruments again, checking the frequency and the coding for Alison's shuttle. They hadn't docked, changed course, or abandoned ship. He would have picked up their trails at one of the space stations, heard tell of a whore with a remarkable shielding device that made her "safe." Or Fenton's gambling, something guaranteed to piss off blowhard losers like Mig Larshe.

They had virtually disappeared from the scanner, which meant one of two things. Either it had been destroyed—the lack of space debris told him that was unlikely—or engulfed by a larger ship. The star cruiser they'd been traveling aboard hadn't altered its course, despite both shuttle suites disappearing, and he was sure they hadn't backtracked. He would have encountered them.

So an unknown third party had become involved. Intentional? Alison had no friends this far from Earth, and from his research on Fenton, he had never left his sector before. Pulling up the stats for the nearby star systems, he scrolled through the list of known species capable of space travel.

The throbbing started behind his left eye, making him aware of the fact he hadn't ingested anything in hours. Retrieving a bottle of water he downed it in one long pull before settling down with another. If not for his confounded physiological needs, he could work tirelessly. But his body always seemed to need something. Food, rest, water, sexual relief. He'd reached a level of achievement most humans would never attain, it seemed almost criminal to slow him up with such mundane limitations.

The proximity claxon shrilled and he whirled in his seat. Where the frack did that ship come from? He'd been scanning long range continuously; nothing should have come so close so fast.

The lights dimmed and his fingers flew over the instrument panel, checking to see the source of his power drain. It was coming from the other ship. Some sort of weapon designed to siphon off his weapons and routes of escape.

The comm panel went dark and he slammed his fists against the station, irate at this unacceptable failure. He'd kill every last soul aboard that ship and take it for his own if he had to. Death would be their penance for interfering with his business.

A thought occurred to him. Unless this was the same vessel that had taken Alison and Fenton. A power drain of that magnitude would explain why the tracking beacon was no longer functioning, why they had essentially fallen off the grid.

A smile crept over his face. This wasn't a setback; it was his reward. With any luck, Alison and her lover would be squatting in a cell aboard this very vessel, waiting for him to join them. He checked his pack, fingering the hood. Calm settled over him as he imagined Alison's screams as he degraded her lover before her eyes. Sitting back, he popped a protein pack. He'd need his strength, especially if it was a large crew he'd be forced to eliminate.

Steepling his fingers, he prepared to be boarded.

18

Fenton paused in the doorway. Flames danced in the grate and a pot of something delicious hung above it on an iron hook. Alison stared down into it, stirring with deep, even strokes. Her back was to him and he caught a few notes of whatever she was humming, sweetly melodic, her hips swishing to the beat only she could hear.

The sight of her there bewitched him, until a blast of cold air ripped up his back through his shirt and chased him inside toward her warmth.

She turned, a welcoming expression softening her face. "Hi."

"Hi." Unstrapping Ari, he left her in the carrier, not wanting to wake her. "What are you making?"

"Me? Nothing. I couldn't cook if someone had a laser pistol aimed at my head. This is from Gwella and Link, a thank-you for all my help."

"Help with what?" He moved closer and peered at the pot.

"Paperwork, mostly." Dipping the spoon into the orange liquid, she turned and held it to his lips. "Try it."

A moment of hesitation passed and their eyes met. Hers seemed to beg him to trust her, the same way he had done with her last night. Shoving all thoughts of poison aside he took the spoon between his lips. She grinned, clearly pleased, and turned back to the pot.

"I think the empress is lonely."

Fenton turned to the bucket of water she must have carried up herself earlier. "Leaders are often isolated from those they govern," he remarked, thinking of Xander.

"It's more than that. Gwella has had to sacrifice for her people, put her life on hold, and her relationship with her daughter has suffered. Dani is her heir, but from what I can tell they barely speak," Alison commented as she ladled out two bowls of the vegetable stew.

Fenton poured them each a cup of water from yet another bucket. "They don't agree on what's best for the inhabitants of Daton Five. It's just politics."

"Not to Gwella. She thinks it's personal, that Dani has something against her breeder."

Fenton shuddered. "Please don't use that term. It's so . . ."

"Sexist? Derogatory?" Alison raised an eyebrow. "Is it really any worse than whore?"

He loomed over her chair, using his height to his advantage. "I thought we settled that last night."

"Is anything ever really settled with us?" She lifted her chin, unyielding in her position. "Between us then, no demeaning labels. But we have to play our roles here as best we can."

"Agreed." He caressed her smooth cheek, his heart thundering at her nearness. Cradling her wrists he stroked her pulse with his thumb, delighting as it sped under his touch.

"The soup will be cold," she whispered.

"To hell with the soup." He'd wanted to kiss her since he walked through the door. Pressing her back against the wall he feathered his lips lightly over hers, gentling his baser urges that wanted to tear her clothes off and rut like a wild thing with her on the cold stone floor.

Her mouth molded to his, a sweet seal of lush softness and warmth more welcoming than any he'd ever known. His hands went to her hips, hers into his hair. They clung to each other as though it was the most natural thing in the universe.

Just when he was ready to lay her down on the pillows, she pulled away, her breathing ragged. Figuring she'd come up for air, he reached for her again, but this time her hands went to his chest and she shook her head. "We shouldn't."

He frowned. "Because of your cycle?"

"It isn't that. Every time we sleep together it muddies the waters. We end up confused and disoriented. I want you to trust me, and you won't if you think I'm manipulating you with sex."

Her words stunned him. He opened his mouth to protest, but snapped it shut again when he realized he didn't know what to say.

"See?" Though her tone was light, he could tell his lack of faith in her upset her. Turning back to the stove she retrieved the bowls. "Let's eat."

He caught her wrist when she set the bowl down in front of him. "Alison, I'm sorry."

"It's okay." But it wasn't, not really. Her smile was wan. "I don't have any expectations here, Del, okay? I can take care of myself, so don't feel guilty for doing what you have to do."

She tugged her arm back and he let her go, swamped with regret. Her argument made sense, but damn it all, he wanted her.

But not if it meant hurting her.

He frowned as he thought over what she'd said. "Have you ever manipulated me with sex?" he asked when she sat across from him.

Her cheeks turned pink. "Um, yeah."

"When?" He took up the hollowed-out utensil that passed for a spoon and brought some soup to his lips.

Her flush deepened. "That first night. You were so standoffish and I really wanted to get under your skin so you'd take me with you. I would have given anything to get off Pental."

He thought about it. "Yes, but you never told me that. I took you because you knew about the phase split, not because you asked me to. So you didn't succeed in manipulating me because I acted on my own."

She blinked, obviously stunned he saw it that way. "Okay. What about when I bought out the ship's store in clothing?"

He took more soup. "Again, my choice. I could have said no to you at any time. I didn't want to. I wouldn't consider that being easily manipulated."

Pushing her bowl aside, she folded her hands neatly on the table in front of her. "Are you saying I *can't* manipulate you?"

He thought about it as he scraped his bowl. "No. You could, if you employed the right tactics."

"Such as?" She waited patiently.

He just looked at her. "If you believe I'll tell you how to handle me, you don't know me very well."

She licked her lips and his cock shot hard as her gaze seemed to bore through the table, to his lap. Her voice was husky when she purred, "I think I know exactly how to handle you, Del."

Sometimes he thought simply listening to her talk in that throaty tone could make him come.

A soft coo came from behind him. Ari was awake. Alison rose but he patted the air. "I've got her."

"You've had her all day."

Was she really arguing with him about which one of them should tend his niece? It was difficult not to envision the future with her, the way they shared responsibility for Ari. "Finish your dinner. If you still want to take over, then go for it."

"I actually missed her today." Alison said as he unfastened

the straps of the carrier and changed her diaper. "Not the bodily functions or anything, but the weight of her. Her scent. Is that odd?"

"No, I know what you mean. When Gili first put her in stasis it felt like there was a giant hole in my life."

"You never talk about your sister. Does Ari look like her?"

He studied his niece, who grunted, obviously working on soiling her fresh diaper. The bright blue eyes with a mischievous twinkle, the swirl of wispy dark hair, the rosebud mouth. "Yeah, she does."

Alison's hand rested on his shoulder. "I'm sorry. You must miss her."

Actually, he'd been feeling guilty that he hadn't missed looking after Gili. The youngest of the three siblings, she'd been spoiled and wild. She'd had a hard life, working as a camp follower and her death had been tragic, but Fenton could admit to the truth. "I loved her but she was so selfish. She took mind-altering drugs and stupid chances. And she never really looked after Ari, not until the end when she put her in stasis. And even that was selfish, because she didn't consult me." A lump formed in his throat.

Alison lifted the bundle from his arms. "You took care of her, didn't you?"

"From the minute she was born." Stroking the baby's cheek he lost himself in remembering. "It was like a second chance. I screwed up with Gili, lost her to her demons, but Ari . . . I've got to get it right with her."

"Hey, look at me."

He did and was shocked to see the fierceness in her eyes.

"Your sister made her own choices. You aren't responsible for what happened to her. Any more than you are for me, all right? I'm a grown-up and anyone who has ever tried to control me has wound up regretting it. Living is tough enough. Don't take on guilt for things not in your control."

* * *

Alison had no idea if she'd actually gotten through to Fenton. He'd been quiet after her vehement speech, finishing what was left of the soup and disappearing into the bathroom. She hoped he was thinking about what she'd said, at least considering her words.

As she bounced Ari on her knee, she mulled over the wisdom behind refusing sex with him. It wasn't just about trust, though that was a weighty factor. She wanted to see if Del actually had feelings for her. Would he still want to be with her if she was no longer ready and willing whenever the mood struck him? He'd been correct the night before; he'd never treated her like a whore, but neither did he act as though they were really together. Alison had very few romantic relationships in her adult life. She didn't trust tender feelings as they always seemed to lead people to make unwise decisions. Exhibit A, her parents and their goatfuck of a marriage.

But if she was honest with herself, she'd already made dubious calls. The most obvious grunted as she soiled herself. Alison sighed, wishing she could take advantage of the whole matriarchal society and make Fenton wash all the diapers, but knowing she would do her share as the non-warrior women of this community did.

Ari gurgled happily and Alison found herself not minding the mess if the result of dealing with it was a happy baby. Once Ari was bundled up once more, Alison sat on the cushion nearest the fire and hummed a few bars of "Twinkle, Twinkle, Little Star." Ari seemed to like it, cooing happily so she sang it twice more. It made her think of that first kiss she'd shared with Fenton on the bridge under the meteor shower. For others it was a romantic image, but for her the memory was tainted by her own cowardice and desperation.

She'd chosen to become a pleasure companion because of the power she thought she would have over men. Had her body sculpted and contoured to perfection until she resembled a living, breathing Barbie doll, a walking fantasy. A fantasy any man could purchase for the right price.

Being desired held only a fleeting power, though. Once her john came, he had no further use for her. She closed her eyes, troubled by the memory of that first early morning walk of shame, with a bigger bank account and a label that wouldn't ever leave her. *Whore.* Someone who had sex for money. Many of the pleasure companions she knew reveled in the stigma, wore it like a badge. She'd imitated them, but deep down the truth lurked like a monster under the bed. She hadn't spread her legs because she liked sex with a variety of partners. She did it because she wasn't good at anything else and it was the only way she knew how to provide for herself.

That fear made her do ugly things, and if she were honest, it was why she was on Daton Five with Fenton's niece on her lap. Her choice to stay, to keep selling her body for money and security, had driven her up the corporate ladder. For a time the credits she'd earned had sated her need for security that no man could take away. Exactly where she wanted to be, or so she thought. She'd been relieved at first when she'd been promoted out of the field. Until she was brought into the loop about the imprisoned empaths the Illustra board used to manipulate their more powerful clients. By then she was in too deep with the company to walk away.

But what if I had? The thought nagged her like an old fishwife. Could she have gotten out sooner, found something else to do, some other way to take care of herself? The what-if scenarios were driving her batshit crazy.

"You have a lovely singing voice." Del stood beside her, dressed in his fresh change of clothing and smelling scrumptiously of clean male skin.

"She seems to like it." She smiled down at Ari, whose lids drifted down.

"You're good with her." He didn't bother to hide his surprise.

"I like children, always have. I just never wanted any of my own."

He crouched beside her and she could feel his gaze searching her face in that way he had. "May I ask why?"

She shrugged as best she could with Ari in her arms. "Never wanted the responsibility."

"There's more. I can see it in your face," he stated. "You can tell me if you wish to unburden yourself."

"Did you ever want children?" She turned the question around on him.

He shook his head. "I wouldn't want anyone to have to endure the phase split. Better the ability dies with me."

"That's the reason?" Alison scowled. "I don't understand why you hate it so much."

His eyes seemed to glow, absorbing the firelight. "Are there not things you do not like about yourself? Things that others say they find attractive but you would be rid of if you could?"

"Well . . ." She made a disgruntled sound and cast him a dark look. "You win."

He smiled but his expression sobered. "It isn't a game. My ability has decimated my family and apparently this world as well. We are in danger because of it. No amount of additional pleasure or usefulness is worth that price."

She saw his point but refused to concede the argument. "It's not about sexual gratification or the ability to be in two places at once, though I appreciate both. It's a part of who you are, what makes you unique."

"You are wise tonight," he murmured, his hand stroking her unbound hair.

"I have my moments." Closing her eyes she leaned into his touch. Everything about this man drew her like a moth to a flame, ever closer to her destruction. And what was more, she didn't care.

He drew away abruptly and stood. "I'm going out for a little while. Do you need anything before I depart?"

"What?" Opening her eyes, she craned her neck to look up at him. "Did I do something wrong?"

His features softened. "No, lovely. I just have to go."

The words were so sudden, so final. Fear compressed her lungs. "Are you coming back?"

"Of course." He gave her a puzzled look. "I'll only be gone a few hours."

Don't be clingy, Alison. Men hate that. You *hate that.* Closing her eyes again, she fought for composure. "Yeah, we're fine. See you later."

He bent and kissed Ari's forehead. "Be good, ladies."

"No strange men or kegs of beer. Got it." The flippant words were hollow.

It was probably just hormones making her antsy. That, combined with the precariousness of her situation here. Daton Five was one big disaster waiting to happen.

Anyone would feel unsettled in her shoes.

But as she tucked first Ari and then herself in for the night, she couldn't help eyeballing the door, wondering what was so compelling that drew Fenton away from them for the night.

Sleep eluded her. She tossed and turned, rose and paced the small confines of the room. This was what she'd wanted, right? Insight into whether or not Del would still want to be with her if not for the sex. Well, she was here and though he'd said some sweet things, he'd left quickly.

Scowling at the fire, she thought over their conversation. He had departed suddenly, almost as though he had somewhere to be.

Why didn't he tell her where he was going? He couldn't be

out in this cold just walking all this time. It had been over an hour since he'd left. But where could he have gone at this time of night? The patrollers had eased their vigilant watch over them, thanks to her newfound relationship with Gwella, but he was limited to the enclosure, as the helcats prowled just beyond the structure.

A shiver raced down her spine. What if he'd left for good, afraid she'd tell Gwella about his phase split? As soon as that idea occurred she dismissed it. Never in a million light-years would he leave Ari behind. And it wasn't his style to sneak off into the night without a word of good-bye. Del Fenton might not be sentimental but he was honorable.

They had food, clothing, shelter, and a decent place to hide. She doubted the assassin would look at this planet anytime soon, so it couldn't be about him. What, then, would compel him to leave them alone at night?

Sex.

Whirling to face the door, her lips parted as she sucked in a pained breath. She'd refused his sexual advance, thinking they could spend time together with their clothes on. It had been nice last night when he'd just held her. But maybe he wanted more than to talk and snuggle. He was a man, after all, and men got stupid about their needs.

He made her promise him exclusivity, but he had never vowed to be faithful in return. She'd said no, so he went looking elsewhere. It made sense, too much sense for her to ignore.

Ari, oblivious to Alison's turmoil, let out a soft sigh. Alison looked at the baby and her chest welled with resentment. How dare he stick her on babysitting duty when he went to tap some other woman's well? If he expected to find her sitting here waiting for him to waltz in after getting his rocks off with some patroller tramp, he had another think coming!

Bundling Ari back up, she opened the door, intending to

head to Gwella's cottage. The matriarch of this colony would understand. She'd ask for separate living quarters.

With the baby strapped to her chest, Alison left the hut. She hadn't counted on how dark it was with no firelight or stars overhead. She'd almost changed her mind when the sound of male voices carried across the night.

"That alien breeder and Dani . . ." They moved out of hearing range.

The only alien breeder she knew of was Del. She remembered Dani, Gwella's warrior daughter. Could those two men have seen them together?

Her drive for answers compelled her to follow them before she could think better of it.

19

The men of Daton Five trickled into the cavern slowly, a few at a time. He'd scoped out the training area earlier. The terrain was flat and a few stalactites jutted from the overhead ceiling, but otherwise it was a large, open space, perfect for practicing combat techniques. Scanning the gathering crowd, he waited for Dani to introduce him. The names and faces blurred together in the sea of eagerness.

In his time on Hosta, Fenton had seen all sorts of men, all with different abilities both physically and mentally. It was his job to suss out the weaknesses, break them down so he could begin the laborious process of building them back up into soldiers. Many of the men he'd trained had resisted, but he'd always found a way to push them where he needed them to go.

The men before him were both ready and willing to learn all he had to teach them. They led physically demanding lives, and all seemed to be fit physically. But the biggest advantage they had was that they were fighting for their loved ones. In his experience there wasn't a more compelling reason to fight.

Dani whistled shrilly, the sharp sound bouncing off the

granite walls. As the only female in the room full of men, she stood a foot shorter than all, yet she easily commanded attention.

"All right, boys. You all know why you are here."

"To learn to fight!" one shouted, and a chorus of cheers went up.

Dani held up a hand, waiting for them to settle down. "Be aware that this is not an officially sanctioned endeavor. If the empress finds out, the consequences for insurrection will be severe. You must tell no one of this, not your lover, your mother, or your children. It is for their protection we are here, even if they cannot accept it. Might even punish us for it."

Fenton watched the men watch Dani. They respected her, trusted her. She had more to risk than any man here, her position in the militia already secured. She could lose her lover, her mother, and her future, but she believed in them enough to be here anyway. She believed in them, and her actions backed up her convictions.

"Now, I am turning your instruction over to Fenton. He was a soldier on his world."

All eyes fixed on him. He nodded once to Dani, then stepped forward. "Once a soldier, always a soldier."

"Not on Daton Five," a large man crowed from the left. "You're a breeder, just like us."

A few nervous chuckles moved across the crowd. Though he hadn't planned on a demonstration, one couldn't hurt. Slowly he turned and made his way through the crowd until he stood toe-to-toe with the man who'd spoken. "Are you addressing me?"

Dark eyes narrowed. "Yeah, what of it?"

Keeping his posture loose, Fenton stared the other man down. "You will address me as Commander Fenton or sir. Understood?"

"What if we don't?"

The insolent words had barely left his lips when Fenton's leg whirled out. With a quick spin, he took the other man down like a felled tree then planted his boot on his chest.

"Then we'll have a problem. What's your name?"

"Ev." The man struggled but couldn't dislodge the boot on his solar plexus.

Fenton leaned down. "Do we have a problem, Ev?"

Those eyes met his again. "No, sir."

Fenton nodded once, then raised his voice to address the crowd. "Alright, everyone. Learn from Ev's mistake. You will respect the chain of command. Do you understand?"

"Yes, sir." The words were fired back at him in a chorus.

Though he was pleased, he was careful not to let it show. Releasing Ev, he helped the other man regain his feet. "The first thing you need to learn is how to move like soldiers. You are strong but clumsy. Brute strength is almost worthless on a battlefield if you don't know how to move. No wasted motion, every muscle strong, but fluid and intentional."

Hopping up on a flat rock, he demonstrated some balance poses, flowing from one form to the next. He stopped and stared down at them. "What are you wasting time for? Let's move."

He demonstrated again and the men followed him. Their successes varied greatly, but after twenty minutes, all had the forms memorized, if not perfected.

"Practice these exercises whenever you can. It will increase your stamina."

"Never had any complaints there," a man in the back hollered. A few others laughed nervously, but most waited to see what Fenton would do.

"Do you think this is a joke? Do you think I'd rather be standing here sweating in this dank cave with you than at home with my woman? I'm doing this so we don't all die. And that's what will happen if you don't shut your damn mouth and learn how to defend your village."

Only the sound of water dripping broke the silence.

"Now pair up. We're going to practice grappling and throws."

Over the next few hours Fenton moved between pairs, adjusting stances, giving pointers and, in a few instances, praise. The thud of big bodies hitting the floor, along with male grunts of pain and frustration, filled the space. They worked tirelessly, falling into line faster than he could have hoped. They knew the risks, knew what was at stake, and they were determined to succeed.

"You know what's out there," he told one of the younger males who had lost against every opponent he'd been pitted against. "You think the helcats are going to give you a breather?"

"No, sir." The boy wheezed and lunged again. There was a dull thump as his opponent flipped him, but he got up faster, circled. He'd be bruised to hell by morning, the hard cave floor completely unyielding. Fenton actually preferred it that way.

"Wait for your opening. Keep out of range until you see it. Remember to move your feet, not just your shoulders. A helcat can cut you off at the knees as easily as at the neck. Both will render you useless, and I have no room for useless."

The boy charged again, this time ducking his opponent's fist by feigning right and taking the other man to the ground with a center strike. The bigger man tapped out.

"Excellent." Fenton clapped the young man on the shoulder. "What's your name?"

"Dav." The boy had big hazel eyes, very similar in shape and color to Alison's.

"I like your courage, Dav. Practice your forms and you'll be unstoppable."

Dav looked down at his gaunt frame. "I'm not as big as some of these guys."

"Neither are the patrollers, yet they are in charge. Why do you think that is?"

"The chem whips?" Dav asked.

"Partly. But more so because they've been taught how to assess a situation, neutralize threats."

"That's right." Dani joined their conversation. "And we were taught how to do it, Dav. It's a skill, and skills can be learned, mastered. Learn how to use your body, and it will be your ultimate weapon."

The boy flushed a brilliant red. "Yes, ma'am."

"I think he has a crush on you," Kel teased.

"Do you blame him?" Dani raised an eye.

"No," the big man whispered. "I've had a crush on you since the moment I first saw you."

They shared a look so intimate, Fenton actually felt heat creeping up his neck. He thought of Alison, waiting for him back at the hut all warm and soft, and he had to turn away to keep from humiliating himself with his budding erection.

"Wait," Dani called out to him and he looked over his shoulder at her, discreetly adjusting himself before he turned to face her.

She jogged to his side. "I might be able to procure some weapons for them to practice with, if you think they are ready."

Fenton thought it over. "Some, like Kel, are. Others need to build their confidence and awareness before I would feel secure arming them."

"We could split them into two groups. I could do weapons training with the advanced students while you continue your work here."

Fenton nodded. "Sounds good. Should we meet again tomorrow night?"

A small scuffling noise from the mouth of the cave drew his notice. Craning his neck, he peered around the corner but didn't see anyone. Probably a bat or some other cave-dwelling creature. The patrollers wouldn't lurk, but rather charge in bashing skulls as they went.

"I'm not sure that's wise. We don't want to rouse any suspicions."

Del understood her concerns and voiced his own. "We don't know how much time we've got either. If we're discovered it all comes crumbling down. I don't know how much longer I can lie to Alison. She deserves better from me."

Alison grit her teeth. She wanted to storm in there and smash his handsome face. She sure as hell did deserve better than a cheating, no-good, scum-sucking, phase-splitting jackass who couldn't keep his dick in his pants.

If you don't want to be called a breeder, then don't act like one!

Seeing Fenton with Dani was difficult enough, but it was the fact he had an obvious hard-on, in spite of the room full of men told her everything she needed to know. She considered storming in there, handing Ari over to him, and spitting on the little man-stealing patroller bitch.

But she had to be careful. Dani was next in line and she'd spent too much time shoring up her position with Gwella to do something rash and get herself banished. Right now she needed to get away, clear her head so she could think. So many things didn't add up. Like, why was there a cavern full of men here? What did they have to do with Del's affair? She'd arrived late, having lost her way in the tunnels and having to backtrack. The breeders looked sweaty, but she had no idea what they'd been doing to get that way.

Carefully, she moved away from the entrance to the cave as Del turned to address the men. She wanted to hear what he was saying, but she had a feeling they'd be leaving soon and the last thing she wanted was to get caught. The only thing going for her was the fact that she knew about Del and Dani but they didn't know she did. If they busted her, all bets were off.

Ari fussed, clearly uncomfortable after spending so much time in the harness. "I'm sorry, sweet baby," she crooned softly. Looking up, she saw a fork in the tunnel ahead. Crap, had that been there before? Her eyesight sucked in this kind of dark, and the small, glowing bioluminescent from Ari's carrier barely made enough light to see five feet ahead. Which way was the way out?

Taking a deep breath, she picked left. Though she hoped she'd made the correct turn, there was no way to be sure. Her guts churned with anxiety. Maybe she better go back.

The image of Del and Dani, the beautiful, competent warriors, made her push onward. The hard-soled slippers she wore slid on some wet rock, and she steadied herself before falling on her ass. *Gotta be more careful.*

The air was damp and cold, seeming to cut right through her clothes. Ari's fussing turned to wailing as she struggled to free herself from the carrier.

Unwilling to continue on listening to the little one scream, Alison stopped and sat on a large, flat rock.

"Ssshhh, it's okay." She took the baby out of the carrier and tried to comfort her.

Red-faced, Ari went stiff as a board, her mouth open, tears rolling down her cheeks. No amount of rocking or singing could calm her. Alison put her over her shoulder, tried to rub her back in a soothing motion, willing the little one to calm down. A brief moment of silence and then Ari emptied the contents of her stomach all down Alison's back. She'd made herself sick.

Ignoring the mess, Alison laid her out on her carrier and placed her chilled palms against the baby's forehead. Her skin felt hot to the touch.

With a jolt, Alison realized how selfish she'd been. Ari was sick and she had no idea what was wrong with her or how to help her. Several unmarked vials were stowed inside her carrier pack, but with no labels, Alison didn't know what they did or if they could help the baby.

To hell with her shattered pride. Picking Ari up, she promised her she'd only be in the carrier for a little while longer, which didn't faze the screaming child one bit. Carefully, she strapped the little girl in and donned the pack before retracing her steps.

Disorientation grew as she walked farther and farther, with no sign of the tunnel she'd taken. With so little visibility, she couldn't keep track of landmarks.

Ari's caterwauling should have caught someone's notice by now. She stopped, tried to listen for the sound of voices, but beside the baby's angry diatribe, there was nothing.

They were lost.

20

Fenton frowned when he saw the fire in their living quarters had burned down to embers. Maybe she was in pain again. Guilt flayed him for leaving her to cope with his niece by herself when she was already hurting. He couldn't make out either Alison or Ari amidst the mounded-up pillows. "Alison? Is everything all right?"

No answer. He listened but didn't hear any sounds of breathing. Heart pounding in his chest, he stalked forward, calling her name again.

The place was empty.

Adrenaline spiked as he whirled around looking for a note or data pad, looking for an explanation as to where they'd gone. Nothing. Had Gwella found out about his part in Dani's underground army? Perhaps she'd taken his females as hostages. Ari's pack was missing, which meant they had time to prepare for their departure.

He considered alerting Dani, but dismissed the idea, instead charging toward the empress's lair. Best not to jump to conclusions. Alison and Gwella had a friendship of sorts, and if anything was wrong, she would have turned to the empress for help.

His keen night vision aided him in following the path through the tree-farmed woods to Gwella's doorstep. Patrollers were stationed at the corners of the porch, and both moved to block his path. "What's your business here, breeder?"

Though he didn't want to have to explain himself, a lash from a chem whip would slow him down more. Dropping to one knee, he bowed his head in a show of respect. "Please, my females are missing. Does the empress know where they are?"

"What's going on?" Swathed in a blanket, Gwella stepped over her threshold.

"Forgive the interruption, Empress. This breeder says his females are missing."

Gwella waved the patrollers off. "Alison's missing?"

Her reaction appeared genuinely concerned. "Yes, Empress, and Ari as well."

"How long?"

"I am uncertain. The fire had almost gone out completely by the time I returned." He ducked his head, hoping she wouldn't ask where he'd been. It was one thing to keep her in the dark about his and Dani's actions, but another entirely to lie to her face.

Luck was on his side because Gwella turned to address the patrollers. "Go to Alison's domicile and search for signs of a struggle."

"There were none, Empress," Fenton offered.

She eyed him shrewdly, then waved the patrollers off. "Follow my orders."

"Gwella?" A large, hulking shadow lurked in the doorway. "What's the matter?"

"Alison's breeder is here. He says she's missing, along with her young."

Still on his knees, Fenton tuned them out. Where could Alison have gone if not here? His blood chilled as he considered that the assassin had come for her, waited until she was alone with his helpless niece, and spirited them both away. Regardless of her dislike of him, he needed to tell Gwella about that possibility.

"Empress, forgive me but there's something you need to know."

She held up a hand to silence him, and he turned his head as the patroller she sent returned.

"It is as he said, Empress. No signs of a struggle and her clothes and the supplies for the child have been packed."

Gwella glared down at him. "Why would she have left? Were you fighting?"

"No." They'd actually been getting along better than ever, or so he'd believed. They talked openly and honestly, shared thoughts and feelings. She'd seemed contented, at least until right before he'd left. Though her no sex edict might have been wise, he couldn't help responding to her, his body aware of hers on a primal level. He recalled her puzzlement over his going out, the stunned look on her face. She'd been curious about where he intended to go. Had she followed him? He recalled the disturbance he'd heard at the end of the training session and consequently dismissed. If it had been Alison, why wouldn't she have made herself known?

The more he thought about the events of the evening, the more sense it made. Alison didn't leave her fate up to chance. She was smart and she would have known he kept something from her. He winced as he realized the vastness of his mistake. By not informing her of his plans, he might have inadvertently put her in danger.

Meanwhile, Gwella was barking orders to her breeder and the patrollers. "Call a meeting in the town square. We need every able-bodied person to help in the search effort. Double-check at the gates and make sure she didn't leave the compound."

The patroller ran off and he got to his feet.

"We should check the tunnels and caves," Fenton spoke up, his worry for Alison and Ari overriding his customary caution. "She may have thought to escape that way."

"How do you know about the tunnels?" The empress glowered at him.

"Dani informed me." He held her gaze, unwilling to back down with everything he held dear at stake. "She discussed strategy with me earlier this morning."

"My daughter knows better than to go to a male for advice. Especially an alien male," Gwella spat.

"She is not burdened by your prejudice, Empress. Ask her if you don't believe me."

"Insolent breeder!" The remaining patroller backhanded him. His head hardly moved, but the blow would undoubtedly leave a sizable bruise. "How dare you overstep your role!"

"Enough!" The big man moved forward. "My love, this will not help your friend. He knows her better than anyone, and if he says to check the tunnels, I say we should follow his advice."

Gwella's eyes shot daggers at him but she nodded. "Fine. But this is not over, breeder. Your disrespect will not be tolerated. And if any harm comes to Alison, I swear I will hold you responsible."

Bowing his head, he closed his eyes, listening as she gave out orders for a few breeders and patrollers to accompany him into the tunnels. If either Alison or Ari were hurt, her loathing would be nothing compared to his self-inflicted wrath.

Ari finally quieted when she fell into a fitful sleep. Exhausted, Alison closed her eyes and leaned her head back against a rock, holding the baby to her chest for warmth. How could she have been so damn stupid, so selfish? She might as well have asked Gwella to open the gates and feed them both to the helcats. At least that would be a fast death, instead of slowly dying from exposure.

No matter how tired she was, staying here wasn't a good plan. Better to stumble around in the dark and hope she came across the way out than to sit here and freeze. Her beautiful clothes were grubby and in no way adequate for the chilly tunnels. She had nothing to ignite a fire for either torch or light.

With a groan, she rose to her feet, ignoring her stiff muscles and various aches and pains. Forward. Or backward. Either way the exertion would help keep her warm rather than sitting on the cold stone floor.

The knowledge that she was going to die was secondary to the thought that she'd hand-delivered Ari's death sentence. Probably Del's too. He'd devoted his life to his niece's care. If Ari died, Alison could easily envision him crawling through the hole in the redwood fortress and out to face a helcat with his bare hands.

His magnificent body would be torn in two, ripped to shreds by one of those monsters. The picture still etched in her mind from the death of the other patroller. And as he breathed his last, he would curse himself for not being strong or capable enough to save his niece.

Or to save her.

Hot tears spilled down her cheeks at the thought of him dying like that. Did it really matter if he had shagged someone else when she'd essentially driven him to it? What kind of whore was she that she ignored the basic nature of a man, hoping to change him into her girlish dream of Prince Charming, faithful, loving, and all that rot?

A dumb whore. Soon to be a dead whore.

Her throat ached, dry with lack of water. Though the stone walls were wet, she didn't see any standing water. Probably just as well; with her luck she'd infect herself with some sort of alien microbe and end up hosting a colony of angry killer insects that would eat their way out of her body.

Stop blaming luck; own your own shit.

She was responsible for everything wrong in her life. It was time to stop blaming her father, her mother, the johns, the universe for her misfortune. Her fat was in the fire because she sat in the wrong spot and was too stubborn to move. It broke her heart to see Del take ownership of all the bad things that had happened to his family when he'd done nothing except survive. He hadn't hurt anyone else for profit.

She wanted to tell him that, to confess all her sins. Hell, if she made it out of this cave and found a way off this world, she'd go with him to the empaths' homeworld, turn herself over to them for punishment. The assassin could piss directly off—she didn't owe him or Illustra anything, and the thought of dying by way of one of his mind fucks was worse than calling it quits in this maze of tunnels.

"Please," she begged whatever deity might be listening. "Let me get Ari out of here. I'll fix all my mistakes, just let me see her safe."

The tunnel inclined sharply, and her breaths huffed out faster. This definitely wasn't the right way; she would have remembered a steep grade when coming in. Exhausted and teeming with frustration, she sat down hard, probably bruising her tailbone in the process.

Where had she gone wrong? This whole experience was like one big, screwed-up metaphor for her life. Stumbling around in the dark, making bad choice after bad choice, all shortsighted decisions because she was ill-equipped to see beyond the end of her nose. Wiping the tears away with her grubby sleeve, she tried to summon the strength to turn around and try again.

A weird scratching sound broke her from her mental flagellation. "Hello?"

No answer. Ari stirred against her breastbone, leaving a trail of sweat. Her fever had broken and Alison breathed a might easier. The scraping noise came again.

Climbing to her feet, she decided to investigate. Moving slowly, she climbed up the steep hill, bracing one hand on the wall to help her balance.

Up ahead, a mountain of rock loomed. Scowling, she moved closer so the bioluminescent light from Ari's pack highlighted what was obviously a cave-in. The scraping sound came again, from the other side of the mounded-up stones.

"Is someone there?" she shouted, hoping someone might be trying to dig through.

Still no answer.

"If you can hear me, I'm trapped in here with an infant!"

As if to underscore her statement, Ari started to cry again.

An eerie cry pierced through the stone and her blood flash-froze. That wasn't a person trying to get through the wall of rock; it was one of those helcats, looking for dinner. Could it smell her?

Heart pounding, she backed up, spinning around as the tunnel sloped back down. If she wasn't so afraid of tripping and landing on the baby, she'd sprint through the darkness. As it was she moved much faster, putting as much distance between them and the predator as possible.

The sound of rocks being dislodged made her scream in terror. The creature was breaking through. "Help me!"

"Alison!" The male shout came from up ahead, the most beautiful thing she'd ever heard.

"Del! I'm here!"

"Stay where you are. I'm coming!"

Her feet stilled and she waited, afraid to take yet another wrong turn, more afraid he wouldn't reach her before that thing managed to break through.

The one good thing about Ari's nonstop crying, it made for

an audio trail of bread crumbs, easy for him to follow. The welcome sight of a torchlight glinting off the wet cave walls filled her with relief. "Over here!"

Then he was there, running to her for all he was worth. He hugged her, careful not to squish Ari between them.

"Thank the stars," he breathed.

The relief in his voice filled her with remorse. "Del, I'm so sorry."

"Later," he muttered, shoving the torch in her hands. He unfastened the carrier, trying to soothe the angry child. "She's burning up. Did you give her anything?"

More guilt, layered so thick it choked her. "I didn't know what was what."

"Let's get out of here. The others took different paths. We'll meet up with them and get the hell out of here." He strapped Ari back in her carrier and reached to take it from her.

The sound of tumbling rocks from behind her made them both jump.

"What was that?" Del grabbed the torch instead of the baby and turned.

The howling cry filled the space. "It's a helcat. It's trying to break through the cave-in back there."

Del swore as an angry roar bounced off the walls. "I think it just did. Quick, give me Ari, we need to get to someone with a weapon."

Oh, hell, she hadn't thought of that. Of course Del wouldn't be armed, and while he might be able to lead them out of here, all he could do against a helcat was die with them.

She shucked the carrier and he strapped it on quickly, taking the burden of the helpless infant off her shoulders and gripping her hand. "Hold the torch, my eyes are better in the dark."

She took the wooden torch from him and held it away from her face. After stumbling around with only the bioluminescent pack to guide her way the light actually made her eyes water.

"As fast as you can." With one arm wrapped around a frighteningly silent Ari and the other holding on to her, Fenton led her back down the tunnel. He bypassed several forks along the path, not even hesitating.

In the distance a voice called her name. "Who's with you?"

"Dani and a few of the patrollers under her command."

She stiffened at hearing the other woman's name but vowed she wouldn't make an issue out of it.

"What's wrong?" Of course he picked up on it.

"It's not important."

"Alison, if you know something—" He cut himself off as another roar resonated from behind them. "We don't have time for games. Tell me what made you tense up like that."

From his demeanor, she knew he wouldn't let it go until she told him. "It's you, sneaking off to be with Dani."

Hopping over a pit she would have stumbled into, he pulled her across, flush against his side. "I was trying to protect you. If you didn't know I didn't think you'd be hurt."

Though there was nothing funny about their situation, a laugh escaped. "Right, like me being ignorant of you sleeping with another woman makes it all okay."

He stopped dead in his tracks and she slammed into his back. "What?" His voice was low, quiet.

"I saw you. With her."

He shot her an incredulous look. "You were *jealous? That's* why you followed me here?"

Another roar filled her with panic. "Later, we'll hash this out later."

Torchlights spilled from the cavern up ahead. Picking up his pace, he practically yanked her arm out of the socket dragging her forward. "I found them, but we have a bigger problem."

Dani strode to his side. "Report."

"Helcat trying to break through at the point of the landslide."

Dani cursed heatedly. "If it gets through, not only are we dead but so is the entire village."

"Options?" Fenton patted Ari's back. The little girl sniffled but was otherwise quiet.

"We have to collapse the tunnels completely. Does anyone have explosive compound?"

Three of the patrollers dug in their packs.

Dani's eyes met Alison's. "My mother would banish us from the village if she knew we had this sort of technology."

"She won't hear it from me."

"Good. Then let's head back out, find a weak point far enough from the village that we can blow the whole thing."

"What about training?" Fenton asked.

"The whole point was to save the people. They can't train if they are dead. We'll have to convince my mother to let the breeders fight or evacuate. If the creatures are desperate enough to dig through rock, our fortress won't hold them much longer."

Without another word they charged up the tunnel. Fenton never let go of Alison's hand and she knew she was slowing him down.

"Save yourself and Ari," she panted. "Don't wait for me."

"Shut up," he grunted, his grip tightening on her arm.

She had no idea how far they traveled, only that her lungs and legs were burning from overuse. She fell at one point, but Del hauled her to her feet, barely breaking stride.

"Here," Dani called at a bottleneck in the tunnel. Several others converged at the same point. "Give me the explosive and detonators."

A roar echoed through the walls and the ground seemed to shake. "It's through!" one of the patrollers shouted.

"Chem whips at the ready." Dani knelt down. "As soon as this is armed, we need to run."

Despite her exhaustion it took all of Alison's willpower not to bolt, knowing that thing was barreling down the darkened pathways, sniffing them out.

"No," Dani breathed, pounding her fist on the wall.

"What's wrong?" Fenton asked.

She turned to face him, her expression grim. "The delay won't work. Someone has to stay behind and set it off manually."

Another roar, even closer this time.

"I'll do it." Del started unfastening Ari's carrier.

"No!" Alison shouted. "She needs you, let me stay."

"Both of you are going so shut up." Dani turned to one of the patrollers. "Tell Kel I love him."

The woman nodded and clapped Dani on the shoulder. "May peace find you."

"Dani, no." Fenton shook his head. "Your people need you."

She turned to face him, face them both. "Yes, they do. They are getting all I have to give. It is up to you to convince my mother of the danger. Safe journey, alien warrior, protect your blessings."

Instead of the embrace Alison expected, Del thumped his hand over his heart then grabbed Alison's hand. "Let's go."

She followed him, the patrollers bringing up the rear. Her heart thudded with every step, but she ran for all she was worth.

The opening to the sanctuary was in sight when entire tunnel shook. Del moved faster, gripping her sweaty hand in his as dust and smoke billowed out around them, choking them.

Del covered Ari's face with one hand, the other still holding hers. "Drop the torch and cover your face—" He broke off, coughing.

The tunnel spit them out onto the lawn, still rumbling from the explosion. Del tugged her down onto a mossy patch, still hacking. The patrollers collapsed nearby. As the dust settled, all eyes turned to the opening.

"Nothing could survive that." Even as she said the words she hoped they weren't true.

People moved closer, men and women coming to gawk at the carnage. Gwella pushed through the gathering crowd. "What happened? Report!"

The patroller with the shorn hair, the one Dani had instructed, stood up. "A helcat broke through the rockslide. Dani brought the mountain down to make sure it wouldn't get to the village."

"Where is she?" Gwella's voice was hollow.

"Empress, I'm sorry, she stayed behind to ensure our escape."

Gwella swayed on her feet as though the ground still shook. Her eyes appeared unfocused. Alison rose and moved toward her. "I'm so sorry." She tried to wrap her arms around the distraught woman, but Gwella wasn't having it.

"You! You and your breeder did this. Cost my daughter her life!" she spat, her voice full of venom. Turning to her patrollers, she ordered, "Seize them."

21

"Del? Can you hear me?" Alison's soft voice and cool hands on his face pulled him out of the fog he'd been floating in.

He groaned, wishing she'd left him there. His bones ached, his head pounded, and his mouth felt gritty, as if he'd been eating sand. Opening his eyes, he squinted into the gloom. Beneath him the floor felt hard and cold. They were in a stone room, a heavy wooden door the only exit. "What happened?" His voice was weak and reedy.

Her hands smoothed his hair back from his face. "What's the last thing you remember?"

Struggling to sit up, he fought his body's weakness. The effort nearly exhausted him. Alison wrapped her arms around herself. He blinked at her in the darkness and guessed she couldn't see at all. He wavered slightly but considered it a victory when he didn't fall flat on his face. Propping himself against the wall, he searched his mind for the last thing that had happened.

"Dani, in the caves." He closed his eyes, remembering her sacrifice. He'd left soldiers behind before, but this had been different. For one thing, he hadn't been in command. If he had he would have ordered her to safety. They'd made it out, him with Alison's hand in his and Ari strapped to his chest—

His eyes flew open. "Where's Ari? Is she still sick?"

"She's upstairs and she's fine. I can hear her crying from time to time. Gwella's breeder is looking after her."

He sagged, grateful for that much. "What was wrong with her?"

"The same thing that was wrong with you, whatever it was. Some kind of viral infection by the look of it. It took you down almost as soon as we were brought here, almost a week ago by my count."

A week. No wonder he felt so awful. He turned to look at her, saw her barely repressed fear. "You've been taking care of me alone all this time?"

"I did the best I could. With what they gave me, which wasn't much. Gwella's still irate." She paused and cleared her throat. "How are you feeling?"

"Like a meteor landed squarely on my head but I'll live. Are you all right?" He fought back the storm of worry that he'd left her and Ari unprotected for a week.

"I'm fine. I was just scared."

Scared that he would die and she'd be alone. He imagined what it would be like for him if she wasn't here. Unbearable didn't begin to cover it. "Thank you."

She didn't say anything, just looked toward the door. "What are we going to do now?"

He rose to his feet, bracing himself on the wall. "Maybe I can phase—"

She exploded to her feet and clapped a hand over his mouth. "Don't even think it, Del. We're in enough trouble already. Gwella's talking about banishing us."

He moved her hand aside. "We can't let that happen. If we don't convince Gwella to leave, the helcats will do us all in.

That one who chased us through the tunnels was starving, desperate, and it broke through a rock wall. How long will this settlement hold against a dozen of them?"

She hugged herself even more tightly. "This is all my fault. If not for me, you and Ari would have gone to the empaths' homeworld and be safely settling in to a new life. I'm sorry, so sorry I fucked everything up for you." She slid down the wall and put her face in her hands.

He sat next to her, grateful for the excuse to be off his feet. Wrapping an arm around her shoulders, he pulled her tightly against him. "Hush now."

Sobs racked her entire body, a week's worth of pent-up fear and frustration finding an outlet. He held her and let her cry, occasionally murmuring that it would be all right.

He lost track of how long they sat there, but gradually the haze over his mind dissipated, leaving him able to remember.

She'd quieted but he sensed she hadn't fallen asleep. The last thing he wanted to do was fight with her, but his need to clear the air compelled him to speak. "Do you really think I was sneaking off to have sex with Dani?"

Her posture stiffened and she sat up, turning to face him. He saw her eyes scanning, searching for him in the darkness. "I didn't know what to think. All I knew was that you left and it was obvious you were hiding something from me."

As the remembered fear surfaced, his grip on her tightened. "So instead of waiting to ask me about it, you risked your life, Ari's life, and for what? To confirm your suspicions? You never trusted me at all, did you?" His voice grew louder with every syllable.

She tried to pull out of his grip, almost succeeded thanks to his weakened state. "Don't yell at me. I know I fucked up."

Seething, he released her and rose to his feet. His weakness didn't help ease his ire. "That doesn't begin to fix this. We're going to die, Alison. With Dani's help at least we stood a chance of convincing Gwella, but now that she's gone . . ." He shook his head and ran his hand through his hair.

"I'm sorry," she mumbled again, a huddled tribute to misery.

Closing his eyes, he tried to find his calm center. Shouting at her wouldn't do any good. She recognized her mistake, and it was his as well. Was it right to ask her to trust him when he'd kept things from her? The woman had spent the better part of a week caring for him, cleaning him, spoon-feeding him, and doing her best to ensure he lived long enough to give them a fighting chance.

"I'm sorry too. I should have told you what was going on with Dani and Kel and the breeders. Don't assume all the fault is yours."

She nodded and rested her head on her knees.

Standing here thinking about all the ways they went wrong wouldn't help either of them. After another slow breath he forced his weakened body to move.

Instinctively, he fell into the first of his forms, then another and another. His motions were slow, choppy, and it took longer than usual. He was sweating, muscles shaking but he pushed onward.

A scuffling sound drew his attention. "What are you doing?"

It was lighter in the room when he opened his eyes, and the way her gaze fixed on him indicated she could see him. "My training forms. Helps me regain my balance, hone my body in preparation to fight."

Slowly, she rose to her feet. Her beautiful clothes were in tatters, and clean streaks reminded him of her recent tears. "Teach me."

"What?" He stopped mid-form and stood, facing her.

"I'm sick of being useless. The women on this planet are supposed to be strong, capable. Teach me how to live up to their expectations. I want to fight by your side, not be a damn liability that slows you down."

It took a moment for him to realize his mouth was hanging open. Sincerity flashed in her eyes, her willingness to let him teach her to fight radiating from her posture. She was determined.

She took his breath away.

"I don't know how long we have," he rasped.

She moved into a stance mimicking his own. "Then we'd better get started."

Every muscle in Alison's body was limp from fatigue. How sad was it that Fenton came off of a week of illness and he was still in better shape than her? She couldn't remember the last time she'd worked so hard at anything. Probably never.

But she had to admit, her body felt better for the exertion. When the patroller opened the door to deliver the tray with their morning meal, she nearly collapsed in exhaustion.

She wrinkled her nose in disgust. "You two reek."

"And you're observant," Alison said with false sweetness. "How about you ask if we can shower at some point?" The waste receptacle in the small room had no chemical foam. She'd made do with a bucket, unwilling to risk Gwella's wrath. After a week she'd grown used to the smell. Who'd have thought?

"It'd be a public service. Of course, your stench might slow the helcats down, so maybe you want to go on stinking."

"Get yourself kidnapped and come back with some new insults. I've heard them all."

The door banged behind the patroller, and Alison caught Fenton eyeing her. "What?"

"You did well with the forms," he murmured after the patroller left. "Most people don't have your focus."

"I'm highly motivated." She gratefully took the cup of water he extended to her.

Fenton eyed her as he drank from his own cup. "How long since you last slept?"

She'd been napping spooned up against him every night, sharing her warmth right after she sponge-bathed him as best she could by using her underwear and cold water from the bucket. They had no blankets, no creature comforts at all. If not for the meals delivered regularly, she'd think Gwella wanted them to rot down here. The only reason she was still sane was because she'd focused all of her attention on seeing Del through his sickness.

Now he was awake and she had a new task. Operation Learn to Kick Some Ass.

Fenton eyed the soup. "Doesn't seem like enough for two."

"It's really not. You have it, you need to regain your strength." Her stomach rumbled as though staging a protest.

He blinked. "You've been feeding it all to me, haven't you?"

Glancing away, she picked at a tear on her grubby pants. "Not all." She'd had a spoonful or two, just enough to make sure she could keep on tending him until he was well enough to look after himself.

"Why?"

"You were sick, you needed the nutrition."

Shoving the bowl at her, he gritted, "Eat all of this."

One look at his face and she knew better than to protest. The soup was bitter, but at least it was hot. She ate about half, then tried to hand it to him. He looked from her to the bowl and back again, glaring.

"I'll dump it out," she threatened.

"I'll force it down your throat," he snarled right back.

A jolt of lust went right through her, like she'd been struck by lightning. He'd defend her, even against herself. He was probably still angry with her about landing them here in the first place, yet he took care of her, sacrificed for her.

Was there anything sexier?

She finished the soup and set the bowl by the door.

"You should try to rest some more. We both should." Fenton scratched at the stubble that grew in around his scar, giving him an even more sinister mien. His hair had grown shaggy since she'd first spotted him, but his shoulders still squared off with military precision. Alison had been with her share of handsome men, but there was just more about Del Fenton. More virile, more rugged, and untamable.

Her face heated and she tore her focus from him. What was her major malfunction? Nothing should turn on her libido when she looked and smelled the way she did.

They took turns using the bathroom, washing up as best they could. Alison went first, scrubbing at the grime until her skin turned red. The water was cold and she was shivering by the time she was done but at least her skin felt clean.

Though she shifted around it was impossible to get comfortable on the icy stone floor. She missed her man-sized pillow and the heat that radiated from him like the sun. If she asked him she knew he'd hold her again, but she didn't want to force him to curl up with her if he hated her, simply out of pity.

"Is your feminine flow over?" Fenton asked from the doorway.

"Yesterday. I couldn't take the device out, though." And she hadn't been about to ask the bitchy patroller to help with that.

He waited, standing to the side of the doorway. It was too dark for her to read his features but his posture looked rigid and his unswerving gaze pinned her in place. "What?"

"I'm waiting for you to ask me to help you."

Hell no. He'd have to pin her down and rip her pants off. Which could be fun but not for the purpose he was intending. She tried to wave it off. "I'm sure it's fine."

Moving closer, he stood directly above her, so she had to crane her neck to look at him. Always considerate, he crouched before her and stared her down. "Those devices were designed the way they were purposefully. So that every female of age had a safeguard, a way to let the breeders around her know she was sexually unavailable. If one was inserted by another's hand it has to be removed by them as well. And it does have to be removed. So again, I'm waiting."

Her lip trembled and she sank her teeth into it to steady it while gathering her thoughts. Neon-blue eyes consumed her, sped her heart until it raced. "I don't want you to feel obligated to do anything for me. I know you must hate me, that it's probably pure torture for you to be locked up in here with me after what I did. Honestly, Del, I hate myself for endangering Ari and landing us into this mess. If I had the option to get away from myself, I would take it."

"Alison," he breathed, crouching down until their eyes met. Tight lines formed between his eyebrows, the smallest show of concern on his otherwise implacable façade. His eyes, though, were always the first to heat. Or maybe they never stopped burning with his deeply guarded passions. His arms reached for her. "Come here."

Stepping into his embrace was the most natural thing in the world to her. He held her head against his chest and she listened to the steady thrumming of his heartbeat.

He didn't say anything, just cradled her. Slowly her shoulders lost their tension, relaxing into the heat of him. She might have fallen asleep, even standing up if he didn't sink to his knees before her.

She sucked in a breath when he hooked his thumbs around her waistband. How had she forgotten his intention?

But she did want that thing removed from her body, and if he knew how to do it, had volunteered for the task, she would ignore her mental discomfort.

Cool air caressing her bare flesh made her shiver as he pulled her pants off. Running his hands up over her legs left a trail of heat to combat the chill. He always seemed to know exactly what she needed, and deliver it unflinchingly. How could he be so altruistic?

"I'm really not," he murmured, his gaze fixed at the juncture of her legs. "In fact, right now I'm feeling very selfish."

With a start she realized she'd asked the question aloud. The way he skimmed his hands over the backs of her thighs made her sigh. He inhaled deeply, as though filling his lungs with her woman's scent, and a masculine growl escaped.

From the possessive way he gripped her ass, Alison knew what he was thinking. He was a man with his face inches away from a woman's bared sex. He might be coming off of a week of illness but that only meant he'd be more driven for sex.

But she didn't want to be his warm woman's body, damn it. She wanted him to want her, not sex. "Just take it out quickly, please. It's cold in here."

Nuzzling her mound he rasped, "I could warm you up."

"No." Squeezing her eyes shut, she shook her head. "Let's just get this over with."

"As you wish." Blunt fingers probed the entrance to her body, deftly separating her folds. He tried to insert a finger but barely got the tip inside. "You have to relax, lovely."

"I'm trying," she said through gritted teeth.

He withdrew and looked up at her. "Alison, look at me."

Sinking her teeth into her lower lip, she shook her head. She was such a wreck; she wanted him so badly, but at the same time she didn't want him to want her back if he only wanted a quick nail and bail.

"If you don't look at me, I'm going to bury my face in your cunt and lick you within an inch of your life."

Her eyes flew open.

"Better. Now, what's going through your mind? I've never seen you so tense."

All of her anxiety bubbled up. "I'm scared to death we'll die in here. Or that Gwella will exile us and we'll be the appetizers, or that the helcats will break through and kill everyone, or that the only reason you're doing this is because you're still stuck with me and I'd give you some space if I had any to give—"

"The hell with it," he growled and gripped her ass, pulling her toward his face.

22

"Del," Alison gasped as he traced the seam of her body with his tongue.

He loved the way she said his name, his first name, especially on a breathy exhale as she shivered with need. Talking to her was getting him nowhere. They both wanted this, needed a physical release. Why she fought him on it was a mystery.

Her hands threaded through his hair as he licked her deeper, more insistently. She could talk all she wanted, but his course was set. He'd make her come until she started making sense.

"Stop, don't do this." Even as she spoke, her hips bucked forward, urging him on.

What was with the token protests? He wanted her wanton and wild, the way he knew she could be, full of sexual confidence and totally without inhibitions. This game playing wasn't like her. Pulling back a bit he stared at her flushed face. "Really?"

Her eyes were bright, her cheeks pink, her lips parted in desire. She didn't pull away and he took advantage of her inner turmoil like the shameless bastard he was.

Using his thumbs to part her labia, he thrashed her clit with his tongue. Her back arched, her hands fisting in his hair. He eased off, but only slightly, elongating his strokes to cover more wet feminine flesh. Damn, but she tasted good, sweet with a heady woman's musk that made his head spin. He wanted to spread her out and feast on her pussy like a starving man given a last meal. Every puffy pink bit of flesh a delicacy to be savored.

Wetness spilled from her tight channel, a fresh gush of lube to ease his way.

"Please," she whimpered when he stroked into her body with his index finger. He didn't know what she was asking for, but he was on a mission. She made no sounds of pain, only desperate pleasure. Later they would address her numerous worries, after he made her come.

Her channel softened, elongated as her arousal increased, but was still a tight fit. Removing his hands, he cupped the fleshy globes of her ass cheeks, holding her in the perfect position. Stabbing his tongue deep into her well, he tasted the exotic flavors of her body at its source, no perfumes or chemicals, just pure Alison. His dick throbbed, demanding its own taste but he ignored it.

Nails bit into his scalp, a sweet stab of pain that told him she was getting close. Zigzagging a path over her vulva, he moved upward, toward that greedy little bundle of nerves that beckoned him even closer. Tracing one hand down her crease, he moved his fingers back to her feminine opening, but didn't enter. He wanted to let the anticipation build just a little longer.

Her body trembled in his hold, poised on the edge. He licked all around her clitoral hood, careful not to make contact. The bud seemed to swell, as though reaching for him, yearning for contact.

"Please," she begged again as he massaged the swollen tissues, teasing her body shamelessly.

He caught her gaze, held it as his lips closed over her tender nub, sucking it into his mouth. She bucked and he saw it there, the rapture sweeping across her features as his fingers drove deeply into her. Vaginal muscles milked them and she cried out as wave after wave of release crashed over her until she sagged against him, totally spent.

He let go of her clit, but his fingers kept going until they bumped into the device nestled against her womb. Pinning it between two fingers, he pulled it slowly from her quaking channel, now lax from her powerful orgasm.

Setting it aside, he held her steady while pulling her pants back up. It was one thing to pleasure her against her will to help her, another entirely to force himself on her if she didn't want him.

She blinked at him, lines forming between her drawn eyebrows when he moved away from her. His balls ached with the need for release. Wiping sweat off his forehead, he caught a whiff of her scent. Her sweet lube still coated his taste buds. His cock was rock-hard and ready to explode. Gritting his molars, he fought the urge to phase split and take care of himself.

Soft hands caressed his face. "Are you all right?"

Fenton couldn't answer without snapping at her. He closed his eyes so he didn't have to look at her, but it didn't help with her sweet feminine aroma surrounding him, driving him to the edge of his control.

You are more than the sum total of your urges. Think of Ari, of escape, anything else but driving into her.

That proved impossible when her hand gripped his cock through the fabric of his pants. "Let me ease you."

He wanted to jerk away, but found himself thrusting into her hold. "No."

A smile curved her lips. "And how far did that get me?"

"It was the only way—" he protested, not wanting her to think he was ignoring her wishes.

Her free hand settled over his lips. "Helping me made you like this. Let me return the favor."

"It's not a—" The protest broke off on a ragged groan when she freed his throbbing shaft from his pants and lowered her face until her soft breaths fell on his sensitive crown.

"Tell me what you want," she whispered. "You look ready to explode."

His hands fisted in her hair. "No teasing. Take me deep."

No sooner had the words left his mouth than hers engulfed his shaft in a warm, wet stroke. A hoarse noise escaped and he thrust up, unable to control his baser urges when they were so close to the surface. It took all his energy not to phase split and hold her in place so he could fuck her face.

Her cheeks hollowed as she sucked him deep into her wet heat, her eyes closed as she concentrated on the task. More sweat popped out over his skin. He was burning up, ready to blow, fighting the urge.

"It's okay," she whispered, her soft exhale tickling his wet shaft. "Do what you need to, I can take it." She took it in again until the head of his shaft hit the back of her throat.

Her permission broke the yoke of his control. With a bellow he snapped his hips back and thrust forward, losing himself in the wet cavern of her mouth. Again and again, completely untamed, wild in his drive for release. She took it all, relaxing her throat when he surged deep, sucking him on the withdrawal. Her eyes shone with satisfaction and trust as she watched him use her mercilessly.

He came with a guttural roar, spilling down her throat, emptying himself until all that was left were the aftershocks, every cell in his body twitching and shuddering.

She slid him from between her lips, refastened his pants. He wanted to thank her but speaking was too much effort. Still, he slid down until he lay flat on his back, uncaring that the floor was cold and hard beneath him when he had a warm Alison draped over him.

His eyelids felt heavy but lifted when she tried to move. "Stay here."

"You need sleep. You're still recovering."

He'd sleep better knowing he cushioned her, warmed her, and kept her safely nestled against him. Too many words to string together. "Stay here," he muttered again.

With a heavy sigh she did, relaxing into him, covering him like a living blanket.

He smiled and the words popped out. "Love you."

Oblivion claimed him.

Love you. Alison had been drifting off when Del sighed those words and then passed out with no consideration of the devastation his half-conscious declaration had wrought. Damn him, she wanted to knee him in the groin and make him explain himself.

Did he mean that? She wanted to believe him so desperately it shocked her. Yes, she cared for him, knew he cared for her. Judging by his determination to help her regardless of his own discomfort, she assumed he still did. But love was another star system altogether. Something more permanent, more life-changing than simple caring. There was commitment and acceptance implied with such an avowal and she craved both from him. When had that happened?

Probably when I fell in love with him too.

She rolled her eyes at herself. The assassin was still tracking her, starving mutant beasts were bearing down on them looking for their next meal, Ari was in the hands of pissed-off feminists with a grudge against them, and here she was worried whether Del meant it when he said he loved her.

I am such *a girl.*

She shivered, and though he was dead to the world, he tightened his embrace. His strength took her breath away, yet it was his gentleness that had captured her heart. Even here in the middle of an icy hellhole with their futures uncertain, he treated her like a queen. Or an empress.

No matter how badly she fucked up, or how irrationally she behaved, he didn't hold it against her, even when she thought he should.

It was like he'd been given an instruction manual capable of navigating her specific breed of crazy. And the way he touched her, aroused her, drove her out of her mind with lust, almost as if he'd been tailor-made for her. Her sex clenched when she remembered exactly how well he fit inside her, how they moved together. Alison had experienced plenty of sex before but sharing her body with Del was so much more than the colliding of body parts like a wreck in space. It was . . . celestial.

But that didn't mean it would last beyond the moment.

Exhaustion crept over her, blunting the sharp edge of her worry until she dozed lightly on top of his broad chest.

The scraping of the cell door woke her even before the voice said, "How precious."

"Drop off the tray and be gone." Alison didn't budge.

"Not this time. The empress wishes to speak with you."

Heart thundering in her ears, she slowly sat up. This was it.

"Del." Alison shook him. "Wake up. Gwella wants to see us."

Crystalline-blue eyes opened and fixed on her. Though he barely moved, she felt his arms tighten in a reassuring squeeze. "Then we shouldn't keep the empress waiting."

He sat up, helped her to her feet before standing himself. The patroller eyeballed them both with obvious distaste before turning on her heel and marching them through the dark basement. Another patroller stood at attention, waiting to bring up the rear.

Del gripped her hand in his. She knew he saw better in the dark, and he guided her safely forward. She had a difficult time swallowing, her throat was so dry. Her heart beat so fast, and she felt a little dizzy, probably from lack of food.

She expected to be led to some kind of throne room or maybe the table in the dining area where she'd done paperwork what seemed like a lifetime ago. Instead the patroller led them to a bathroom, a real one with chemical foam showerheads.

"You have two minutes to clean your hides and dress in fresh clothing." She nodded to a storage container with beige and gray fabric sealed within.

"And if we're not ready?" Alison couldn't help but prod.

"I'll whip you both and drag you naked before her." The glimmer in her eyes told Alison she'd enjoy it.

The second the door closed, she and Fenton raced to strip. Having more practice getting naked, she won and smacked the button on the wall. The cleansing foam rained down on them.

He spit, and she giggled as she moved to him, eager to help him clean up. To get her hands on his magnificent body. After spending a few hours trying to keep up with his workout routine, she knew exactly how those muscles could move. And how much work he'd done to hone them so precisely.

"If I didn't know better, I'd think you were enjoying yourself."

Skimming her hands over his body, she arched when he did the same to hers. "It'll go faster if we wash each other."

"You think so?" he rumbled, his touch traveling over her back, down to her ass. He liked it exactly as it was, despite the jiggles, the larger size. Proof-positive grew hard against her belly while he cupped her overly padded backside.

"Maybe not, but it's definitely more fun." Perhaps it was the finality that was only moments away, but Alison felt almost giddy as he explored her body. The tingling foam evaporated, leaving her feeling clean for the first time in a week.

"I never considered fun"—he rested his forehead against

hers even as his hands kept up their busy work, half-cleaning, half-playing—"until I met you."

"It seems so frivolous. We have no idea what's going to happen after we leave here."

"No sense worrying about that." His hands moved to her front, cupped her breasts, weighing them, then moved to her shoulders. "You are so lovely."

"I never felt this way before, not until you looked at me the way you do." She slathered his chest and down over his eight-pack of hard muscles.

"One minute!" The patroller banged on the door, shattering the sweet moment.

"What way is that?" He ignored the patroller and scrubbed her hair thoroughly, while her hands went lower. His erection pressed into her fleshy midsection, leaving a drop of precum on her skin. If they were anywhere else, she'd work him into a state until he took her hard and fast. But they didn't have the time. Instead she cleaned his ridged flesh, the sac hanging heavily beneath, then skimmed down his legs.

To her this little ritual wasn't about getting clean, much as she wanted that. She wanted to say good-bye. With that thought in mind, she worked her way up the backs of his legs over the firm globes of his ass and down the crease in between. "Like I mean something."

Using what was left of the foam, she worked her finger into his opening at the same time she swallowed his cock whole. He wasn't expecting it, didn't tense up, and she wiggled the digit until she found the hard bump of his prostate, pressing hard, pushing him toward release with an insistent massage even as she gulped down the ridged staff, milking him with her throat muscles.

With a strangled yell he came, shooting down her throat just as the bitch patroller shouted, "Thirty seconds!"

Though she didn't want to, Alison released him and finished washing herself as best she could with the remaining foam. He went down on all fours looking utterly shocked. She dove for the container and ripped open the lid, pulling out the fabric within. A long-sleeved dress for her and shirt and pants for Del. The foam had almost evaporated, though he hadn't moved.

"Here, put these on." Flinging the clothes at him she yanked the dress over her head. It wasn't the most flattering thing in the world, more like a shapeless sack and without any undergarments the coarse texture abraded her still tingling nipples.

Del barely had the pants up over his hips when the door opened.

"Time's up. Hope you made good use of it." The patroller waved them forward.

Alison blocked the other woman's view of Del with her body and put her hands on her hips. "Couldn't think of a better one." She smirked.

He made a strangled sound behind her. She cast him a quick look and was glad to see he had pulled the shirt on. Good, no whipping. Patroller bitch would just have to get her rocks off elsewhere.

The patroller's eyes narrowed. "The empress is waiting. Move it."

23

Fenton clasped his hands behind his back, hiding them from the patroller's scrutiny. Alison had blindsided him completely with her little surprise seduction. One second he had been busy washing her, and in the next she had driven him to his knees, gasping to recover from the most explosive orgasm of his life.

He hadn't seen it coming, hadn't anticipated her abruptness or his potent reaction to her shocking touch. Embarrassment at his lightning-quick reaction churned under the surface. Sure, he'd been aroused, he usually was when he was so near her, but the way she'd taken charge, demanded his body obey, took sexual gratification to a whole new level.

No one else could have toppled his control. Only Alison had ever crept past his defense grid to his command center. She'd taken over and he couldn't wait for her to do it again.

Just like her jealousy, it warmed him to know she wanted him so fiercely, had as much trouble keeping her hands off him as he had keeping his away from her. He owed her an orgasm, though, and he licked his lips as his eyes absorbed the swaying of her backside. So many possibilities to even the playing field.

Now is not the time for this.

But the moment would come and he planned to take full advantage of it.

Gwella had visibly aged since the last time Fenton saw her. She sat at the end of a long table. The seats to her right and left remained empty. Kel and the man he recognized as her personal breeder sat facing one another. Ari was nowhere in sight.

"Where is she?" Fenton's voice was calm, but even so, the patroller who'd escorted them up hit him on the back of the head with the end of her chem whip. It hurt, but he barely flinched. The time of pretending to fit in with this society was at an end.

Alison glared at the patroller. "That was unnecessary."

"Your breeder speaks out of turn." She sneered.

Alison's hazel eyes narrowed, her tone filled with warning. "Don't call him that. He's twice the warrior you are, you rancid bitch."

"Enough!" Gwella smacked her hand on the table. "Patrollers will leave now."

The sadistic woman's jaw dropped. "Empress, they are dangerous—"

Gwella cast the woman a dangerous look. "I have their offspring. They pose no threat to me. Be gone, before I order you whipped for insubordination."

Bowing low, the women turned and departed. Gwella's glare fixed on him. "You. You have incited revolution."

"What do you mean?" Alison asked. "How could he do anything? He's barely been conscious in the last week."

Kel cleared his throat. His gaze went to Gwella, who scowled, but he spoke anyway. "The breeders are gathered by the gate, demanding to be let out. It seems they would rather face the helcats with their bare hands than continue to live in subjugation."

"You are their representative?" Fenton asked.

Grief shadowed the other man's face. "It's what Dani would have wanted."

"How dare you speak for my daughter?" Gwella snarled. "She was the greatest warrior ever to be born."

"But she didn't want to be!" Kel stood up and faced down his lost love's irate mother. "Do you know what she wanted? To spend time with the young ones, to nurture and teach them to grow things. Her heart was that of a caretaker, not a warrior. She did what she did out of love and duty, but she hated every minute."

"Lies!" the empress snarled. "I think I know the heart of my own child better than some half-wit breeder!"

"Enough!" the other man thundered, causing Alison to jump. Fenton put his hand on her arm to reassure her and she cast him a nervous glance.

"Link," Gwella started but he rose to his full imposing height, clearly irritated.

He narrowed his eyes at her. "Is that really how you see us? See me? As some intellectual inferior?"

"No, of course not," the empress stammered. "It's them, not you."

Planting his fists on the table, Link steamrolled her. "I am one of them! I agree with them, the same way your daughter did. Do you want to know why we never got along? It had nothing to do with her sire. She didn't respect me for not standing up to you, for being your faithful hound instead of the man I could have been."

Gwella wrapped her arms around herself, shook her head. "That's not true."

"It is, whether you accept it or not. She came to me, begged me to talk to you. I refused, told her I believed you would make wise decisions and do what was best for your people. That I owed you my support. I thought we had an understanding, that there was mutual respect shared between us. I see now your prejudices make that impossible. No man alive took part in the creation of the helcats, yet we are continually subjected to your disdain. How is that just?" Link squared his shoulders and moved toward the door.

"I will not be coerced, by you or anyone else!" Gwella shouted. "This colony's welfare is my responsibility, not yours."

Link turned back to face her, to face them all. "Then you have condemned us to death. And if I'm going to die, I'll go out fighting."

Gwella's lips parted as she watched him go, her expression truly stunned. "Treason."

"Empress," Kel said softly. "It doesn't have to be this way. Allow the men to fight, at least those not tied to the care of off-spring. We can reach a compromise."

Fenton noted that Kel didn't mention Dani again, a wise move since Gwella appeared overwrought as it was. Sinking into a chair, she put her head in her hands.

Alison moved forward and knelt before her onetime friend. "Gwella, he's right. The men want to fight, they were training for it, with Del."

"I never should have brought you here. We were con-tented," the empress murmured, almost to herself.

"We were dying," Kel responded. "We still are. Commander Fenton gave us a fighting chance."

"An act punishable by banishment." Gwella's gaze locked on his. "Do you have anything to say for yourself?"

Fenton squared his shoulders and clasped his hands behind his back. Looking her directly in the eye, he said, "I did what I had to do in order to protect my loved ones. Dani and Kel had the right of it, things could not keep going the way they were. The genetic mutations are starving, and a starving animal will take greater risks. Like the one that dug through the tunnels.

You need every able-bodied individual fighting if you want to survive."

"He's right." Alison spoke quietly, putting her hand over Gwella's. "Those things are hungry and desperate. If there aren't enough people holding them at bay, this haven will fall."

The empress stared at each one of them in turn, then her gaze went to the door.

"Please, Empress," Kel implored. "Don't let her sacrifice be for nothing."

Gwella stood and paced the room. Alison rose but Fenton put a hand on her shoulder, holding her in place.

The empress turned and her chin went up. "Fine. Tell the breeders . . . the *men* . . . that those not tied to the care of a child less than ten may take up arms. Commander Fenton will instruct them how to fight."

Kel's head lowered. "Thank you, Empress. It is the wisest choice."

"I will lead the vanguard, if that is your wish," Fenton volunteered.

"You will do no such thing," Gwella snapped. "Did you not hear what I said?"

Alison's eyebrows drew together. "Del is probably the best warrior on Daton Five."

"Which is why I want him training our patrollers, male and female. But he is responsible for a young life and therefore he must remain behind." She smiled, but it was cool and carried a malevolent message. "No, you, Alison, will take my daughter's place and lead the attack."

"What are you doing?" Alison moved to the small table where Fenton worked. Ari was asleep in the next room, what had become her own residence at Gwella's. Though they'd both been beyond relieved to see the little girl was both healthy and happy, the reunion had been bittersweet, made stressful by the empress's announcement that Alison would lead the vanguard attack against the helcats.

Fenton didn't answer her, didn't look up from the small device he was picking apart, and she wrapped her arms around herself. "Del?"

"Training starts tomorrow. Get some sleep, you'll need it."

Covering the hand he was working with, she murmured, "I'll sleep when I'm dead."

"That's not funny." He jerked away, stood up, and ran a hand through his shaggy hair. She wished she had the skills to cut it for him as the longer locks seemed to irritate him.

"I know. Sorry, just trying to lighten the mood." It was clear that Gwella was still irate, as only a grieving mother could be. Though the conditions had improved, they were still prisoners, and Alison was to take the brunt of the punishment for Fenton's hand in leading the insurgents of the men of Daton Five.

He paced the small room. "I can shift, disguise my other self and go with you, protect you."

She shook her head. "And what if you're caught? She'll have us both put to death, probably Ari too. This is the only way, Del."

"No. I won't accept that." He sat back down at the table. "There has to be another solution." Again he picked up the tools and started fumbling.

Alison eyed the device he'd been picking apart since she put Ari down for the night. The attack was scheduled for two days from now, at midday. The last thing she wanted to do was spend her last precious hours of life watching him fiddle with whatever that was.

She moved closer and looked over his shoulder. "Is that . . . ?"

He held up the device, the one she'd had inside her body for almost a week, and heat crept up her face. "Should I even ask why you kept that or why you felt the need to dissect it?"

"It's like a demoleculizer, breaking matter up into its basic atoms. I thought, in conjunction with your shield, that I could weaponize it."

She frowned. "My shield? You mean my health guard?" The one she'd forgotten to use not once, but twice earlier when she'd taken him into her mouth. Sure, she could blame the situation, the constant surges of adrenaline that left her either jittery or exhausted, but deep down she knew the truth. She wanted Del's flavor on her tongue, wanted to be marked by him in that primal way. It made her feel powerful, desirable, and no technology should get in the way of that.

"Yes. If we modify it and tie it in to the frequency of your shield, it will amplify the effect so that any living thing you touch will be obliterated, its DNA unwoven."

She blinked, imagining herself as a walking force of destruction. Her lack of military prowess would be irrelevant; the helcats wouldn't stand a chance. "You can do that?"

He bent over the device once more. "I need to find something that will boost the power."

She left him to it and went to check on Ari. The little one lay on her stomach, her head turned to the side. Alison was still taken aback by how much she'd grown in the last week. She'd put on weight and was starting to wiggle more and more. She actually pushed herself up onto her hands and knees earlier.

"You are so beautiful, little princess." Tears burned behind her eyes. Part of her wanted to pick Ari up, to hug her and breathe in her distinct baby smell. She wanted it fresh in her mind when she went up against the helcats.

"She sure is."

"Link." Alison turned toward the man leaning against the doorjamb and wiped her eyes. "Thank you for taking such good care of her."

"It was my pleasure." He waved her out and shut the door so they wouldn't disturb Ari. Deep, dark chocolate eyes fixed on her face. "I want you to know I volunteered as your first in the vanguard."

"Why?"

"Because it pissed Gwella off, although not enough to have her rethink this madness, unfortunately."

A wry smile worked its way out. "I don't blame her. If someone caused Ari any harm, I'd want his guts for garters."

He flashed her a brilliant grin, that seemed to glow in the dim lighting against his dark skin. "That's how mothers are."

"Oh, I'm not Ari's mother."

"In all the ways that matter, you are."

She closed her eyes. "I never wanted a child."

"Why?"

Normally she'd deflect or ignore the personal question altogether. But with the sands running out of the hourglass, she couldn't remember why. Opening her eyes, she met his gaze. "I'm selfish, always have been, always will be. I don't make sacrifices for others, not without resenting them. It's not pretty, but it's the truth. No child should grow up with someone like me for a mother."

Behind them a door closed, and she stiffened, sensing Del's presence. How much had he heard?

He stopped behind her and though he didn't touch her, she could feel him in every cell of her body. "Would you excuse us?"

"Have a good night." With a nod, Link disappeared downstairs.

"Come back inside." Del took her hand and pulled her into their room.

She looked at the thing on the table, which seemed to still be in as many pieces as when she'd left. "Any progress?"

Slowly, he nodded. "I think so. I hooked it to the biomechanoid from Ari's pod. Carbon life forms generate heat, which can be converted to energy. In theory, it should work but that's not why I dragged you back in here. I owe you an apology."

"Whatever for?"

"Not paying attention to your needs. You wanted to talk and I distanced myself. The cause was just, but I don't want you to think you are alone." Blowing out a breath, he sank onto the pile of cushions. "This isn't the way it's supposed to be. I don't know how to be left behind."

He looked so miserable and it tore at her heart. "At least you and Ari will be safe, might even have a chance to get away. By all rights you should hate me for what I've cost you."

Stroking the side of her face he whispered, "I could never hate you. Haven't you figured out yet that I'm in love with you?"

She sucked in a sharp breath, but when she released it, the question popped out too. "Why, for fuck's sake?"

He grinned. "It might be your elegant way with words."

She shoved him. "Don't jerk me around. My sanity is dangling by a thread here."

Sobering, he moved closer again until the back of his hand stroked her face. "I'm sorry, I'm no good at lightening the mood either."

"So, it was some kind of joke?" She refused to cry, not over that, no matter how much she wanted his love, his acceptance, and the knowledge that she mattered to him for whatever time she had left.

"No. Stop twisting my words. You asked why. Maybe because you accept me and all my faults? Or how about the way you take care of Ari?" He put a hand over her mouth, the knowledge of her protest in his eyes. "It was a mistake, Alison, a bad judgment call. I know you didn't mean to put her in danger."

He took a deep breath and lowered his hand. "I'll be honest, I like your jealousy. Not the result, but that you felt strongly enough about me to be so possessive . . . no one ever cared so much about me. And waking up to discover you've been caring for me for a week, when I know you've never done that for another person in your life. It was an incredible feeling."

Her heart thundered and the room spun. "It wasn't a sacrifice. Not really. I just wanted you to be well."

His gaze smoldered across her body. She could feel it like a touch and her libido responded to it. Nipples tightening, sex moistening, preparing her for him.

His eyes met hers again. "I'm well now. So what are you going to do with me?"

Licking her lips, she thought of the best way to answer when the clang of a bell drew their gazes to the window. Del was on his feet in an instant, shoving the window up. Screams and shouts drifted from the area by the gate, along with the roar of a helcat.

"One got in somehow." Grabbing the device, he turned to face her, his expression dire. "Time to see if this thing works."

"And if it doesn't?"

Taking her hand in his, he brought it to his lips. "It has to. I won't lose you now."

24

Ari was irate at having her sleep disturbed only to be lashed into her carrier, and her screams made conversation impossible. Fenton thought his eardrums were bleeding by the time she finally settled down.

"You could stay here with her," Alison whispered when his niece stopped wailing. "It's probably safer here than anywhere else in the compound."

Fenton didn't argue, just strapped Ari to his back. "I'm more comfortable on the move."

It was a lie. He'd be most comfortable taking the danger on himself, instead of sending Alison out to face down one of those horrors with nothing but his muddled mess of technology that might not even work properly. He admitted to himself that he didn't know what he was doing. He was a soldier, not a tech. True, he'd personally handled all the repairs and upgrades to the equipment at the base, but he'd never built a weapon from scratch before and her germ shield was unlike anything he'd ever dealt with. If there was any way to take on the weapon himself, he would, Gwella's orders be damned. But removing her shield and trying to recalibrate it to his genetic code would take more time than they had.

A furious roar punctuated that thought.

Alison's eyes met his. "What do you want me to do?"

What he wanted and what he'd ask of her were two different things entirely. A lump formed in his throat. "Activate your shield. I need to calibrate the demoleculizer to your genetic pattern. Once it's activated, do not touch anything you don't want to annihilate."

Looking down, he fussed with the power source. "These things are used to living in a colony. I'm not sure how long they'll hold out on their own. If they fade out, your energy source is depleted. If that happens I want you to get yourself to safety. Climb a tree, dig a hole, whatever it takes, but do not engage those creatures. I will find you, but you have to get away first. Run as fast as you can, got it?"

"Yes. Del?"

He looked up just as she moved into him. Reflexively, his arms went around her and her arms went around his waist, her head pressed against his chest, next to Ari's. She was shaking from head to toe. He closed his eyes and buried his nose in her fragrant locks.

"I wish we had more time. I wish we had a lifetime to get it right."

His throat closed up. Never enough time. They never hit the right chord, followed the same wavelength. Instead they had to fight their way from one dead-end situation to the next and hope they made it out intact.

He held her to him. With both his females safe and whole in his embrace, he begged the universe that it wouldn't be for the last time.

Alison pulled away first. "Okay. Hook me up." Her fingers depressed the trigger on the inside of her elbow and her health guard snapped to life.

Scanning the energy signature, Fenton calibrated the device he'd constructed, praying it would be enough to keep her safe. Once he was certain he breathed, "It needs to stay in contact with your skin."

"I'll hold it. I wouldn't know what to do with a chem whip anyway." One pale, trembling hand reached forward and she picked the small thing up between her thumb and index finger.

They both sagged slightly when she took it and he didn't vaporize.

"Should we test it on something?"

He pointed to a small evergreen sapling off the corner of the porch. "There."

Cautiously, she moved forward and he held his breath when her hand reached out, her index finger pointed at the topmost branch. He waited, unable to draw a breath and beseeched whatever deity might be listening.

Please let it work, please.

There was no noise, no flash of light to indicate something miraculous had happened. One second the small tree was there and the next it was gone. Erased, as though it had never existed.

"We did it!" She whirled and took a step toward him before she remembered they couldn't touch. "How do I shut it off?"

"Put it in your pocket and deactivate your shield. But don't, not yet. The extra stress might kill the bioluminescent microbes more quickly."

She nodded. "Time to annihilate some helcats, then."

"Lead the way."

The forest around Gwella's house was deserted, not a single patroller left behind to guard them. They moved quickly, Alison several paces in front of him. The path through the woods seemed to take a lifetime to traverse but when it finally spit them out by what had once been the town green, Fenton wished it had taken longer.

The huts were ablaze, fire licking up the sides, engulfing five homes up. A helcat stood at the gate, all the patrollers and several dozen breeders lashing out at it with their chem whips, trying to drive it back out. Each lash made it roar in fury but it kept on. People ran everywhere and three helcats circled overhead, their large wings almost spanning the humongous dome. What had once kept the inhabitants of Daton Five safe had become their tomb. The outline of ribs poked through layers of fur. Dani had been right. They were starving, and hunger made them even more vicious.

"Del, up there!" Alison pointed six huts up. The staircase was covered with smoldering debris and two little boys were trapped above. The helcat's cry sent a chill to his marrow.

"I need to be in two places at once," he warned Alison. "I can't take Ari up there."

Her gaze met his and he saw understanding flash in her eyes. "Stay safe."

"You too." Taking a deep breath he turned away from her and focused on his split.

His double appeared in the vacant hut above the trapped children. The helcat swooped down, spotting what it thought was easy pickings. Fenton rolled over the edge, gripping the staircase with his fingers and rocking his legs to build momentum.

"Stand back!" he shouted, hoping the children inside could hear him.

Another shrill call and the helcat came for him again, its razor-sharp claws whistling just above his head a second before he swung himself into the hut below.

The place was thick with putrid black smoke and he heard coughing from a far corner. Dropping to his knees, he crawled farther into the alcove home. A cough alerted him. The children were huddled together in the farthest corner.

"It's okay," he soothed them, moving closer to the frightened pair. The oldest couldn't be more than seven, his face still round with baby fat. He wondered if the helcats had picked off their protector. "Are you alone?"

"The breeder left us to fight," the older one whispered. "He said we'd be safe here."

Tamping down his ire at the stupid male who had thought it noble to abandon his frightened charges, he said, "I'm here now and I won't leave you."

The floor beneath his palms grew hotter by the second. It wouldn't be long before the entire infrastructure went up in flames. They needed to get to lower ground now. Glancing around, he took stock of the contents of the room. "I need you guys to help me. Toss as many pillows as you can out the window into a big pile okay?"

"What about the beasties?" The younger looked at him with wide-eyed fear.

"They can't see through the smoke." Fenton genuinely hoped it was true. "Stay low just in case."

The boys worked quickly, dragging the pillows and cushions to the opening and throwing them out. Del went into the lavatory and began ripping the metal sheets off the wall into the longest strip he could manage. The material was thin, but sturdy. It would hold the children at least.

The sounds of battle chilled his blood, the screams and shouts enhancing his worry for Alison. Neither version of himself could see her, the air thick with smoke and the stench of death. The children had to be terrified, but they bravely plodded on until every pillow and cushion lay mounded on the ground below. "Nice work," he said and the oldest boy grinned, baring a gap between his teeth.

"Now, here's what we're going to do. There's a man down there and he is going to hold the bottom. You'll recognize him because he looks a lot like me and he has a baby with him. You do exactly as he says, all right?"

"Is he your brother?" the youngest asked.

"We're very close." Fenton unrolled the metal sheeting and held it down. Down below, his other self aligned the slide with the cushions.

"You have to go one at a time." He held the sheeting down, placing his full weight on it.

The youngest one sat on the ramp. His eyes were huge as he gazed down the massive drop.

"It's okay, he'll catch you. Try to stay to the center as best you can. Just push off and it'll be over before you know it."

The boy looked to his brother, who nodded. "Go on."

He pushed off, screaming in terror the whole way down. He landed face-first in the mountain of pillows.

"Are you all right?" the Fenton with Ari asked him.

"Can I go again?" The boy grinned up at him.

Back at the top, Fenton indicated the older boy should go ahead.

"What about you?" The child looked from where he stood holding the top portion of the metal down the ramp, quickly figuring out that there was no one to hold the slide in place for him."

The floor beneath them groaned, hot even through his boots. This place wouldn't last much longer. "I've got another way down. I'll see you soon, okay?"

Another scream and then the second boy was safe an instant before the floor gave way beneath his feet.

Getting close enough to touch one of the helcats without accidentally bumping into one of the patrollers or breeders fighting the massive creature was incredibly stressful. Alison had already had a couple of near misses with patrollers who had backed up suddenly to avoid the snapping jaws as the beast pushed forward.

Her shield hummed at the ready and Fenton's little invention was grasped tightly in her sweating palm. To her right, Gwella drew her chem whip back and lashed the creature, landing the blow just short of its massive eye. It screeched in outrage, trying to spread its enormous wings and take flight. Overhead the circling helcats called back. She eyed them ominously, but they remained aloft.

The wood around the gate had begun buckling with each push the beast made to break through the bottleneck. She had no idea why the ones overhead weren't picking off the fleeing people below like fish in a barrel. It made no sense, they wanted in, they were starving, so why wait?

If she could get to Gwella, perhaps the empress would order the patrollers back and give her room to work. Picking a deserted path behind the melee, she goose-stepped around the fallen warriors, unwilling to cheat their loved ones out of closure or expend more energy than her little demoleculizer could spare.

"Empress!" she called but the helcat roared in outrage at the same moment, drowning her out. She needed to get closer.

A few more steps forward and, hauling in a substantial lungful, she bellowed, "Gwella!"

It worked. Gwella glanced over her shoulder, scowling and sweating from exertion. "What are you waiting for? Grab a chem whip."

"I have something better." At least she hoped. "Can you call everyone back from the gate?"

"Have you lost your mind?" Another lash from Gwella's whip hit its mark, this time the great beast's left eye. Rearing up, it let out another of those soul-disturbing cries. "If we pull back, it'll take advantage and break through."

"Just trust me!" The words came out before she realized how foolish they sounded. Of course Gwella didn't trust her; it was why she was here in the first place. "Listen to me, I'm so, so sorry about Dani, you'll never know how sorry. But I can help. Del and Ari are here too. Please, I wouldn't ask this if I didn't genuinely believe I could do this."

Gwella pulled back and stared directly into her eyes. Squaring her shoulders, Alison held her gaze, hoping her sincerity would shine through and convince the empress to listen to her.

"All right." Gwella nodded once, then whistled. The patrollers instantly fell back, and after a moment the breeders, realizing their female counterparts were retreating, followed suit.

The half-blind helcat roared and those circling above did as well. Hands shaking, Alison stepped forward on its blind side, alone against the massive beast. She had to do this, had to get rid of this thing that never should have been. The idea of touching it scared her to death, but every second she wasted collecting her courage was another second that it could break free or the others could attack.

She had just put her hand out when the creature jerked toward her, somehow sensing her presence. The remaining golden eye gleamed and the paw came down, ready to cut her in half. She screamed and brought her hands up to protect herself from the deathblow.

Contact. But instead of her being cut into pieces on the ground, the monster had simply vanished.

Righting herself, she stared at the bent gate, at the helcats above and the fires licking up the giant trees. The warriors all stared at her, stunned with disbelief.

"What did you do?" Gwella whispered, her eyes wide.

"Saved your people." She looked around for Del and Ari, but she couldn't see them in the chaos. "This place is going to collapse in on us. We need to evacuate."

"There might be more of them out there," the bitchy patroller who had been her guard protested.

"Well, there are definitely more of them in here. We need to get to a cave or something, get the hell away from them. I'll lead the way." She swallowed hard when she looked at her device. The helcats were enormous, and if she wasn't mistaken, the bioluminescent light had faded.

Eyeing the sky, Gwella nodded. "She's right. Get everyone over here, now."

The piercing screech of the circling helcats punctuated her point.

As the patrollers and breeders ran off, Gwella turned to Alison. "If I get everyone aboard the ship, can you and a small group pick off the rest?"

"I hope so."

Gwella nodded once. "Right. I'll call the ship to set down in the clearing there. Once we're ready, we'll have the patrollers form a perimeter to keep the beasts at bay long enough to evacuate."

"Make sure they know not to touch me. This device won't discriminate between friend and helcat." Alison eyed the beasts overhead. "Why aren't they attacking? They are obviously starving, so why wait?"

"I don't know, but I plan to take full advantage of it." Gwella removed a small communication device from her pocket. "The ship has been in orbit for several days now. I had a feeling everything would come to a head. Go out into the clearing. If there are any more nearby, the scent of blood will draw them here."

Alison had wanted to wait for Del, to make sure he and Ari were safe, but she was just rebuilding the trust between the empress and herself, so she simply nodded and moved through the open gate.

Everything outside was eerie and still, with only a slight breeze rustling the dead leaves on the forest floor. Clutching her device she walked the tree line and scanned the skies. Perhaps there had only been four helcats left, the four that had at-tacked. Her demoleculizer ought to hold off the last three. She hoped.

The great roaring of engines overhead caught her notice and she saw the massive ship, still fighting gravity, maneuver to the indicated spot for extraction. Again her eyes went to the trees, heart banging against her ribs like it wanted out. If it wouldn't waste whatever juice her bioluminescents had left she'd start zapping trees, just to be sure nothing lurked in the shadows be-tween them. The hair on the back of her neck stood completely on end.

With a groaning of metal, the ship set down, the rear hull separating like a giant mouth preparing to take a bite. And like krill to a whale, the remaining inhabitants of Daton Five spilled forth, eager to be the appetizer.

You're losing it, Alison. The ship is safe, the monsters are be-hind them.

Patrollers moved forward, chem whips at the ready, fanning out around the ship, ready to die if it meant their loved ones would be safe. A few met her eye and nodded, a show of re-spect she'd seen them give to Dani. It warmed her that these warrior women had accepted her.

She nodded back once before slowly circling back to the gate.

Men held on to children or carried elders to speed up the process. The helcats alternately screeched and roared from within the crumbling village. Her apprehension grew. If there was one universal truth it was that nothing was ever easy and this evacuation was going way too neatly. Those things should be swooping down on the people, blocking their paths and keeping them from escaping. Their food source was fleeing and yet they did nothing to stop it.

"Del!" she called out at the swarm of people bee-lining for the ship. Several heads turned in her direction but none of them were his. "Del Fenton!" He understood much more about strategy than she did and she wanted his take on what was happening.

The last few trickles of humanity spilled from the gate, Kel and Link bringing up the rear. "Unless there are people in hiding, that's everyone. We'll do a head count once we're airborne."

Nodding, Alison backed toward the ship. "Go make sure Del Fenton and Ari are onboard."

"I'm sure they're fine," Link rumbled.

Not taking her gaze off the burning village, she gritted, "I won't leave without them."

A silent communication passed between the men and Link bowed. "You are just as strong as any patroller defending her personal breeder."

They ran off and Alison gestured to the patrollers still guarding the trees to get aboard.

Too smooth, too seamless. Nothing is this easy.

As though hearing her mental criticism of their tactics, the helcats thumped down, the ground actually shaking as it absorbed the shock of their substantial weight. They were smaller, sleeker, or perhaps simply further along the road to starvation than the one in the gate because the first ran right through, wings tucked in to streamline its motion as it charged her. It hit her shield mid-roar and the noise was cut off instantly as it was atomized.

The second was in hot pursuit and she barely registered the dim glow from the bioluminescent colony before it was upon her. This time, however, only the front half of the enormous mutant beast vanished, its hind legs and tail twitching.

The lights had gone out completely, the little critters worn out and probably dead. Tossing it aside, Alison turned and bolted for the ship. The roar behind her spurred her to move faster than she ever had.

Del. Where is Del? Somewhere in the corner of her mind that wasn't completely frozen in fear she registered the oddness that Kel and Link hadn't called out to let her know he and Ari were safely aboard. Perhaps they hadn't found them yet or Gwella had forbidden them from leaving with the helcats bearing down.

The ramp was in sight and she swore she could feel the creature's breath on her neck but she didn't turn to look, afraid she'd trip and it would be all over.

Heart pounding, muscles burning, she charged up the ramp and kept going even as the thrusters fired up, lifting them off the ground.

Someone caught her and she turned to stare as the helcat's wings beat against the shifting air currents, intent on catching her. The metal doors clanged shut. Her whole body shook. That was too close.

"Don't worry, it won't follow past the atmosphere, I've seen to that." The voice was soft, reassuring, and at the same time struck a chord of terror in her that only one being ever had.

Slowly she turned to meet the soulless gaze of the assassin.

25

Fenton's arm was killing him.

He thought it might be dislocated. He hadn't phase split himself back together before the floor had collapsed, and he'd bashed both his shoulder and ankle on the way down. The ankle made walking painful, but with the welfare of Ari and the two little boys he'd rescued on the line, he had sucked it up and run as fast as they could go to the center of the forest, back to Gwella's, and down into the basement where he and Alison had been imprisoned.

"It stinks down here." The younger boy wrinkled his nose.

"You'll get used to it. This is the best place to hide from the beasties." He was banking on Alison to get rid of the beasties before they came looking down here.

The older boy tugged on his sleeve, jarring his injured side. "What about your brother? Do you think he got out?"

"He's fine, just a little banged up." Fenton winced as he unstrapped Ari's carrier and set her down against the wall. The little girl's eyes were wide though she didn't make a peep. "He's out checking to see what's going on and he'll let us know when it's safe to go back above ground."

In fact, he'd been attempting to phase split since the moment they entered the cabin, to leave one version of himself standing guard. Unfortunately, it hadn't worked. It must have something to do with his injury. "What are your names?"

"I'm Thom and this is Rand," the older boy said.

Fenton stuck out his hand. "Good to meet you, Thom. Rand. I'm Del, and this is Ari." His niece yawned, obviously not a fan of the pleasantries.

Looking around, he admitted that the underground cell might become their tomb. While there was only one way for the helcats to get in, there was also no other way for them to escape. Another dead end. Not wanting to upset the children, he kept that bit of information to himself.

"Are you bound to a patroller?" Rand asked.

"No." He was beginning to second-guess everything. It was too quiet up there. If this was such a brilliant hiding spot, then why wasn't anyone else here?

Doubts about the demoleculizer he'd fashioned for Alison almost sent him to his knees. What had he been thinking? He could have killed her before she got anywhere near a helcat. The overlord had always said the Fenton line of males was stupid. Verbal abuse was just another weapon in the dead man's sadistic arsenal, but he'd been taking chances, dabbling where an expert hand was needed. Just because he'd rigged some prehistoric equipment on a few military bases didn't mean he could successfully engineer a genetic deterrent.

"Are you all right?" Thom looked at him with wide eyes.

Keep it together. For them. Make a plan, see it through. You can't control anything else right now. Taking a deep breath, he squared his shoulders and forced a smile. "I'm worried about my female. She's off fighting."

"I thought you said you weren't bound to a patroller."

"I'm not. She's not a patroller."

"Then why is she fighting?" Rand prodded.

Children and questions, some things were universal. Good thing Ari couldn't talk yet or they'd have him surrounded. A head-on ambush wasn't working, so he switched to diversionary tactics. "Tell you what. If this is where we're holing up, we need to stock up for a siege. Do you guys know what a siege is?"

Thom nodded, but Rand shook his head. Fenton explained for both their benefits as simply as he could. "It's when you are stuck somewhere for a long time. You need what are called provisions. Food, water, medical supplies, pillows, and blankets. What I want us to do is go throughout the house and collect as much of that kind of stuff as we can. Got it?"

They worked steadily, making several trips downstairs to the basement and back, bringing candles, containers of preserved food, pillows, blankets, warm clothes, and as much water as possible, in case the pipes turned off.

With no one else to tend Ari, Fenton couldn't put his arm in a sling the way he wanted. The throbbing ache and worry over Alison kept him awake long after all three of the children dropped off into an exhausted sleep.

No roars or screeches broke the stillness. If he didn't know better, he'd think they were the only beings left alive on the surface of Daton Five.

Shuffling footsteps came down the stairs and he rose, standing by the open door. "Alison?"

"Sorry." The face that appeared didn't belong to the woman he most wanted to see, but she was a welcome sight nonetheless. "Not who you were expecting."

"Dani?" He grinned, thrilled to see her. "But how? That explosion collapsed the entire tunnel."

"I was transported out at the last second."

Transported? "By whom?"

Her face was grim. "He called himself the assassin. He was looking for your woman."

Fenton cursed, then immediately lowered his voice so as not to disturb the children. "I can't believe he found her. How did you escape?"

"Purely by accident. He's controlling the helcats, using his mind to somehow make them behave however he wants. They're herding everyone onboard the ship as we speak."

"Take me there," he said and then looked back at the sleeping children. "Is there anyone left who can stay with them?"

Dani called up the stairs and another patroller appeared, along with several men, one badly injured. "I came across them on my way here."

"We'll look after the little ones." Though he was covered in ash and sweat, the man stood up and saluted Fenton. "Sir."

He recognized the younger man from training. "Dav, right?"

His face broke into a grin. "Yes, sir. Your training saved my life, sir."

"Glad to hear it." Kneeling down, he feathered a kiss over Ari's forehead. "I'll be back soon, little love."

He followed Dani up the stairs and out of the cottage. The insane roar of a helcat prodded them both into a jog heading directly for the main gates.

He saw two of the creatures and then there was one and a half, with a stunned Alison beyond the carnage. She eyed the monstrosity coming for her and sprinted for the ship.

"Alison! No!" He shouted her name but the cry of the last living helcat drowned out his call. Concentrating as best he could, he tried to phase split, only to have the pain in his shoulder jolt him back together. "Damn it!"

Helplessly, he watched Alison get swallowed up by the ship that headed into the atmosphere, up out of sight. "We're too late."

"Not necessarily," Dani said. "I have your ship. If we can get close enough, you can phase split onto theirs, right?"

Slowly he turned to her. "Where is it?"

She led him out around the burning side of the city, out through the gates. "Keep an eye out for helcats."

Jogging through the clearing, he followed her up a steep incline and through a thick copse of evergreens to where, lo and behold, his shuttle suite sat. "I thought Gwella had this thing stripped down."

"Most of the contents were redistributed, but we hadn't gotten around to stripping your tech." Dani climbed aboard and proffered her hand.

He took it and looked around the opulent space he and Alison had shared what seemed like a lifetime ago. "Everything is exactly as we left it."

Dani moved to the controls. "Hurry, they've already broke atmo."

Keying in the tracking sequence, he waited for the ship to lift and then turned to face her. "This truly is incredible, Dani."

She smiled, but the pleased expression fell away as he stalked closer. "Del?"

"I don't think you understand. I really don't believe it. Any of it. Dani just happens to be alive and just happens to lure me out of hiding in time to see Alison run headlong into danger and *just happens* to have a ship nearby ready for me to give chase? No, I'm not that trusting."

"Del, come on—" Her words cut off when he wrapped his hands around her throat.

"Only Alison calls me Del. Only Alison knows about my phase split and I know of only one person capable of reading that information from her mind. The assassin. So the fact that you know it means you're in league with him. Now, let's try this again. Who. The fuck. Are you?"

The creature pinned in his grip vaporized, leaving him empty-handed.

"Well, that didn't work." The assassin appeared mildly put out as he stared out at a cloud of gold mist heading toward the ship. "Or, more accurately, didn't entirely work. You'll be relieved to know, dear Alison, that Fenton is in hot pursuit."

Alison struggled against the invisible bonds holding her against the wall. "Leave him alone."

"Now why would I want to do something like that?" After tapping in a few commands he prowled the room. "It's all in good fun."

"Del hasn't done anything to end up on your list. Leave him alone."

"Oh, my dear, naïve girl, you think this is about a list? Your name was removed from my list weeks ago. You can go home any old time you like."

"Then why go to all this trouble? Why chase us so far?"

His eyes narrowed even as his lips curled up. "It's what I do. The pay, the list, none of it really matters. I'm in it for the thrill of the hunt, the anticipation of the blood yet to be spilled."

"You're sick," she whispered.

"And you're observant." His gaze went to the viewport. "And he's a worthy opponent. I might have overplayed my hand a bit, resurrecting Dani, but he fell for it. I was hoping for some grand theater, see if maybe the chameleon could entice him into a little romance. You're still envious of that dead warrior woman, so jealous it fills you up. I would have loved to see your reaction if he had taken the bait."

She closed her eyes, trying to block his viciousness out, but it seeped through the corners, permeating her brain. He was in there, reading her thoughts, commenting on them as though he had a right. "Someone should put you down like the rabid mongrel you are."

"Ah, now there's the rub. No one can. I'm completely and utterly invincible." His laugh was bitter. "Believe me, it's not all it's cracked up to be, so I take my amusement where and when I can. And for my next trick, I'm going to fuck your beloved, slit his throat the moment he comes. You'll be soon to follow, of course, coated in his arterial spray like a living tribute to his demise."

Behind him the shuttle suite drew nearer, stark white against the vast blackness of space. Maybe Del had a plan, maybe he saw a way out of this. Distracting the assassin and giving him his chance was the only thing she could do. "And then what?"

"Then you'll be dead."

She made a rude, dismissive noise. "Yes, yes, but what will you do?"

"Kill every single person I stashed down in the cargo hold."

"Just slaughter them, like sheep? That doesn't sound like much of a challenge."

He made a disgruntled sound. Behind him the shuttle suite filled the view screen. She intentionally kept her mind blank, focused on nothing. If he suspected, they were done for. "I still have that space pirate to contend with. And the empath."

"You don't sound thrilled with those options."

He raised an eyebrow. "Why should you care if I'm bored?"

"We were friends once. I'm betting on you to remember that. To show me a little leniency."

Slowly, he shook his head. "No, we weren't. We worked together on some mutually beneficial projects. You were always afraid of me. Smart of you, by the way. I think you're trying to snow me. Bravo for the attempt. However—"

She'd never know what he'd intended to say because the shuttle suite collided with the bigger ship, the sound of grating metal echoing throughout the room.

The assassin whirled, just in time for the hull of the shuttle suite to come flying toward them. She screamed and he roared in outrage as sparks flew.

Her invisible bonds loosened as he dove out of the way of the oncoming wreckage and she ran for the nearest doorway. The control center was already starting to depressurize, the air getting sucked out through the hole and out into the void.

"Alison!" Del was there, wearing zero gravity gear. He held an emergency air mask, which he slipped over her head. "Get to the lower level."

"If he dies, we all die!" She pointed to where the assassin was struggling to maintain his grip on the deck.

"Trust me!" Fenton shouted. He held something she didn't recognize.

She did. The man had risked the demise of the entire sector, including his niece, to rescue her. Pulling herself forward, she shut herself out of the room, then stared through the circular window.

Fenton closed in on the assassin, his zero-G suit giving him the distinct advantage. The assassin shouted something, and Del shook his head, raised his arm.

The thing he'd been holding shattered across the assassin's back. The man's screams froze, as did his body, impotent rage etched on his features.

Fenton dragged him across the floor, a slow, laborious process. Alison stood aside when he reached the door, so as not to be sucked out into the vacuum.

"What did you do to him?" she breathed, staring at the twisted features of the man by her feet. He could have been a grotesque statue and she wouldn't have been able to tell the difference.

Del pulled his helmet off. "It's the cryogen from Ari's stasis pod. The pod itself is used to protect the individual once they are placed in stasis. I wasn't too worried if he got a little banged up. We need him alive, not unharmed." He actually stepped on the frozen man to get to her.

Flinging herself forward, Alison rushed into his arms. "You crazy man, you almost killed us all. What the hell were you thinking?"

Moving a strand of hair aside, he examined a sore spot on her cheek. "That I love you and would risk anything for you."

"I don't deserve you." She clung to him, though.

He pulled back and grinned down at her. "Since when do we get what we deserve? Come on, we need someone to help us figure out how to land this thing without a central command station."

He made to pull away but she stopped him. "I love you too."

Pulling her into his arms, he murmured, "I was wrong. Sometimes we get exactly what we deserve."

26

"You wanted to see me, Empress?" Fenton approached the porch to Gwella's house, the one structure in the settlement that had remained unscathed in the helcat attack.

"Sit down, Fenton." She indicated the steps beside her.

"Where are your guards?" There wasn't a patroller in sight.

"Busy, elsewhere. I hear I have you to thank for rescuing Thom and Rand. They told me an interesting story, about you and your 'brother' rescuing them from a burning building after their breeder abandoned them."

Fenton froze. Damn, he thought the boys had forgotten about that. He offered no explanations or apologies. Having been without his ability for crucial moments, he knew Alison had been right. He needed to accept that part of himself, even if it meant enduring the empress's wrath.

Turning to face her, he raised his chin and waited.

"At ease, soldier." She patted the air. "No one else is dying today."

"I'll leave, if that's what you want. One of the shuttle suites is still intact—"

"And by law, mine, for invading my space. I plan on using that to repair the damage you wrought to my ship and rebuild my city." Her eyes were dark and harder than a winter in the Northern Territories.

Oh, yeah, she was angry.

Again he waited for her verdict. He would acknowledge her wishes as best he could, but Alison and Ari's welfare came first.

Gwella stared out over the trees. "I'm not wrong often enough to acknowledge it gracefully. But I do know when I have made a mistake. If it weren't for you and Alison opening my eyes, there would be no one left to rebuild. For that, I owe you my eternal thanks."

Fenton blinked. His lips parted, but he couldn't think of anything to say.

"Now, for the matter of Rand and Thom. Their breeder was one of the first slain, so they have nowhere to go once they leave here. You seem to have bonded with them, gained their trust. Both boys were very upset when you left. I wanted to offer you and Alison the option to raise them here."

"I'd have to ask Alison first." His voice came out hoarse. She didn't want to have one child to contend with, and now she'd be saddled with three. She'd changed, but so much, so quickly?

Gwella clasped her hands onto her lap. "Good, you do that. I'll keep the boys here another night. Ari too, she's still asleep. They can help Link prepare the meal. For some reason they enjoy sleeping in the cells and playing 'siege.' You wouldn't know anything about that, would you?"

She rose, then placed a hand on his shoulder. "You're a good man. Treat her right."

He planned to, if she'd have him.

At least they had the night to themselves. While walking back through the woods he plotted out the evening. He had no idea where she was or what she was up to. Knowing her, she was in the thick of the recovery process, helping situate people in the undamaged rooms and handing out supplies for the night. She promised to return by sunset to the undamaged shuttle suite and make plans for the future.

Over the next few hours, Fenton did his best to ensure her plans would include him.

Everything was staged and he paced restlessly as the twin moons rose higher and the sun disappeared. The snapping of twigs alerted him to her and he turned, blocking her view of the interior as best he could.

"Sorry I'm late," she said, offering him a tired smile. "There was so much to do and I didn't want to just run out on them. It felt too selfish."

"It's not too selfish to look after your own interests once in a while. You almost died today. Multiple times." He pulled her into his arms, glad to have her back, whole and safe.

"You'll be happy to hear the last helcat is dead. Patrollers found it a few hours ago. From what they saw, it suffered some sort of brain aneurism, probably from the mind control."

"The assassin actually did us a favor then. If he weren't buried in the tunnels in stasis, I might thank him."

She hugged him fiercely for a moment, but pulled away abruptly. "Your shoulder, I forgot. Did I hurt you?"

He waved her off. In truth he hadn't thought about his shoulder in ages. "I feel no pain when I have you near."

She smiled, then stood on her toes, attempting to look behind him. "Is Ari napping?"

Caressing her face with the back of his hand, he whispered, "She's at Gwella's. We're alone tonight."

Wrapping her arms around his waist, she tilted her head back to look at him. "Really? What shall we do with ourselves?"

Stepping aside he showed her the interior of the shuttle suite. Lit with hundreds of candles surrounding a steaming tub of water and a real bed. She turned and her jaw dropped at the sight. "Oh, Del."

"I love the way you say my name." He nuzzled the side of her face, then cupped her jaw and turned her lips toward his. "This is for you. I want to be sure you understand that. We don't have to make any decisions tonight."

"Decisions? About what?" she murmured, her soft lips following the line of his jaw, up to his scar.

The coarse fabric of her dress irritated him. He wanted to strip her out of it, to touch soft, smooth skin. But he didn't want to pressure her either. She was tired and he didn't want her to feel coerced or pressured. He wanted her to stay with him of her own volition. To choose him, in spite of the three children he'd probably be raising.

Clenching his fists, he swallowed, ignoring the throbbing in his groin. "About the future. Where you want to go from here."

Her palm cupped him through the fabric of his pants. "Right now, I want us both to strip out of these clothes and get into that big bath. After that, to the bed and we'll wing it from there. Does that sound like a plan you can live with?"

He growled and before Alison could move he had whipped the dress over her head, scooped her up into his arms, and carried her to the steaming tub. Reflexively her arms went around his neck. "Del, your clothes."

"Fuck 'em," he muttered. Sitting in the water, he held her facing him so he could trail kisses along her collarbones. He pulled her flush against him until she felt the solid length of his shaft pressing into her belly. Fingers traced the bumps of her spine, down to her crease.

Her breath hitched as she stared down into his face, knowing instinctively what he wanted. "I'm yours, take whatever you want from me."

Another set of hands cupped her breasts from behind,

pulled her off his lap and against a very naked and familiar male form. "I don't want to take anything from you, only to give, to share with you," he breathed into her ear.

His doppelgänger shed his clothes in record speed and before she could blink, she was the filling in a Fenton sandwich, surrounded by his heat, his scent. Calloused hands swept over her skin. Like she was a feminine *pasha* being ministered to and cleansed by her sexy bath attendants. Her head fell back against his shoulder. He held her breasts on display from behind even as his lips closed over the peaks of her stiffened nipples. The thrash of his tongue over the swollen little buds made her sex clench in need.

A small bottle of oil sat on the lip of the tub. She focused on it when he switched to the other breast. "Is that . . . ?"

Following her gaze, he nodded. "It's yours. I snagged it that first night. I'll never forget the scent or the scene that drove me out of my mind with lust."

"And for a while I thought it didn't have any real effect on you. I thought I wasted it, my last tie to home, on a bad bet."

Taking the bottle up, he rubbed it between his palms. "Oh, I'm a bad bet, all right. I intend to use my superior numbers to keep you interested, pampered, and spoiled on this backwater planet for the next twenty years at least. Because, lovely, you do have an effect on me. Here." Taking her hand, he placed it over his heart.

The steady thrum of his heart drew her forward until she was inches from him. Fisting his hair in her other hand, she let their mouths meld together until their tongues danced together in a fierce mating until she ground against his cock, needing it inside her, craving the feel of him inside her as deep as he could go. "Don't wait."

The version behind her took the bottle of lube. She expected to feel him prodding against her ass but as usual Fenton surprised her. His fingers dug into the tense muscles of her shoulders, prompting her to break the kiss on a moan.

"Don't rush me. I have a strategy." He smiled, then climbed from the tub, dried himself, while she melted in a puddle of goo under his hands.

The warm water and his deep tissue massage relaxed her to an almost comatose state, so much so that when he whispered, "Time to get out," she groaned in protest.

Chuckling, he helped her from the water, swathing her in warm towels. With two of him on the job, she was dry in no time.

Candlelight danced across his features as he pressed her down onto the bed, brushing his lips over hers. "Spread your legs."

She did and shivered as cool air made contact with her wet sex. Then his mouth was there, warming her, flicking over the blood-engorged tissues, sucking her juices and licking around all her tingling nerves. The other Fenton watched, his gaze hooded, and it was his sharp, intense focus that sent her hurtling over the edge.

She'd barely come down when he pulled her limp form up and settled her across his lap. His cock aligned perfectly with her clit. "Put your shield up, lovely."

She thought about it for half a second, then shook her head. "No."

Two sets of cerulean-blue eyes went wide. "You could get pregnant."

"I hope I do." Taking advantage of his astonishment, she gripped his shaft on one hand while raising her hips. "I told you, I'm in this for good. No more lying, no more running. Me and you, it's a done deal."

He kissed her then and drove deeply inside her at the same moment, cementing their arrangement. Pulling her down until she was astride him, she almost forgot about the other man until he gripped her ass cheeks, spreading her wide.

The maneuver helped him fuck more deeply into her, at the same time exposing her puckered ring to his other self. Teeth sank into the rounded curve of her buttocks, a little hint of pain tightening the coil inside her. Then the wet rasp of his tongue across her clenched muscles, coaxing her to open for him, pressing inward with what felt like his thumb.

Her body yielded to his onslaught, letting him in. She'd expected discomfort but there was only the odd sensation of being filled. The stretch of her muscles around various parts of his body, the scrape of a callus over her sensitive flesh. All of it designed to make her aware.

The thumb invaded her, massaged her, pressing against the thin wall where his cock filled her. He moved completely in tandem, working her body over with his. Every time she sank down, the cock and digit went deeper until she writhed. It wasn't enough.

"More," she gasped, throwing her head back and staring down into his eyes. "Give me more."

The thumb retreated, only to be replaced by two oil-slicked fingers, driving deeper. Her body contracted sharply, adjusted. It wasn't enough to send her over, though. She wanted his heat pressed against her back, his rod thick and spearing deep inside her, filling her to capacity.

She told him so.

Pulling her down against him again, the Fenton buried deeply in her pussy kissed her while the one about to penetrate her ass slathered his cock with oil. Then the crown pressed in, gripping her hips to hold her still. She'd thought she was ready, but he was so big, the ridged flesh unyielding.

He stopped, sensing the revival of her tension. She could hear him grit his teeth and broke the kiss. "I'm sorry," she gasped.

"Ssshh. None of that. Rub your clit, lovely. Come hard on my cocks."

She nodded and taking a deep breath, wound her hand between their bodies. Her clit was hard and stiff. It jumped beneath her fingers.

"That's it." He swept her hair back from her face. "Make yourself feel as good as you make me feel."

It wasn't a challenge when surrounded by a patient, sexy man. Just a few strokes sent her over the precipice, the clenching of her muscles drawing him deeper into her pussy and ass.

They moved in unison then, retreating slightly before plunging forward, gaining more ground. Ever the soldier, the tactician, his strategy worked, and she let him conquer her body fully, just as he had her heart.

With a dual roar he came, fountaining hot jets of cum inside her. She bucked, orgasming again, this one shaking her from head to toe until she nearly blacked out. He held her to him as the form behind her was drawn back to himself. His softening cock remained inside her and she held still, not wishing to dislodge him.

"I love you, Alison."

Lifting her face just enough to see into those hot blue eyes, she grinned, knowing she would feel his love for a long time to come. "I wouldn't have it any other way."